THE SEARCH ANGEL

The Search Angel

TISH COHEN

HarperCollins*Publishers*Ltd

The Search Angel
Copyright © 2013 by Tish Cohen.
All rights reserved.

Published by HarperCollins Publishers Ltd

First edition

No part of this book may be used or reproduced in any manner whatsoever
without the prior written permission of the publisher, except in the case of
brief quotations embodied in reviews.

HarperCollins books may be purchased for educational, business,
or sales promotional use through our Special Markets Department.

HarperCollins Publishers Ltd
2 Bloor Street East, 20th Floor
Toronto, Ontario, Canada, M4W 1A8

www.harpercollins.ca

Library and Archives Canada Cataloguing in Publication
information is available upon request

ISBN 978-1-44341-082-3

Printed and bound in the United States of America
RRD 9 8 7 6 5 4 3 2 1

For Max and Lucas

Prologue

1959

The woman in the next bed nursed her baby in the dark. Isabelle listened to wet suckling, to rhythmic sighs so faint they might have come from a day-old sparrow. If the dividing curtain was open, Isabelle would see the outline of tiny fingers batting against an engorged breast, a mother's palm cupping her infant's head in wonder. She would see the blackened shapes of helium balloons bobbing against the ceiling. The mother, Beatrice, said her daughter was born two weeks early but healthy as a horse. "A boy and a girl now," Beatrice said to Isabelle as her visitors filed out. "The million-dollar family."

Isabelle shifted onto her side and fixed her gaze on the glowing exit sign over the door. Her breasts ached. The hot compresses the delivery team recommended hadn't done a thing.

The baby was kissed loudly and wheeled away by a nurse. When the covers stopped rustling and Beatrice finally lay still, when the cadence of her breath slowed enough to reveal the woman was asleep, Isabelle placed bare feet on cold linoleum and stood up. She untied her gown, soaked down the front now, and reached for her clothes, folded neatly on the chair next to the bed.

"Don't give him a name," the chaplain had said in the labor room, gold cross strung from her neck. With her stout frame, in white suit and hose, sturdy beige nursing shoes, she could be a carton of milk. "Makes them too human."

The corridor was lit only by the glow of a coffee machine and a goose-necked lamp at the nurses' station. No sign of life, other than a tired doctor waiting for his cup to fill with bad coffee. Finally he left and Isabelle stepped into the hall.

She'd promised herself she wouldn't do this.

"Don't look at the baby, not even for a second," the chaplain added when Isabelle was instructed to push, "or you'll see that face first thing every morning for the rest of your life. You'll never move on." Isabelle had allowed them to take her son away the moment he was born. The weighing, the Apgar test, it all was done in another room. The baby hadn't made much sound. One angry squawk when they bundled him off, that was it.

Behind the neonatal station was the nursery—a shallow viewing room that displayed babies like pansies in a window box. Isabelle tied her long hair in a knot and focused on the glass before actually looking through it. Someone should give it a wipe with vinegar, she thought. The fingerprints and nose prints blurred the view.

Finally, she allowed her eyes to skim the bassinets. Pink blanket. Pink. Blue. Pink. Blue. Blue. All swaddled up tight like pastel burritos. She wandered along the window's ledge, reading the index cards taped to each bassinet. *Stephanie*

Blaskovic. Ayushi Kapoor. Ian Bell. Jenna Fennessey. Baby Jenna was so big she could start nursery school soon. Isabelle, six feet tall herself, mentally wished the girl well.

The next card read only: *Baby Boy Santos.*

She stopped. Let her eyes travel up the blanket to rest on a flick of wavy hair, a sleeping face the color of baby aspirin. His cheeks weren't as plump as the others'. You could see what he would look like as a man. Earnest and sad. Resigned. As if he'd peered through the glass and somehow gotten a glimpse of his future.

The chaplain was right. Seeing the child's crumpled brow and pursed lips, his fists balled and ready to fight, it was a mistake.

Isabelle walked. Down the stairs. Past the candy machine. Out into night air that smelled like water. With shaking hands, she lit a cigarette. Pulled her coat tight and marched toward the bus stop.

Chapter 1

2010

Eleanor gazes out into the darkened gloom of Newbury Street thinking it's about time to close up shop. A flash of movement catches her eye. There, with rush hour traffic battling the rain behind her, a trench-coated woman stands beneath the tree and takes turns looking from her feet to the window.

She's trying to work up the nerve to enter.

They feel they have no right, these women. As if having a fully functioning womb were required to even step inside Pretty Baby and if they're caught without one, an alarm will sound throughout the store. Eleanor knows the feeling well. She steps back from the door, busies herself with a piece of lint on her otherwise pristine white shirt. She took extra care with her appearance this morning. Polished her boots. Ironed her jeans. Folded a vintage hankie and put it in her vest pocket. This isn't just any Tuesday.

The blonde outside has made her decision. She holds her purse over her head and steps out from beneath the dripping elm.

It doesn't happen all that often, that an infertile woman enters Boston's most exclusive baby shop to torture herself with all that could have been, but when it does, it's always the same. She slips through the door and winces when the bell chirps her arrival. She avoids eye contact with Eleanor and her assistant, Ginny Hardwell, and wanders along the battered wooden floor toward the back, taking care to stick to the store's periphery where the larger baby equipment is displayed—chunky jogging strollers that look like miniature ATVs, cribs that justify their exorbitant prices by later converting into daybeds. Then, when she no longer feels the weight of anyone's attention, the woman wanders along the antique shelving, pausing to examine a Baby Mozart CD or a vanilla-scented plastic giraffe. These objects don't hold her attention for long. What stops her—what stops this woman today—are the newborn sleepers.

The look on the blonde's crumpled face as she holds up a tiny onesie says it all. Wanting anything this small cannot be too much to ask of life.

Pretty Baby was born of need. Eleanor Sweet's need to have a baby of her own. When she opened the store some nine years prior, she knew what she was doing. In stocking the shelves with organic hemp diapers, Swedish soothers, and washable bibs made of antique linen, she was collecting the most elaborate layette an infant could ever hope for.

Her own baby never came.

"Just because it happens for others and not for you," the doctor told Eleanor and Jonathan last year as he closed her file, "doesn't mean you've failed as a woman."

It wasn't easy for Jonathan to accept. Even in the most unpredictable of jobs—emergency room physician—Jonathan took comfort in what he could count on. That the ER would empty out the night of an Olympic gold hockey game. That childhood injuries would peak at 4 p.m. after kids tumbled home from school. That Christmas break would see at least one couple exaggerate an elderly parent's symptoms so they could fly the kids to Orlando with a clear conscience.

Trying to get pregnant is a game of odds and the odds stack up quite nicely for the average couple. Given a year of enthusiastic trying, eighty to ninety percent of couples will conceive. It never seemed a thing to worry about, until it didn't happen to them.

But none of that matters anymore. Finally, Eleanor and Jonathan Sweet are to have their baby. Eleanor checks the cash in the till. The paper in the register. She's never left the store for an entire week before and she wants everything to be perfect.

The store's atmosphere is paramount to its success. The nine months a woman spends pregnant are made up of moments. Moments in which the mother-to-be holds the secret: that hers is the most special baby ever to be conceived. Pretty Baby is set up to reinforce this. Classical music—often Beethoven's cello sonatas for their deep, calming tones— wafts through the air.

The decor is soft and romantic without being precious— one wall is brick painted in matte white, the other two are dressed in blue and white toile du Jouy wallpaper depicting scenes of pastoral country life in which a sailor-suited male pushes a nymph on a rope swing. Off to the side, a baby— their baby, it must be presumed—chortles and kicks fat feet from a Moses basket. That the repeating pattern represents fertility did not happen by accident. Eleanor hoped, rather than believed, her ovaries would be kick-started via tasteful visual suggestion.

The store's shelving is artfully distressed in a creamy white finish. Scattered throughout are sumptuous white denim chairs with matching ottomans upon which tired mothers-to-be can rest their swollen feet. Chandeliers heavy with Austrian crystals sparkle and wink from above.

Eleanor is well aware that a pregnant woman is determined that her infant will be cared for like no baby before. She wants to provide her progeny abundance, luxury, and purity. All this, Pretty Baby provides.

Decorative objects, such as silver piggy banks, heirloom clocks, and dolls are displayed in threes or fives as odd numbers offer greater visual interest. Baby towels and facecloths are plenty and languish in fluffy pastel piles throughout the store. Lamb-soft cashmere and Italian wool blankets are rolled and stacked in pyramids for a calming effect on the psyche. The walls and shelving are dotted at regular intervals with the gleam of something silver. A clock, a tissue-box cover, a photo album meant for baby's first year.

Even the air's scent has been given careful attention. Throughout the store are tiny bowls full of roses doused in essential oils. The fragrance is decidedly subtle—the hormones of pregnancy can make a woman's olfactory senses hypersensitive and Eleanor does not want to offend.

Pretty Baby is an oasis of calm for the expectant mother.

Now, Eleanor approaches the trench-coated woman under the ruse of adjusting a stack of receiving blankets. The blonde, whose purse is cracked at the edges, whose coat is torn beneath one arm, starts. The white sleeper slips off the hanger in her hands and onto the wet floor. When the woman picks it up, she's horrified. The sleeper is stained along one side.

"I'll pay for it," she says.

The gesture makes Eleanor want to put her arms around the woman, who reminds her of herself—mid-thirties, hair the color of vanilla ice cream, mouth slightly too big for her face except when she smiles. "It gets easier, sweet pea," she wants to say. "Once you stop hoping, it gets better."

The day after Eleanor learned she'd never bear a child, she took a newborn sleeper from Pretty Baby upstairs to the two-bedroom walk-up above the shop that she and Jonathan have shared since he finished med school. He didn't know it, but she slept with that Velour, zippered onesie under her pillow for three weeks.

"You know what?" says Eleanor. "Just keep it. Wash it with a bit of vinegar and it'll come out just like new."

The blonde looks at it, her mouth twisted with desire. "I could never." She fumbles with the ninety-eight-dollar price tag that twirls on a pale pink ribbon.

"I insist."

Before Eleanor might change her mind, the woman thanks her and is gone, the Genova sleeper tucked inside her vinyl handbag—maybe later, beneath her pillow.

Eleanor feels a nervous flutter in her stomach. The flight is in less than four hours. It's time to go upstairs and finish packing.

"Ginny," she calls as she marches to the back of the store, "if I leave you instructions not to torch the place while I'm gone, can I trust you to follow them?"

Ginny sits in the staff room filing invoices into an accordion envelope, her shirt so rumpled it could be a used Kleenex.

Ginny's attire is always better from a distance. Eleanor has spoken to her about the benefits of a crisply ironed blouse—Pretty Baby customers should feel they're being cared for by consummate professionals—but having a police-officer husband who does shift work and three hyperactive boys under the age of five, Ginny once explained, bumps her wardrobe down on her own personal hierarchy of needs. When you're scraping last night's lasagna from the dining room wall, bleaching spit-up stains from the shoulder of your sweater drops dramatically on the list of priorities.

"We could keep clothes here for you," Eleanor says. "Like a Pretty Baby uniform you change into when you arrive. And you would never, ever wear it home."

Ginny looks up at her boss. "Would I have to dress like you? Turtleneck, blouse, vest. I could get you a parka too."

Eleanor smoothes her shirt. "What? Layers are fashionable."

"Not when the store is heated by radiators." Ginny stands up and checks the thermostat. "Seventy-three degrees in here."

"I'm leaving. If anything comes up, I'll be checking my e-mail every day—as long as I have service. Just remember to lock up at night. If you pop out for lunch, put a sign on the door. And don't forget the Kleinmans are coming in next week to pick up the furniture order. Mr. Kleinman said he'd assemble the crib himself, but based on the way his tie was done up, I'm pretty sure he'll need your help. So if you don't mind heading over there—"

"Hey." Ginny looks up casually. "Can I book a week off over Christmas?"

"Didn't you use up your three weeks over the summer? You went to Ted's parents' place out on the Cape? You brought me back one of those snow globes but it cracked in your suitcase and was empty when you gave it to me?"

"It's the thought. Remember that." Ginny blinks at her boss. "And you gave me four weeks when you hired me."

"I'm pretty sure it was three."

"Honestly, Eleanor. You should write this stuff down."

It's possible she did forget. She has been mentally wrapped up in the adoption. And before that, the battle to get pregnant. God knows, Jonathan keeps pointing it out. "Okay, then. Christmas is fine with me."

With a triumphant grin, Ginny punches a number into her phone. She turns to Eleanor and covers her mouthpiece. "Do you mind?"

"Oh. Of course." Eleanor gathers her bag from the closet and heads to the front.

As she goes, Ginny says into the phone, "Hon? I just scored an extra week's vacation!"

Eleanor stops, hoists her bag farther up her shoulder. She should fire the woman. Anyone else would. Ginny is unkempt. She can't stand her own kids, let alone anyone else's. And she's surly to customers. But who else would hire her? And with the three boys, Ginny and Ted struggle financially. The Hardwells need the job.

"Ginny?"

Her assistant's dark ponytail pokes through the doorway as she leans way back in her chair. "Yes?"

"I was just thinking. What if she doesn't like me?"

"Not possible. Babies are hardwired to love their mothers, no matter what. I can't even pee without at least two of them following me into the bathroom and you know what kind of mother I am."

Eleanor smiles. "Yes. A terrible one."

"Exactly. Now get your skinny butt on that plane and go pick up your kid."

With a wave goodbye, Eleanor heads out the door.

Chapter 2

The suitcases line the entryway like well-behaved children waiting for recess. Eleanor sets her purse atop the tallest and pulls on a jacket. The cotton isn't warm enough for the cab ride to the airport, not on a rainy night in October, but she won't need a coat once they land. It'll be ninety degrees, and when they land in Palm Springs, the last thing she'll want is heavy wool outerwear for the long, dusty drive to El Centro, California.

"Hurry up," she calls to Jonathan, who hasn't come out of the bathroom since she got home.

Plane tickets, birth certificates, keys.

She stares at the bags—the largest of which props open the apartment door—and secretly hopes the elusive Valerie across the hall or one of the guys from the third floor will appear and ask where she and Jonathan are headed.

It doesn't happen.

Okay. Focus. Eleanor does a mental tally of what she's packed. It's important to think in terms of bodily zones. Otherwise things get left behind. You forget, say, the entire region of feet. Then you're left with no socks on a hiking trip. Or you may remember your face—soap, moisturizer, toothbrush, floss, lip balm—but neglect to consider hair. Now you're stepping out of a shower after a windy afternoon in Chicago with no comb.

"Trim that cool-guy stubble before we go," she shouts to the bathroom door. "It's prickly when it gets long and I don't want to meet her with a chafed chin. We're going to neck like teenagers over Louisiana. I once read in a book they had quicksand there. Whatever happened to quicksand, anyway? It's like the Bermuda Triangle. As a danger it just sort of vanished."

One bag sits at the front of the lineup, smaller but most important. This taupe Gucci-knockoff carry-on is Sylvie's. It contains the most precious cargo. Diapers. Formula. A doll. A crushable rattle. A muslin swaddling blanket. A pink ruffled dress with matching bloomers. A Kissy Kissy matching bodysuit, cardigan and hat. All sized for a child six months. They've been warned that Sylvie is tiny.

"I can't believe she's going to be ours," Eleanor calls to Jonathan, who still hasn't appeared. "What am I saying? She *is* ours."

Angus, a massive black Great Dane that better resembles a baby dinosaur than a dog, pants at her feet, huge bony elbows and knees jutting across the foyer. His uncropped ears work to catch any sound that might signify departure. Every minute or so he whines accusingly at the suitcases— the source of his distress. If they'd just stayed under the bed where they belong, his humans wouldn't be leaving. A growl emanates from deep within his barrel.

"Poor baby." Eleanor pauses to rub his nose. To Jonathan: "Don't forget, we have to drop him off. Cab driver should love a dog this size in the car almost as much as Angus loves the vet." Angus looks up at her and pleads with a thwack of his tail on the floor. "I need to get rid of my guilt. What was it you told me about dogs and their sense of time?"

He doesn't answer.

"Something like, they can sense when it's four o'clock every day but not the passing of hours, whatever that's called?"

Jonathan has a mind for scientific facts no matter what the species. "Linear time. That's a construct of a more developed type of brain."

"Right." She tickles the velvet of Angus's floppy ears. "We could be gone half a day to him, right? Not a whole week."

Silence from behind the bathroom door.

"Jonathan?"

"Mmm."

They got the news three weeks ago. A large envelope from California, the stamps depicting the state flag. Holding her breath, she tore open the envelope and scanned the letter. It was the news they'd been waiting for. Their adoption had been approved. The baby girl she and Jonathan had only seen in one photograph was theirs.

The infant's story is tragic, and unusual after a quake that injured many but only killed five. The Baja California earthquake happened April 4 in Mexico, earning it the nickname the Easter Sunday Quake. The epicenter was just off the coast of the Gulf of California and while Mexico was hit hardest, with the sides ripped off buildings, fallen telephone poles, and cracked roads, it was the strongest quake to hit Southern California in eighteen years. Skyscrapers shook in San Diego. Sporadic power outtages. Broken water mains.

In El Centro, in the far southeastern corner of California, the damage was largely limited to gas leaks, collapsed chimneys, and sheds. There were many injuries, but only one death: a young Irish-Vietnamese woman named Tia Kim, who had just moved into a forty-year-old apartment building. She'd been sunning herself on her main-floor balcony when the three balconies above collapsed on her and her three-month-old infant.

Sylvie Kim had no father on record, though with her pale green-gold eyes, caramel freckled skin and wild kinky hair that ranged from deep brown to blond at the hairline, she was clearly a striking mix of races beyond her mother's unusual background.

With only a disabled aunt as a family member, the infant was declared an orphan and placed in an already crowded foster home with five other children. There, she shared a room with two other babies. Eleanor and Jonathan saw her photo at Back Bay Adoption here in Boston. Eleanor took one look at the girl's cute-as-a-button face, stunning eyes wide with wonder, tulip-bud mouth half open, impossibly tiny white teeth, and fell hard.

They met all the requirements through the partner agency in California, including the paperwork and a home visit by the Boston branch to save precious agency dollars. Everything is finally in place. They've been approved and will finally have their little girl.

Now, two beeps from outside have Eleanor racing to the living room window. There on the sill sits a fat wooden picture frame she bought specifically for the stock photo it came with. A photo of a toothy family, all windswept and bare-toed and brunette, all in jeans and black T-shirts on the grass in front of a lake. Not posed stiffly either. This is no boring family. These people frolic, laugh, piggyback. As if this is life all the time, not just when a professional photographer is poised to immortalize them on a stock photo website.

This family is either whole, or doing a damn good job of pretending. Which is fine. She'll replace them with one of her own family soon. Herself, Jonathan, and Sylvie. And Angus, of course.

She leans over the photo to look down at the street. There, double parked, is a yellow Boston Cab glistening in the rain. "Car's here." She rushes to the kitchen to make sure the window is locked tight, then to turn off the lights throughout the apartment. "Jon!" She drags all the bags into the outer hallway. Another beep from the street. "It's rush hour. And we have to stop at the vet's first. Then we check in. Fight our way through the lineup at check-in . . ." One quick stop in the bedroom to make sure she hasn't left anything on the bed, to find she left something on the bed. She grabs the car seat and rushes it to the door. "Then the plane. Then the mile-high make-out because we're going to be parents but we're not going to be dull. Jonathan, hurry. *Sylvie!*"

A click. A thunk. The bathroom door creaks open. Her favorite room in the apartment. Deep porcelain tub, black and white hexagon floor tiles, many of which are cracked from a near century of use. The freestanding sink still has separate hot and cold faucets—a feature Eleanor finds charming and Jonathan does not. Keeps burning his hands, he says. He steps out from behind the door wearing nothing but boxers.

She stares at his bare feet, arms, chest. "You're not even dressed!"

He leans against the door frame. He doesn't speak.

"Hurry. Throw on some pants. We have to go."

A movement so small she doesn't realize right away that he's shaking his head.

"What? What's wrong?"

More honking from outside.

"Jonathan. Talk to me."

"I just. I can't do it."

"Can't do what?"

He doesn't move. Doesn't speak. She doesn't breathe. For what seems a lifetime, he stares at a spot on the wall just over her left shoulder. The front door is wide open and a chill from the stairway makes her shiver. A series of clicks as the heat kicks on inside the apartment. The honking has stopped.

Finally, Jonathan motions toward the bags and car seat in the doorway, the airline tickets on the hall table, the bedroom awaiting their adoptive daughter. "Any of it."

Chapter 3

Her first instinct is to bolt. To get on the plane without him. Without a word she grabs her purse, her passport, the car seat, then her bag and Sylvie's, and heads down the narrow staircase. She trips halfway down and her suitcase and the car seat somersault to the bottom, where the seat lands on its yawning face and the bag bursts open. Ignoring her T-shirts and panties splayed out on the tiny landing beneath the row of mailboxes, she rushes out onto the street to stop the driver from leaving.

The cab is gone.

It's okay. She'll repack her bag. Hail another cab. She'll get to the airport if it kills her. She marches back into the building to stuff sundresses and flip-flops and a tampon box back into the suitcase as Jonathan tries to stop her.

"Don't be ridiculous. You can't just show up as one half of the adoptive couple and take her with you."

"Oh yes I can."

"Eleanor, be real. We need to talk about this."

"I'll go get her, bring her back, then we can talk."

The case won't zip up. Eleanor shoves sleeves and stray

socks back inside the bag and leans her weight onto it. Tugs on the zipper.

"Eleanor. Forget it."

She tugs harder and harder on the zipper until part of it breaks off in her hand. Dropping back onto her heels, she sinks to the floor and stares accusingly at the metal slider on her palm. The scream inside her head comes out as a whisper. "How could you?"

A half hour later, they're back upstairs. Jonathan lowers himself onto the bed and leans over his thighs, rubbing his jawline. "Cassie Shreve from ICU's been telling us all these stories about her sister. Adopted a boy from Russia. Now the kid's a tween and a total horror show. Shoots coke, smokes in the house. He's barely fifteen and grabbed the car keys one night. Took off until the next day; they had no idea where he was. It's a nightmare. They have two other kids and thought they'd give back by taking in this orphan. Now their lives are ruined. Cassie said specifically: *don't do it*."

Eleanor sits on the other side of the bed. Reaches for a pillow and presses it into her abdomen.

This bed, king-size. She didn't say anything about children when they picked it out; there'd been too many miscarriages at that point and Jonathan had placed a moratorium on baby talk. "Every conversation doesn't have to be about how great our lives would be with kids," he'd said. When they lay side by side on the display mattress, he spoke about the way the pillow-top sunk down just enough that it felt like a full-body hug. He asked the salesgirl if it came with a warranty. If it was included in the Spring Price Wars promotion.

Eleanor didn't care about the price. She was busy imagining their baby on a Saturday morning, all fed and changed and happy, crawling around between them and giggling when the downy surface knocked him off balance. Or her. She hadn't shared her fantasy with Jonathan until the bed was delivered. He kissed her hand then and said they were going to have that one day. They were going to have it all.

"That's one case," Eleanor says now. "One boy. We don't know how they raised him. What mistakes they made."

"Their other two are honor students. Dream children. But their lives are being completely messed up by this Pavel kid."

"When did this conversation with Cassie even happen?"

He shrugs. "A while ago. Couple of weeks."

"And you've gone along with everything. Painting her room. Booking the flight. Letting me think you were onside."

"I guess I thought . . . I don't know what I thought. I'd change my mind or something. Getting this baby seems like it will fix everything. Like it will be the same as our own child, but it won't."

"Of course it will."

"You don't know what you're getting. It's too risky. The attachment bond is broken at the infant stage. Once that's severed, there's no repair. Not even with years of therapy."

She says nothing.

"The child can grow up to have difficulty forming meaningful relationships," he says. "They can reject those who love them and chase down those who don't in an attempt to win back the mother who rejected them. The damage can last a lifetime."

Sylvie's curly pigtails. Those sweet, streaky pom-poms above the tiny whorls of her ears. Eleanor will never get to touch them. To pull out the elastic bands and see what her hair looks like loose and wild. To bury her nose in Sylvie's neck and inhale the smell of her own child. To stare into those incredible eyes. "This is a *young* baby."

"Doesn't matter. Attachment is everything." He reaches over to squeeze her fingers. "It's not as if we're trained to handle this, even. We'd mess her up for sure."

She pulls her hand away.

"It would be different if she were our own."

"We can't have one, Jonathan."

"But why destroy our lives by taking on someone else's problem?"

"*I* was someone else's problem. And *I* turned out fine."

He hesitates a moment too long.

"I didn't turn out fine?" she snaps.

"Ever since we started dating, you've asked over and over if I'm going to leave you. And over and over I tell you I'm never going to leave you. Our entire relationship you've been certain I'll take off, like your birth mother did. How is that fine?"

It was true. Eleanor always knew he would leave.

They met at a pet store not far from the shop. Eleanor was still in business school and wanted a low-maintenance pet, something she could say good morning to and good night. She'd spent half an hour studying a little brown mouse working to tunnel through the corner of the aquarium, his furious efforts creating an impressive mound of cedar shavings behind him. There was something about his desire for more that she found admirable. As she priced out cages, a man with a narrow nose and a headful of black curls lifted a sack of dog food over his shoulder, only to have the bag rip open and kibble scatter across the floor like marbles. She rushed to help him, feeling her cheeks heat up when his green eyes were upon her. His wild hair, his Saturday-morning stubble, his lazy grin—men like this did not pay attention to Eleanor Prue. So when he asked her for coffee after, her instinct was to say no. But she didn't.

Ever since, through the engagement, on the honeymoon, and well beyond, she's been certain he'll come to his senses. Figure out she isn't worth his time. He'll suddenly notice something that escaped him before. Like how flat her hair is in the morning. Or that she can never pick a good movie. That her nose looks bigger from the left.

But he hasn't.

From the start, he said he loved the way her focus followed him, like a spotlight. Even if he left the room, left the apartment, he could feel her thoughts, her affection still with him. He was raised the middle child of five, by parents too busy trying to keep their framing shop in the black to pay one studious child much attention. Jonathan did well in school, he didn't cause trouble. The others just needed more. One with dyslexia, another partied away his future. Jonathan could raise himself.

Eleanor not only had time for him, but made time for him. And that was something he'd never before experienced.

Once in a bookstore he was riffling through the magazines while Eleanor debated between two just-released novels. She felt his eyes on her and looked up to find him staring, an odd expression on his face. *That's it*, she thought. *He's realized he's made a horrific mistake and wants out of the marriage. He's trying to figure out how to tell me he doesn't like my laugh and that he's done.* Instead, he came closer, draped his arm over her shoulders and said, "God, I'm lucky."

She would concoct scenarios in which she left him and he pined for her. Oh, how he pined! In one make-believe, oft-repeated sequence, Jonathan wakes up from a nap in the living room to find she isn't in the kitchen making her same old spaghetti with ground turkey that she always overcooks. Instead she's made ginger-soy glazed mahi mahi and spooned it onto platinum-edged plates she doesn't even own. He gets up and searches the apartment for her, baffled. Eleanor never goes anywhere on a Sunday night.

Then he sees it. Tacked to the inside of the front door is a note he can barely read through his tears.

> *Dear Jonathan,*
> *I'll always love you. I'll always wish you well.*
> *Goodbye,*
> *xox*
> *Eleanor*

"Baby, let's just go," Eleanor says now. "Meet her in person. Then decide."

He lets out a heavy breath.

"You may feel differently. You can't make a decision this big until you see her."

Jonathan gets up, moves to the window. Outside, a neighbor's balcony light goes on. Then off. Blurry red and white dots in the sky mean a plane lowering itself for a landing in the rain at Logan. Minutes pass, or hours. Maybe years. Finally, he turns.

"It's not just Sylvie."

Eleanor doesn't breathe.

"All these years of thinking about getting pregnant and trying to get pregnant. The thermometer and the sex that was no longer about sex but about a goal. And then the adoption frenzy—where from, and are we good enough, and home visits, and meetings with Nancy. You and me, we just vanished. Or you did."

"I didn't."

"When was the last time we had sex?"

"Sex? I don't know."

"Well I do. It's been a month and five days. And it had been two months before that. Almost three before that. I ask and I ask. And you keep saying you're tired."

"It's been rough, this process."

"We used to sit at the kitchen table on a Saturday morning and do the crossword puzzle. You actually looked at me when you spoke. And when you spoke it was about something other than ovulation charts or adoption agencies. You were right there with me. Present. You once faked a sprained ankle to surprise me in the ER, remember? And you'd snuck in a bottle of champagne in your purse." He laughs. "Damn near got me fired."

"That's not gone. We've just been living this battle for a baby."

"But that shouldn't break us. That shouldn't ever have taken over and replaced what we had. What we were."

"It hasn't. Don't you see? Once we have her, it'll fix everything. We'll be just like before."

"That's not the way it works, El. You don't get a baby to fix your life. We need to fix us first. Then we can see."

"I can't do it that way. We'll lose Sylvie. They'll give her to someone else. People are clamoring for her, you know that."

He slides his hands into his pockets and leans against the window frame. "It's the only way I'll even consider it."

"You're telling me to choose between you and my baby?"

"I'm telling you I'm no longer sure."

"About me, or about the adoption?"

"About anything."

The rattle of his keys as he stuffs them into his pocket. The sweep of air as he moves past on his way out of the room. From the hall, as the door swings shut, a sharp click, then footfalls down the apartment stairs.

She walks into the second bedroom and stares. The walls they painted yellow so the Boston climate would feel sunny to Sylvie, even in the dead of winter. The stuffed penguin poised atop the change table to offer her something to play with during diapering. The vintage trunk Eleanor covered with cotton batting and striped fabric, the lid of which Jonathan rigged with a safety hinge to protect small fingers.

She sinks to her knees and rests her cheek on the floor. The adoption approval had made Eleanor feel solid in her marriage for the first time. She doesn't know what about this evening is worse. The irony or the tragedy.

Chapter 4

Eleanor pushes the covers off her face and struggles to sit up. A slice of light made of dust motes travels drowsily across the bed, over Angus's bony legs, and along the bathroom floor. Nearly eleven, the digital clock says. If all had gone according to plan, she and Jonathan would now be nervously pacing in a motel room in El Centro, moments away from having Sylvie in their arms.

For the fourth, maybe fifth time since he left, Eleanor rushes into the bathroom and leans over the toilet, her stomach knotted from dry heaves. Like he did the other times, Angus clamors to his feet, gallops over, and watches, the tip of his tail twitching with concern. She drinks from the faucet and returns to bed, wiping her mouth with the back of her hand. She needs to call Nancy, her caseworker at Back Bay, but not before she comes up with a better excuse than the possible—probable—dissolution of her marriage. A marital separation at this moment is certain to stop the adoption process dead.

Sylvie's face haunted her all night long. Worse than Jonathan backing out, far worse, is the scene she can't get out of her mind.

Her foster mother, Cathy Siebert, the forty-something former factory worker Eleanor and Jonathan have never met, bouncing the child on her hip, telling Sylvie her mother and father are coming to get her. Their caseworker from the California agency, a young Hispanic man named Luiz, telling Sylvie she has a family now. A home. That she'll be getting on a big airplane and flying somewhere far away. That she is lucky. That she is loved.

Sylvie cannot possibly grasp the magnitude of what is surely going on, but she must feel the atmosphere crackle with excitement. At ten months of age, she must be able to understand that someone is coming for her. That this day belongs to her.

The anticipation builds. Any second now the happy couple will walk in to claim their most precious of prizes. But as the wait creeps into twenty minutes, Cathy and Luiz start to wonder. Luiz calls the agency. Asks if they've heard anything.

Thirty minutes stretches into an hour. Sylvie is placed back in her playpen or crib while Luiz and Cathy huddle over a desk or coffeepot and wonder aloud what kind of about-to-be parents simply don't bother to show up.

But it's the image of Sylvie sitting in the middle of her mattress, not knowing how badly she's wanted, that renders Eleanor unable to breathe.

Now, she punches Nancy's number into the phone and waits, her heart hammering in her ears.

"Nancy here."

"Hey. It's Eleanor Sweet." Her mind races for an explanation big enough to excuse missing the flight. Death in the family is too traceable. Illness, perhaps. Something swift and sure. But quickly curable, should Jonathan change his mind. Nothing comes to mind. She coughs into her hand.

"What's happening? I just got off the phone with Luiz," Nancy says, confused. "You guys didn't show?"

"I'm so sorry. Of all the timing—I'm sick. Haven't gotten out of bed except to throw up." At least that part was true. "The doctor said it's a sinus infection."

"Oh dear."

"Fever of a hundred and two. Everything hurts, even my fingernails." What if Nancy expects Jonathan to have gone without her? She quickly adds, "Jonathan got it first, then me."

"Huh. I didn't think you could catch a sinus infection." A pause. "Wait. You mean you're still in Boston?"

"We couldn't make it to the airport."

"Okay. You two focus on getting better. I'll sort things out on the other end."

"I'm devastated, Nancy . . ."

"With life comes puke. It can't be helped. I'll call you back in a few hours to rearrange things. Don't worry."

Eleanor hears a click and lets the phone drop into her lap. *Don't worry.* If only it were possible.

The cold morning air hits her like a slap. Eleanor stumbles out onto the foggy sidewalk and stands perfectly still, wrapped in a vintage cape she plans not to remove. Ever. The wool-blend tweed may be only thing holding her upright.

Part of her wishes she'd tried harder to make it to the airport. Maybe if she'd arrived in California as planned, maybe if the people there met her, if they saw Eleanor and Sylvie

together, they wouldn't care about Jonathan's sudden with-
drawal. They'd know, as Eleanor does, that this adoption was
simply meant to be.

Jonathan's exodus sits like a knife in her left shoulder,
of all places. There's something weak and needy about her
frame. It absorbs emotional pain and funnels it straight into
her trapezius. She wraps herself tighter in the cape.

The agency will nullify the adoption. Even if they allow
singles to adopt, would they give an already vulnerable infant
to a woman whose marriage combusted during the process?
Where's the stability in that?

Another pain pierces her shoulder.

A group of teenagers peer through the window of the
place next door, vacant since her beloved neighbor Birdie
Gross died, bringing the close of the tea shop she ran for
twenty-seven years. Eleanor looks up. Now, replacing the
flowery Birdie's Tearoom sign is a black backlit sign reading, in knife-slash font, death by vinyl punk, funk, and junk.
The logo is a d stylized into a skull, and inside the store, two
mohawked males graffiti a wall with spray paint.

Birdie would die a second death.

Music thumps from the new store. As Eleanor unlocks
her own door, she finds the music even louder inside Pretty
Baby. "Bohemian Rhapsody" by Queen. Loud enough to hear
Freddie Mercury's murderous confession to his mother. She
flicks on the lights and sinks onto the stool behind the cash.
It was wrong to come in. She should have stayed home to
come up with a plan. What to tell Nancy. How to save the
adoption.

Outside, Ginny fumbles with her keys, her eyes practically closed, a steaming coffee in her hand. That the door

wasn't locked escapes her notice. She walks in to drop her coat on the floor beside the diaper pails. Eleanor at the counter doesn't register at all. It's the light switch that does it. She looks up, confused that the lights are already on. Finally, she sees Eleanor and her mouth drops open.

"You won't believe it . . ." Eleanor begins.

But Ginny wanders over and touches Eleanor's clothes. "A cape? Are you freaking kidding me? And what's with this wool skirt over pants? And a scarf?" Ginny says. "It's like you're trying to sneak a new wardrobe, several new wardrobes, past Customs."

Eleanor is willing to admit she overdresses. But only to herself. "Runway models dress exactly like this, for your information." She pulls her cape closed. "Anyway . . ."

"Careful, I see a bit of skin here," Ginny mumbles as she tugs Eleanor's sweater sleeves down over her hands. "And here." She pulls Eleanor's scarf higher up her neck as Eleanor swats her away. "Wait a sec. Aren't you supposed to be somewhere warm?"

"He bolted."

"Who bolted?"

Eleanor shoves her hands into her pockets and feels around for bits of thread, paper. Anything to busy her fingers with. "Jonathan."

"What, he left?"

"He . . ." Her voice cracks. Somehow relaying the story to Ginny is making anger bubble up her esophagus. "I'm going to kill him."

It was almost morning when she heard the front door open—after four o'clock. Jonathan had come back. Eleanor lifted her face off the pillow in the dark, her neck tight and sore from sleeping on her stomach—though she wasn't really sure she had slept more than a few minutes at a time.

Instead of calling out to him, she laid her head down again and closed her eyes. Waited. Prayed.

Silence, then he was in the room. He must have tiptoed across the squeaky floorboards in the hall. She felt his gaze travel over her bare shoulders, the tangled mass of hair still damp from the scalding shower she calmed herself with before bed.

The pain of his silence was exquisite.

Say something. "*It was all a mistake. I'm in. Let's go.*"

The clock flicked to 4:12. If he spoke, she decided, she would refuse to say anything back. Nothing short of "Let's get on the next flight" would draw a word from her. *He'll realize*, she thought. *He'll see just how badly he's damaged things.*

The sound of him scratching himself. She forced herself not to look.

Say something! She wanted to scream it.

He moved away in the dark.

Hangers clinked softly in the closet. She opened her eyes. Watched the blurred shadow of him pull out a clean shirt. Dress pants. He disappeared into the bathroom. Came back with what sounded like his shaving kit.

If he wouldn't speak to her, she certainly wasn't going to speak to him. "Jonathan. Talk to me."

"Not right now." And he padded out of the bedroom and down the hallway—no tiptoeing this time—and left the apartment they'd shared since college.

Ginny stares at her as she scrubs at an ink smear on the wooden counter. "Seriously, what happened?"

"He doesn't want the adoption. Basically said it's Sylvie or him." Actually, that wasn't true. He said he didn't know about anything. Including Eleanor.

A rat-a-tat-tat of increasingly violent *no*'s from "Bohemian Rhapsody" next door, loud enough that Ginny covers her ears. "Holy . . . is that guy deaf?"

The bell tinkles to announce two women who can only be sisters with their red-brown hair, soft jawlines, and heavy eyebrows. Second only to their husbands or partners, the people Pretty Baby customers bring in most often are family members—sisters, mothers, mothers-in-law. Some familial similarities are obvious to everyone: similar coloring or a tendency toward heaviness or leanness. It's the more subtle likenesses that escape most observers, and every family has them. A squareness at the tip of the nose, a certain boxiness to the chin or marionette lines flanking the mouth. A narrowing at the tips of the fingers, most often with papery, oval-shaped nails. An upward tilt to the head when walking. A slight hesitation before speaking. These are the habits Eleanor has learned to look for.

In the way a person who has always been overweight might watch the naturally thin, or someone who has never been married might have a fascination with weddings, Eleanor cannot help but stare. She knows of no blood family at all. If there's a person on earth who shares her features, she has yet to set eyes on them.

The sisters wander toward the display of wicker bassinets next to the cribs—all of which are marked twenty percent off. The pregnant one, who looks like Ali McGraw, has a hand on her belly, a massive diamond glittering from one finger. Her shoes are black velvet slippers; the kissing *G*s of Gucci gleam from the toes.

"Are the bassinets on sale too?" she calls out to Eleanor from where she examines an oversized round bassinet designed more for style than function in a nursery.

Eleanor switches to automatic pilot. With a forced smile, she points out the safety features of the cradles and explains that they are not, in fact, discounted, but bassinets are a convenience the customer will appreciate at three in the morning, when baby wakes up for the third time. But when Ali McGraw makes a face, Eleanor adds quickly, "Of course, an infant can feel just as secure in a full-size crib if properly swaddled and that's a great way to keep nursery costs to a minimum."

Ali grins a toothy smile and reaches for her sister's hand, places it over her stomach. The sister—far less pampered-looking in batik skirt, lined forehead, and worn suede boots—nods. She looks familiar, but Eleanor cannot think where she's seen her before. "Yup," she says. "He wants to meet his Auntie Faith. Come for a sleepover." Faith yawns into her hand. "If Auntie Faith gets a full night's sleep ever again."

"Still?" Ali asks.

As Freddie Mercury screams an increasingly louder series of *no*'s, Auntie Faith looks at Eleanor. "I live right above that store."

"Seriously?" says Eleanor. "I don't think I've ever seen you."

"I work nights. Cashier at a twenty-four/seven. It's all very fancy. Anyway, the guy kept me up all day today."

Ginny grunts. "I bet he's ancient. And deaf."

"The place is called Death by Vinyl," says Eleanor. "I doubt the owner is ancient."

"If he keeps up with this, I don't know what I'll do," Faith says.

"I think I'm getting a migraine." Ginny rubs her temples

so hard she stretches her eyelids. "Frenetic sound is dangerous to my system. It mimics my children."

"We could call the cops," Faith says.

"I could bring my kids one afternoon," says Ginny. "Set
them loose in his place. No one can survive them for three
straight hours. Not even me."

"Oh, we'll give him noise," Faith says. "He'll regret the
day, believe you me."

"You can't get even with a deaf guy by making noise," says
Ginny. "We have to go drastic."

"No one's going drastic," says Eleanor. "I'll talk to him.
I'm sure he's reasonable."

"And if he isn't?" asks Faith.

Ginny grins. "That's when we go drastic!"

Faith glances through the front window. "Speak of the
devil."

They crowd the window display to gape at a tall man in
his late thirties, hair like a teddy bear that's been through
the wash a few times, dressed in requisite music-store attire
of ripped jeans, Band of Horses tee, and motorcycle boots.
With a rag in hand, he walks across the sidewalk toward the
road.

"Definitely not elderly," Ginny says, her brows raised.

Ali leans over a change table for a better view. "No
indeedy."

He wipes the night's rain from the hood of a black Audi.
The trouble is, the sky has started dripping again. No sooner
has he wiped down the roof than the hood is wet again. And
once the hood is gleaming, the trunk is splotchy.

"It's going to be a challenge," says Eleanor. "Catching
every raindrop before it hits the car."

Ginny turns to her in mock disgust. "I can't *believe* you just made fun of a deaf man."

"He was out here last night, doing the same thing," Faith says. "Walked round and round before it started raining to wipe off the aerospheric detritus."

"He's darling," Ali McGraw says. "In a slept-in-the-backseat kind of way."

As the rain grows heavier, the new store owner gives up and lopes back to his store for shelter. The women quickly feign interest in the change table they've been leaning over, lest he realize they've been staring. Only Ginny doesn't budge. She sucks in her stomach and waggles her fingers in coquettish greeting. He glances over them, completely disinterested, and disappears into his shop.

By noon, the rain has cleared. Nancy from the adoption agency has called three times. Eleanor has hidden from every call. Nancy's going to want to talk rescheduling and Eleanor doesn't trust herself to not burst into tears. She'd hoped Jonathan would have realized by now that this was simply a poorly timed case of cold feet; according to what Nancy said during their earlier visits, it happens all the time. Particularly to husbands. But with every hour that passes, this explanation seems less and less likely.

Jonathan hasn't called once.

She busies herself with inspecting diaper creams and baby lotions from an exclusive French supplier named La Jeune, pulling out several blue boxes wrapped in a rubber band. The tag identifies them as free samples. Oui ou Non, they're called. French pregnancy tests.

"Bohemian Rhapsody" continues to obliterate her cello music. Ginny's been complaining all morning about her head-ache. Faith from upstairs has passed by the window several times miming aural agony by cupping hands over ears and making a face. So when Eleanor sees the new store owner out front again, she puts away the samples and heads next door to find him kneeled on his own threshold, taping a Buzzcocks concert poster onto the door to cover Birdie's hand-painted cupcake. Not that his store appears to be one note. Below the Buzzcocks are an Andrea Bocelli poster, a notice for the upcoming Classic Christmas on Frog Pond, and a gigantic sticker of a black crow.

Eleanor arranges herself behind his Sex Pistols T-shirt. The Buzzcocks poster is crooked. Before she can open her mouth, Ginny booms from behind her, "I'M GINNY, THIS IS ELEANOR. WE'RE PRETTY BABY."

"Noel Bannon."

His face is actually quite pleasing with its Labrador brown eyes and library-book softness. It catches Eleanor by surprise and she struggles to regain her former anger. "We're just having a bit of trouble with your music. The volume."

"The volume's not high."

"I LIKE YOUR SHIRT. SO COOL." Ginny points to her own top. Then, in case he missed it, even louder, "COOL."

Two giggling preteen girls in puffy jackets and UGGs stop on the sidewalk and squeal. One claps her hands over her mouth and the other calls out, "Are you open yet?"

"No!" says Noel.

Disappointed, they walk away.

Eleanor turns back to Noel. "We can hear your music from inside our store."

He tapes down the corners of his crooked poster and Ginny thumps Eleanor in the shoulder. "YOU HAVE TO TALK LOUDER SO HE CAN HEAR YOU."

"I'm not deaf, Ginny!"

"IT'S HEARING IMPAIRED."

"He isn't hearing impaired. He already introduced himself."

"Why do you think he keeps his hair so long. To cover his hearing aids." To Noel she motions toward her ears. "YOU SHOULDN'T BE EMBARRASSED."

Mortified, Eleanor continues as if Ginny isn't there. "Could you turn it down a bit more? Ginny's getting migraines—she spent the entire morning lying in the staff room with the lights off."

Ginny reddens, smiles at him. "NOT THE ENTIRE MORNING."

"My customers are complaining—there's a woman who lives above you who works nights . . ."

He has the sweet, dusty-cotton smell of a house closed up for the winter. "I'm setting up my speaker system."

"By playing the same song over and over?"

"It's my test track. Has it all, the cappella, soft piano, thumping base, guitar riffs that could melt your face off. I can't go playing something else mid-setup. I'd have no way to compare my adjustments."

"I DANCED MY VERY FIRST SLOW DANCE TO THAT SONG. TIMMY RICHARDSON. IT HAS SUCH SENTIMENTAL MEANING TO ME."

"You don't like 'Bohemian Rhapsody'?" he asks Eleanor. Noel and Ginny seem to be examining her for signs that she's uptight, unsophisticated.

"Of course I do. I lost my virginity to it."

"Wow," says Ginny. "That is so not appropriate."

"And don't even get me started on Mercury's voice," says Noel.

"I *love* his voice," says Eleanor. "I saw him sing live a couple of years ago."

Noel blinks. "Mercury died in '91."

"Oh my God," Ginny whispers.

Eleanor feels her cheeks flash red. "Can we please just ease up on the volume?"

"I'm only playing it loud enough so I can hear it and make adjustments. I honestly do not have it turned up." He affixes the last corner of the poster and stands back to assess it. "Does that look straight to you?"

At the same time, Ginny says "YES" and Eleanor says "No."

With a grunt, he peels the poster off the door and starts over, this time taping it up even more crooked than before. "Something as random as the placement of my shelves can make the sound skip. It's a delicate process."

"OF COURSE IT IS."

The tinkle of a bell announces a woman wandering into Pretty Baby. Eleanor nods toward the store. "Ginny?"

With a goodbye to Noel that Eleanor fears might turn into a blown kiss, Ginny heads inside.

Eleanor turns to him. "So how long do you expect this delicate process to take?"

"As long as it takes." He tapes the poster up again and steps back to reassess.

His arrogance infuriates her. She snatches the poster off the door, sticks it back on perfectly straight, then marches

THE SEARCH ANGEL ❧ 39

back into Pretty Baby. As Ginny's customer inspects a wooden rattle painted in bold black and white graphics, Eleanor overhears her staffer say, "This is the kind of overpriced dreck you buy for your first kid. By the time you're on your third, you're handing them an egg carton and telling them to soften the cardboard by gumming it before they swallow."

Eleanor drops into a chair in the break room and her cell phone pings from her pocket. An e-mail.

Hey guys,
I spoke with Martina down in Palm Springs; you know how she can be. I want to give her a date just to keep things moving. Please get in touch as soon as possible.
Nancy

Chapter 5

After closing the store, she lets Angus out. Offers him dinner—which he ignores—and invites him to lie with her atop the bed, an honor he has never before been bestowed. He refuses, retreating instead to the dining room. Jonathan has been gone only twenty-four hours, but already the dog is upset.

Eleanor kicks off her layers and climbs under the cold sheet in camisole and panties. It's too empty, the bed. She stretches one leg across the expanse and tucks it close to her body again. She'll never be able sleep well without him here. Every night, without fail, she lays her head on his chest, wraps her leg over his thighs. It makes her feel safe. She reaches across for his pillows now and stuffs them beneath the sheets alongside her. The king-size for his hips and legs, the regular pillow for his chest. Pillow Jonathan looks lumpy and flat, so she fluffs him up to better simulate a man. Once she's satisfied, she wraps herself around him and stares at Jonathan's nightstand, the stack of books he's been trying to read for years but cannot get through more than a page or two before falling asleep, worn out from another long shift. There, on the bottom. *Crime and Punishment*. She bought it for him at a used bookstore.

It was a bitterly cold Sunday in January, before the strain of failed conceptions had tainted their lives. Snow on the sidewalks squeaked beneath their boots and taking even a shallow breath of outside air cracked the lungs. Tree branches were brittle with ice. The slightest pressure snapped them. Even the apartment seemed to have shrunk from the cold. Cupboard doors refused to stay shut and hot water taps ran warm at best. Eleanor and Jonathan needed to get out.

Bundled in big coats, jeans, and boots, takeout coffee in Jonathan's MG's cup holders, they blasted the heater and left town. The radio was broken and they were both too groggy for chatter, so they traveled along the I-95 with nothing but the snapping of road salt hitting the convertible's underbelly to entertain them.

They had no particular destination, just an unformed plan to wind up somewhere vaguely amusing. When they passed a sign for Otterville, they got off the highway. The town, really more of a hamlet, was surrounded by velvety hills dotted with sheep and cows, and consisted of a handful of historic cottages set right at the edge of the road, and two stores: Otterville Dairy, a tin-ceilinged shop with shelving original to the 1840s store, and The Book Nook, a labyrinth of small rooms that made up the main floor of a narrow Victorian. The restroom and kitchen, fully intact, groaned beneath used books and mismatched shelving that soared to the ceiling.

The prices were high. No book, no matter what its condition or size or obscure nature, was priced below ten dollars, and Jonathan and Eleanor determined ten dollars was too high for a used novel. The owner, a burly man in a fishermen's sweater, was in and out of a door that led upstairs. Every time he came back down he carried with him the sound of young children.

They might have spent an hour or more looking for books they could afford, sipping lukewarm coffee from Otterville Dairy, where they trust you to return the mug when you're finished. At one point, when the bookstore owner was shuffling papers from behind the counter in the store's living room, there came a thud from upstairs, then a wail. The man was up the staircase in a heartbeat. Minutes later he returned with a tear-stained boy on one hip. He set the boy, who was sucking in a chocolate chip cookie, on the glass counter where he could keep an eye on him as he worked. Eleanor turned back to the Classics section, looking for a copy of Jane Austen's *Emma*. They couldn't walk out without buying something. God knew how rare it was that anyone came to Otterville. Jonathan nudged her. Motioned toward the living room. Silhouetted by the large drizzly window, the boy had leaned forward, put a hand on his father's shoulder. He was holding his cookie out, watching while his dad took a small bite. The cookie went back into the boy's mouth and the moment passed.

Eleanor pulled *Crime and Punishment* off the shelf and peered inside the cover. She held it up. "Nine ninety-nine."

"I've been wanting to read Dostoyevsky."

"Let's pay for it and go."

"I also want that." Jonathan was still watching the father and son.

She pushed hair behind her ears. Smiled. "When?"

He took the book and headed for the cash. "Now."

As they say, that was then. This isn't. The sharp quill of a feather pricks her eyelid and she sits up, claps a hand over the stinging pain. She stares down at Pillow Jonathan, her eye watering. His abdomen, suddenly so downy and self-satisfied, infuriates her. Her well-being should not be dependent upon a man made of feathers! As hard as she can, she punches him in the gut. When the flattened pillow starts to inhale into the shape of him again, she unleashes her fury—kicking and punching until Pillow Jonathan lies in three battered lumps on the floor.

The phone rings from the nightstand. It's him. She picks up without saying a word.

"Hey," Jonathan says, the sounds of traffic in the background. A siren in the distance.

Breathing feels like a risk. Like a deer in a meadow, he could bolt if she makes the slightest sound.

"Are you still up?" he asks.

From beneath the dining room table, Angus stretches out and groans in his sleep. "Yes," she lies. "Just walked in."

"Did you get in touch with Julie?"

"I said you gave me a sinus infection."

"But sinus infections aren't—"

"I know!"

He's silent while she fiddles with the phone cord. In the background she hears the static of a car engine, then the tick-tick of a turn signal. He's driving. Maybe home.

"Where are you staying?" She tries to make it sound casual.

"My parents'. I thought about you all day."

She realizes she's been holding her breath and exhales. "Me too."

"I know how much you want her."

Eleanor's pulse quickens. She tucks her knees in to her chest.

"No one would make a better mother than you. You mother *me* even, making sure the blankets don't slide off me in bed. Checking the weather before I leave the apartment."

She tries not to look at the pillows on the floor. "I love you. That's why."

"I love you too, baby."

The sound of the engine in the background cuts out. Eleanor jumps out of bed to look out the window. Maybe he's down on the street. About to get out of the car and come back to their bed. Their life.

A few cars drive past in the dark. No sign of his Jeep.

"I'll call you tomorrow," he says, and hangs up.

Eleanor tilts her face up to let the shower pelt her eyelids. The pain is distracting. In the hour and a half since Jonathan called, she has left him three messages she now regrets. She couldn't help it. Why was he out at nearly one in the morning? Where was he coming from? Or, worse, where was he going? She tries not to think about the way the young nurses look at him and who may or may not have invited him to sleep on their sofa.

The best thing to do would've been to go silent. Not care. Isn't that what they say? That makes men come back. Or maybe it makes them chase you in the first place. They cannot resist your resistance.

She could back down about Sylvie. Just tell him, tell Nancy, that she's changed her mind. He was right. They were good before the pregnancy attempts.

When they found out she would never conceive, they walked out of the obstetrician's office and into a May afternoon bursting with life. Sidewalks glowed green beneath an umbrella of leaves. Downtown flower beds grew wild with heavy perfume. Office workers lounged on the benches, steps, handrails, winter skin hungry for the sun.

Eleanor hadn't said a word since they heard the news. She stood in front of the medical arts building, blocking people's exit from the revolving door. Jonathan gently led her off to one side and sat her down beside the fountain. He didn't suggest they stay hopeful. Hope was gone; they'd seen the ultrasound. He didn't try to distract her with suggestions of movies or dinner. He didn't try to talk.

He held her.

It was hours that they sat on that granite ledge. Her seat went numb, she remembers that much. The medical building had emptied out. Most restaurants had closed. But Jonathan continued to hold her. He'd have held her all night if she hadn't stood up. That was Jonathan.

The steam of the shower is too much now. She turns off the water. Dripping all over the floor, she grabs the top item of clothing in the laundry hamper behind the door. Rumpled and holey. Soft. His. She watches in the mirror as dark, wet spots spread across the shirt. She takes off her ring, sets it on the counter. Hates the lightness of her finger. Grabs the ring and slides it back on her finger.

Bundled in the duvet from the bed, wet hair twisted down her back, Eleanor pads to the kitchen and roots through the fridge for something to quiet her stomach. Nothing that requires any preparation. She finds eggs, frozen bagels, a piece of cooked but frozen chicken. All too much work. She takes a container of Häagen-Dazs ice cream, dulce de leche, and spoons it into her mouth.

Smooth cold ribbons of caramel melt on her tongue and she loses herself in the taste, dropping to the linoleum floor. Forget marriage, motherhood. Forget love entirely. All a person needs is dulce de leche and a spoon.

When she calls for Angus, he doesn't respond. She gets up to drag the reluctant animal out from beneath the dining room table and into the kitchen. Forced companionship is better than none at all tonight. She pats the floor until he gives in and lies down beside her on the floor. Watching. To her left his food sits, untouched, in its chrome bowl.

Offered a spoonful of ice cream, the dog crawls closer, elbows thunking on the hard floor in a way that sounds painful, and licks the spoon, then the container, clean.

Her right hip and shoulder feel bruised. Her arm is asleep. The warmth of Angus shifts slightly beneath her. They're still on the floor, the empty ice cream container between them. She takes his muzzle in her hand and wipes it clean with a corner of the blanket. His tongue slips in and out for what's left on his nose, then he stares at her, panting, as if hoping she has a better long-term plan for them than this.

She does.

Eleanor gets to her feet and heads into the bedroom, dragging the ice-cream-stained duvet behind her. Drawers open and slam shut. A hairbrush clatters to the floor. She slips into jeans, a long-sleeved thermal shirt, a sweater. She pulls on boots. If she's going to make a phone call this important, she's going to be well protected.

⫷

It takes until 7 a.m. to get up the nerve to ask. She sits at the kitchen table, phone to her ear, and twirls the cord around her finger. The dazzling sun pouring into the kitchen earlier has gone, to be replaced by a dense cloud cover. But for the amber glow from the oven hood, the kitchen is bruised over with shadow. Suits the moment just fine, Eleanor thinks as she explains and then waits for Jonathan's answer.

When she woke up, it became clear. There are two choices right now. She either walks into Nancy's office and tells her the truth—that Jonathan is gone—and risks never seeing Sylvie again. Or she doesn't.

A long sigh from his end. In the background, the muffled gong of the hospital PA system confirms what he's already told her. That when he called, he'd been on his way to work.

"Is this why you called so many times?" he asks.

No. "Yes."

"It's ridiculous."

"I don't have the luxury of waiting around to see what happens between you and me. Nancy's waiting for us and if she senses any trouble, they could give Sylvie to someone else."

"You're asking me to lie."

"Not lie. Pretend."

"Same goddamn thing."

"It's not like anyone's going to ask any questions," she said. "We look like we're together. We'll go in and meet with Nancy whenever she asks."

"And I fly to California and put on the show of my life?"

"I won't have you do that. We'll have Sylvie brought in with Luiz the way they wanted to do it anyway, remember? You'll just come with me to the airport."

"I'm really not comfortable doing that. Plus, there'll be follow-up stuff. You'll never pull this off."

"Please. I'm begging you."

"I just—I can't make such a big decision right now. I've got two cardiac cases waiting; I've been up all night."

"Just say yes."

"It's a terrible idea, lying to get a child."

"I don't care."

"It would be tough enough raising your own child all alone, let alone this way."

"'No one would make a better mother than you.' That's what you told me a few hours ago."

"Where would this leave *us*, El?" he says quietly.

She lets the moment lapse into grainy silence by staring at a hairline crack in the wall and mentally measuring the length. Fourteen inches, maybe fifteen if it continues behind the shelf Jonathan hung to display her cookbooks. Outside, a truck roars down Newbury. In the next room, Angus groans in his sleep.

"Okay. I'll do it."

Chapter 6

S omeone wonderful enough to know how much we needed you and generous enough to let you go." That was the answer every time Eleanor asked about her birth mother's identity.

Thomas and Marion Prue were in their mid-fifties before they seriously considered adoption. Marion herself, a school secretary, had been born to a mother of fifty-three. It hadn't seemed impossible that it could still happen for them.

They'd been living a hushed life in Hyannis, tucked away in a weathered cedar cottage at the end of a cul-de-sac, walking distance to the water. The house was perfect, they'd thought when they first saw it—waves of the Cape's blue mophead hydrangeas lapping at the split-rail fence that surrounded the property, massive trees providing a watery shade for children to play.

The original plan was this: Marion, a drugstore cashier, would retire early and take the kids to the beach every morning, teach them to swim. Unimpressed with the quality of teachers at the neighborhood elementary, she planned to home-school them. Snack and lessons after the beach, a healthy lunch, then naps all around. Three children they wanted. Two girls and a boy. Or two boys and a girl. In the meantime, as month after month passed without so much as a missed period for Marion, they focused all their attention on prettying up the house. Carefully lifting back the rambling roses from the wooden fence and re-staining it each year. Tugging dandelions out of the lawn with a skewer so as to keep the yard pesticide free, should the children ever come. Building a garden shed that for now would hold their tools, but later could be converted into a playhouse, complete with window that opened onto a covered platform, all ready for someone to play store. No make-believe shop owner worth his salt would allow his imaginary customers to get wet while counting out their pennies.

Hope withered gradually as, month after month, pregnancy tests came back negative. It dropped dead May 3, 1973, on a verdant stretch of freeway with nothing but grass trimmed as short as velvet and oak trees being softly strangled by English ivy gone wild. Marion wanted to plant the dark waxy groundcover in the garden and Thomas slowed to point out just how high up the trees the ivy had climbed.

"It's invasive," he said. "Chokes out the roots of native plants. Grows so thick it topples trees. Takes out entire forests."

"Entire forests?" said Marion. "One tiny vine?"

He made a sucking sound with his teeth. "Well documented. Look it up, if you like. Some states have made it illegal."

"Illegal. Honestly, Thomas." She nobly rearranged her purse on the floor beside her feet and sat back again. "On the house, then. Up the south wall—it's so plain on that side."

"Worse." Thomas stopped playing with the radio and

shot her a look. "Those little tendrils crack the mortar and then you've got moisture and bugs coming in."

They were driving back from visiting her sister in Sandwich, Massachusetts. Anna's husband had just left her for her best friend and she had wanted support while he picked up his things. Marion sat with Anna in the kitchen, while Thomas sat on the sofa, aggrieved, and clicked from channel to channel in search of a football game that didn't exist. It was mid-morning on a Tuesday. Football wouldn't be out of bed until the weekend.

In the car, Marion folded her hands in her lap and stared out the window. After studying a barn so splintered it had sunken in on one side, she grunted. "They don't make the cracks."

"Ivy vines? They most certainly do!"

"They wiggle their way into cracks that are already there. I did do *some* research."

"You should grow tomatoes if you want to keep busy. Can't go wrong with tomatoes."

This she didn't answer.

Thomas slowed the wood-paneled Jeep Cherokee as they approached a dark red minivan at the side of the road. He muttered something about the van being too close to the passing traffic. "See? This is how terrible accidents happen. People don't use common sense."

Marion hadn't noticed. She was busy watching a young mother slide out the side of the van, a boy in her arms, his grasshopper legs wound around her waist. The mother hurried toward the copse of brush to find privacy for her son to relieve himself, his hands bumping against her neck as they went. The Cherokee sped past and Marion turned around.

Mother and son were no longer visible. She settled back in her seat and stared down at the thinning skin on the back of her hands.

It was never going to happen for her. The window had closed.

Chapter 7

DC Manufacturing Inc. She has no memory of an order from such a company. It's happened before—that a manufacturer sends unordered product with an accompanying invoice in the hopes that the harried store owner will assume she's ordered the pacifiers or diaper covers or pillowcases and simply pay the bill. Eleanor has made a point of avoiding such trickery, in no small part because the mystery product tends to be inferior.

As has become usual, Queen thumps through the wall from Noel's place.

She punctures the packing tape with a pop and drags the knife along the length of the box. If the contents prove to be unasked for, she decides, she won't waste the money to return them. Maybe—this might teach the sender a lesson—she'll just place the merchandise on her shelves and sell it. Play stupid, as if she assumed it was a free sample.

Inside the box is one pair of gorgeous, hand-knitted booties. Pale yellow with a satin ribbon woven through at the ankle. Eleanor stares at them and smiles. It doesn't matter that Sylvie is too old for booties. Eleanor will keep them. They're the same yellow as her room.

It's a sign.

Everything is in place. She called Back Bay the moment it opened this morning. Made an appointment with Nancy for two o'clock. Jonathan swore he wouldn't be late.

Eleanor heads to the back of the store with her empty Mass General mug—a stocking stuffer from Jonathan a few years ago—and starts when she sees Ginny lying in a nursing chair, face blanketed with a French crib quilt.

"Don't tell me," Eleanor says. "The sentimentality of 'Bohemian Rhapsody' knocked you off your feet?"

"Grab me one of those nursing pillows, would you?" says Ginny, pointing to a pile of cushions and toys. "My head is going to explode."

Eleanor hands her a faded denim croissant-shaped cushion.

"No. Hold it above me."

Eleanor hooks her empty mug in one finger and holds up the pillow. "Like this?"

"Just press it over my face and hold it down until I stop writhing."

"That's it. I'll threaten him this time."

Ginny struggles to her feet. "Don't say it's because of me!"

Eleanor marches into the break room and sets about making a fresh pot of coffee. "Honestly, Ginny. What do you care what he thinks?"

"Did you see the guy? He's gorgeous. Even his name is gorgeous. Noel. Who's named Noel these days?" Ginny drops into a chair at the table.

"Well. Simmer down. You're married. With children."

"The headaches aren't my usual. These don't start out like typical migraines—no blurry vision or anything. This pain just slams me out of nowhere."

"You don't think . . ."

"What? It's a tumor? That's a nice suggestion."

"No. I just wonder." Eleanor waves toward Ginny's mid-section as she pours two cups of coffee. "You know. Whether you're all . . . babied up again."

"There is no way I'm pregnant."

As Ginny reaches for the mug, Eleanor says, "Maybe you shouldn't drink that until you know for sure."

Ginny cradles the mug to her chest. Her eyes search the wallpaper for confirmation, but the suggestions of fertility and pastoral bliss do nothing to help. "It isn't even possible. We never even had time to look at each other, let alone—" Ginny stops, closes her eyes. "Oh no."

"What?"

"Shit."

"What?"

"One night. There was one night, we had time. Mother of God, it cannot be happening again. It cannot. It cannot. It cannot."

It would be the worst timing of all Ginny's pregnancies. Eleanor's assistant does not suffer pregnancies well. She grows as big as a delivery van and the nausea lasts clear into the third trimester. Sylvie is coming and Eleanor will be alone. She'll need Ginny more than ever.

Without a word, Eleanor grabs a Oui ou Non pregnancy kit from the table Ginny recently labeled *Oops, I did it again.* Testing is a waste of time. Ginny is pregnant again, Eleanor can feel it in her left shoulder. In a few weeks, she'll be complaining about the fizzy feeling in her abdomen; no woman seems to be able to feel her baby's squirming as early as Ginny Hardwell. Feels like drinking too much 7UP and having the bubbles trickle up through your core, she'll say.

Eleanor drops the pregnancy stick into Ginny's lap. "I'm going next door. What'd you bring in your lunch? Anything sweet? Dessert-like?"

"A pecan-raisin butter tart, that's your threat?"

"I'm going to kill the guy with kindness." Eleanor shrugs as she opens the door to go. "If that doesn't work, I'll use my teeth."

"Tell him I say hi!" Ginny calls, ripping open the package and heading for the bathroom.

In the Death by Vinyl entryway, Eleanor stands face to face with a dusty brown ten-foot Sasquatch figure with a hockey mask for a face. A sign hangs crookedly from a chain around his hairy neck: go away. Nice. Good for business. In one of the creature's lifeless hands, being held by a foot, is a baby doll in a nautical playsuit. Behind Bigfoot are panels of chain-link fencing that separate the cash area from any customer foolish enough to believe the owner is remotely interested in trading merchandise for something as banal as cold hard cash.

In her hand is Ginny's dessert, wrapped in a pretty blue napkin. Not that she'll come right out and say the tart is home-made, but she did go to the effort of removing the Auntie Jane's Bakery packaging with its line drawing of a country cottage. Mass-produced baked goods—even those depicting curls of smoke coming from Auntie Jane's stone chimney—don't invoke a feeling of homey comfort. If Noel happens to think she went to the trouble of baking for him, well she'll simply correct him. It isn't as if she's planning to lie.

Noel's floors are much like her own: a beautiful worn stretch of planks mottled to black in spots. The ceiling, however, is painted charcoal, and strung from it are faded album covers that spin in the airflow, old metal fans, and a disco ball. Long plywood troughs hold thousands upon thousands of records, and, beneath the troughs, plastic milk crates hold even more—with handwritten signs prompting customers to *Check out these records too!* with an arrow pointing down. Also beneath the troughs are dusty old record players that seem to range wildly in price from $25 for one assured to not be in working order to $160 for one in "good condition with sweet-ass needle."

The music, no surprise, is "Bohemian Rhapsody."

She catches sight of a framed photo on the cash desk and stops, leans closer. The grinning woman is classically beautiful with deep-set eyes, curly black hair, and an unself-conscious smile. She sits in front of a birthday cake ablaze with candles.

"I'm not open yet." Noel doesn't look down from the top of a ladder. Over his head, a stoplight changes from yellow to red. "Try again next week. Or the week after."

"It's me. Eleanor." She holds up the tart. "I just came by to offer you a pastry. And to insist you turn down the music."

He glances now. "I'm kind of in the middle of something here." He motions with his screwdriver toward the closest speaker. "If you don't mind."

"It's customary, among the humans, to be appreciative when someone brings you a treat."

"I'm not into sweets."

"But I baked it myself. From *scratch*."

No reaction from him.

Her exit is blocked by a stooped man who has wandered in, his hat in his hands as he slows to examine the Sasquatch.

"Do you carry John Coltrane?" he asks Noel. "I'm looking for the album *Black Pearls*."

Eleanor is standing beside the Jazz section and allows her eyes to travel the names. She walks her fingers through the *C*s to *Coltrane* and pulls out the album. "Here it is. It's marked twenty-nine dollars."

"That seems a bit high," the man says.

"I agree. I mean, the jacket is all dinged up." Eleanor pulls out the disk. "The record itself looks pretty good . . ."

"I'm not open for business yet!" says Noel.

"Would you pay nine ninety-nine?" Eleanor asks the man with the hat.

He digs through his pockets and hands her a ten.

"I don't have a penny," she says, putting the album in his hands. "Noel will owe you a penny."

"Is nobody listening? I'm not open yet!"

"It's fine," Eleanor says, shooing the customer out.

The man nods, unsure of what just transpired. With an accusatory glance at Noel and the album pressed tight to his chest, he scurries out of the store.

"Come again!" she calls after him. Once the door is shut, she says, "Well, there's a customer who'll never be back."

"Hey. Sign on the door says 'Closed.' Technically, the guy's trespassing." Noel leans into the screwdriver and gives it a few mighty twists. In a low voice he adds, "As is anyone who walks in here uninvited."

"Excuse me?"

"Thank you for the cupcake—"

"It's a butter tart!"

"Thank you for the butter tart, but I don't eat dessert." He nods toward the door. "So if you don't mind . . ."

Her chest heaves with as much indignation as if she'd been up all night rolling dough. She takes the tart between two fingers, holds it up so he can see it, drops it to the floor, and mashes it with her heel. On her way out, she calls, "Turn down your music!"

"Sound is what I sell. I can't not display it!"

The relative calm of Pretty Baby is a relief after the surreal interior of Death by Vinyl. At least here, things make sense. The items on the shelves are for sale. Customers walking in are encouraged to buy them. The entire place is Sasquatch-free. Eleanor grabs a stack of baby books and arranges them on a shelf, fuming. "What kind of person refuses a tart? Even if you don't want it, you accept it! You don't stare down from your stupid ladder—which was not even positioned very well, I might add—and pretend the person who just walked in with a tart she may have spent an entire evening baking for all you know . . . you don't just pretend she walked in empty-handed. I mean tarts—they're not like cookies. You have to roll the crust, cut it, bake it, and then, once you add the filling, cook it again. I swear to God, I'm not talking to that guy again. From now on you'll do the communicating." When Ginny doesn't respond, Eleanor looks around. "Gin?"

The door to the restroom is still open. The test! Eleanor rushes to the back of the store to find Ginny hunched on the toilet, pants around her ankles, staring at the pregnancy stick. She lifts her tear-stained face and shakes her head.

"Don't tell me."

"I swear, all it takes is the sound of his belt buckle and

there I am. Pregnant again." Ginny looks up, unbrushed hair curtaining a face already puffy with maternity bloat.

A fourth baby for a woman who'd been determined to have none.

The pain is spreading to Eleanor's neck. She reaches up to rub her shoulder.

Chapter 8

Jonathan is late. Eleanor watches the other people in the agency waiting room and tries to stop her hands from shaking. Couples, all except the one who just walked in. There, in the corner, behind a crisp copy of *House Beautiful*, this single woman seats herself, a graceful, olive-skinned creature with bare ankles. With light brown hair pulled off her face and a long neck, she could be a ballet dancer on her day off. There's something self-conscious in the way she keeps checking her watch, swiping nonexistent lint from her lap.

Eleanor picks up *Parenting* magazine and tries to focus on an article about teething, but her attention keeps drifting back to the dancer. Surely there have been other people here in the agency alone, but not until now has Eleanor paid any attention. Why is the ballerina by herself? Could this one have been dumped recently as well? Or is she going it alone? She's delicate, this girl. Unsure of herself. No earth-mother aura to her whatsoever. It gives Eleanor a thrill. If this one can raise a child on her own, so can she.

The cherub-faced man at reception—Miles, Eleanor has heard him called—wearing a modern shrunken suit that exposes leopard-spotted socks, stands up and calls out "the Needhams?" A petite couple, pink-cheeked with excitement, follow him down the back hall to one of the caseworkers' offices. Moments later, Miles is back to set a fresh pot of coffee by the plants on the windowsill. A stack of Styrofoam cups needs straightening and he takes care of it. He nods at Eleanor. "Nancy will be right with you?" She remembers him from her other visits. Phrases every statement as a question in a way that suggests a good-natured lack of confidence. It made her like him right away.

She pulls out her phone and stares at it, willing a text to appear from Jonathan telling her he's looking for a parking spot.

It was over a year ago that Eleanor and Jonathan came in to try to convince Nancy Stachniuk they were worthy. Eleanor nearly buckled under the scrutiny, terrified the agency would come across some minor infraction from the annals of her life, something as benign as an unpaid parking ticket, and use it to prove that nature was, in fact, all-knowing, and that Eleanor was not qualified to become someone's mother.

A twenty-something couple sits across from her with clasped hands. Eleanor recognizes the nervous giggles, the toes pointed inward in submission. The woman, a reddish-blonde with only a hint of a chin, appears more nervous than the man, who is prim and controlled in his fitted polo sweater and polished brogues. He has one arm around her shoulder, squeezing it rhythmically.

The blonde's purse lies on its side between her feet, its contents oozing out onto the navy carpet. Eleanor leans forward and smiles. "Your wallet's on the floor." She motions to the purse. "I just don't want you to lose it."

"I'm a mess when I'm nervous." The woman leans down to pick it up.

Her partner grins affably. "This application process is rigorous, don't you think?"

Eleanor nods. "I was so desperate to appear good I was afraid to put my hands in my pockets in case they thought I'd just stolen a pen."

The door flies open and a tall bearded man in square glasses and turtleneck walks in, catches the eye of the dancer, and hurries to her full of apologies. They kiss and whisper excitedly.

Ballerina Girl isn't alone.

The blonde woman asks, "How far along are you in the process?"

"Approved. We're just sort of . . . working on the date."

"Oh, how wonderful," she says. "To be at your stage—I can only hope we get there." She looks at her partner. "Can you imagine, honey?"

"Dream come true," he says. "Total dream come true."

Eleanor's phone pings. She looks down to see Jonathan has texted: *Sorry, El. Thought about it some more. Not comfortable doing this.*

She sits back, wills herself not to vomit.

Miles calls out, "Jonathan and Eleanor Sweet? Nancy will see you now?"

Eleanor stares at her phone. Texts a response to Jonathan. *I'll do it without you, then.*

"Mrs. Sweet?"

She stands, drops the magazine to the floor, and fumbles to pick it up.

"Are we waiting for Dr. S to arrive?" Miles asks as she approaches.

"Just me today."

The young couple nearly bounce out of their seats with good-luck waves. Eleanor nods her thanks and waves back, nauseated.

She follows Miles's spotted socks along the hall, trying to formulate a new plan. The truth. That's all she has left.

"You remember where Nancy is, love? Second door on the left?"

The entire wall behind Nancy's desk is plastered with photographs of happy clients with their adopted children. These freshly formed families pose atop bicycles, in front of the Eiffel Tower, at the kitchen counter, and lying on their backs making snow angels. Some have faces slathered in chocolate birthday cake, others in spaghetti sauce. But all are grinning.

"So," says Nancy, sipping from a can of Nestea. A droplet lands on her sweatshirt and she frowns. "You're feeling better?"

Eleanor pulls her cardigan closer. "Yes."

"Good. And where's Jonathan?"

"He isn't here."

Nancy's laugh has an edge. "I can see that. He's not well yet, I take it?"

"No. Not really."

There's no benefit to delaying the truth. There's no way around it. The best thing is to just blurt it out and suffer the consequences.

"Poor guy. I had a sinus infection once. Thought my face was going to explode."

"Nancy?"

"Hmm?"

"We weren't really sick."

"I don't understand." The pop can returns to the desk.

"Jonathan left me."

"What?"

"He walked out."

"Oh shit." Nancy's chair squeaks as she slides closer. "Because of this?"

Eleanor nods. She feels sobs coming on and digs her nails into her thighs. She cannot break down. She must appear strong. Fiercely maternal and capable. Able to raise cribloads of babies all on her own.

Nancy reaches out and squeezes Eleanor's hand. "Hey. It happens. It sucks, but something as huge as adoption can break a couple. It's not the first time I've seen it."

"He's all about the attachment problems, what might go wrong . . ." Her voice quivers and she stops talking rather than risk a sob.

"I know. And he has a point. There is a higher likelihood for emotional problems with some of these kids. You don't go into this halfway."

Eleanor reaches for a Kleenex on Nancy's desk. "Last night, I actually begged him to lie to you. To pretend we were intact so you didn't pull the adoption." She presses a tissue into the corner of one eye and then the other. "I shouldn't be telling you this."

Nancy smiles. "Well, I'm glad we didn't go *that* route. Not that I haven't been there before too." She watches Eleanor.

"So. You're here in front of me. It's out in the open. What do you want to do?"

Eleanor tucks her hair behind her ears. "I want to adopt her on my own."

Nancy pauses. Presses her lips together thoughtfully. "It's not the ideal, but certainly adoption by single parents is a growing trend in many countries," says Nancy. "I know of a single woman who had success in China. Russia and some of its former republics welcome singles. It's not typical, singles adopting, but it's happening more and more. Guatemala is another country accepting them."

Eleanor stares at the woman who's been working with her for the better part of a year. What does Eleanor care about Russia or China? "Sylvie's from the States."

"The problem, for single adoptive parents, doesn't just lie in the agency or country's approval. It can be difficult once you bring the baby home. Friends, family, sometimes they jump in with their own judgment. That's something to consider."

"Yes. What about Cali—?"

"Guatemala is really on the forefront. Same-sex couples qualify in Guatemala. Huge draw for gay couples."

"Okay, but—"

Nancy sits forward in her seat and folds one hand over the other. "Sri Lanka doesn't adopt out to singles."

"Nancy. I only want Sylvie. I want to go ahead with this adoption. Not another one."

"We're cool with single parents adopting here. We're good."

Eleanor falls back in her chair. She closes her eyes for a moment to process this, then leans forward on the desk. "So Sylvie's still mine? That's what you're saying?"

"Every agency has their own policy—some don't accept singles at all. But here, we see it like this: Not every couple that adopts will remain a couple. And not every single parent will remain single. We look at a person's strength and character. His or her parenting potential. You own the hottest baby store in the city. It's not everything, but it gives us a certain amount of ease. There will be some new paperwork to fill out, satisfy us that your finances can support a child, that you have appropriate care for her while you're at work, etcetera. But the real thing is: we need to see you have a strong support system—this becomes more important than ever for a single parent. This we do not waver on."

She can have Sylvie. Eleanor allows this to sink in a moment. "By support system you mean child care, that sort of thing?"

"I mean friends and family. You need at least one dependable person who lives nearby, who is going to be there for you day or night. Are your parents close?"

"My parents are dead."

"Siblings? Uncles or aunts? Cousins?"

Eleanor searches her life for middle-of-the-night support. Jonathan, really. He was her support, has been since her adoptive parents died two years ago. There are no siblings. No cousins, but for her dad's second-cousin Jeremy who runs a whale-spotting boat tour out in Maine.

"No siblings. Aunts and uncles and cousins aren't around here. But I do have a friend who works for me. Ginny."

"Okay. She's good with kids?"

"Well, she has three of her own . . . so."

"Is she the kind of person you can call at three in the morning to pick up Pedialyte at the drugstore? That kind of thing?"

"Well, her husband does shift work, but some nights would work, I'm sure."

Nancy frowns and leans over her desk. "You seem to be a bit isolated, Eleanor. I'd be lying if I said I wasn't concerned."

"No, I'm not isolated." Eleanor laughs too shrilly. "I'm surrounded by people all day long."

"We had a similar case a few months back: single woman adopting from Indiana. She was a little fuzzy on who, exactly, would be there for her in a pinch, but she was such a doll and worked as a teacher. Anyway, she convinced us. Four months into the adoption, she lost her job. Had to miss work one too many times because of colds, unreliable child care, a bout of chicken pox. Then she had a huge financial struggle, had to go on government assistance, what have you. Wasn't a great situation. My superior is fanatical now. We do not support single-parent adoptions unless the individual has a reliable support network."

Eleanor shifts in her chair. "So where does that leave me?"

"I can't in good conscience approve you adopting Sylvie on your own if you don't have more support, Eleanor. I'm sorry." Nancy opens a file on her desk and shuffles through the papers. "I know you've already had a home visit, but I'm going to book you in for another now, with this change in your situation." She looks up, her expression grim. "I'd like you to have at least one key support person there. Do you have a problem with that?"

Eleanor stands, slings her purse over one shoulder. "No. No problem at all."

"Oh, and Eleanor?"

"Yes?"

"There's a guest speaker coming next week. Get the details from Miles. I'd like you to attend."

Chapter 9

The package in her mailbox is from El Centro, post-marked two weeks prior. She knows exactly what it is—it's a DVD from the agency in California. Part of the deal through the agency is a video of your child, though Nancy warned them that some of these videos arrive after the child does. On the envelope, above the address, *Mommy* has been written in black marker, obviously by a caregiver. Eleanor races up the gritty stairs to the second floor and into her apartment.

She kneels in front of the DVD player and fumbles to get the plastic disk free while Angus watches from beneath the dining room table. "Angus, come sit with me."

With a forlorn groan, he drops his chin onto his paws and stays put.

She slides the disk into the machine and waits. Nothing happens at first, then the crooked chaos of the camera being held at someone's side, turned on, pointed at the ground. Children shouting, a baby crying, a TV blaring can all be heard in the background. A woman speaks, her voice deep in tone, almost masculine, but it's impossible to hear what she's saying over the din. Then the camera swings up. *There.*

Sylvie.

Moving. Babbling. Looking around.

Eleanor laughs out loud, her eyes stinging with tears. It's magic to see her in motion. To see her come to life.

That smooth caramel skin with freckles scattered across her nose and cheeks. Those eyes! They glow as if lit from behind. Her wild hair defies gravity. With adult hands cupping her underarms, she stands stunned and wobbly in a too-tight sleeper on what is likely her foster mother's lap. Eleanor's breath sticks in her throat as Sylvie looks off to the side, drooling as she sucks on a set of plastic keys.

To see her live like this. It's almost like having her in the room.

The camera pans back and more of Cathy can be seen. She's long-faced and tired in leggings, a big T-shirt, and pastel Keds. From her neck hangs a silver cross. The furniture behind her, it all seems to have been taken from an office. If not for the playpen to one side with two toddlers in it, and the TV blaring, you wouldn't know it was a home. Cathy smiles stiffly—clearly she's not comfortable in front of the camera, but the baby she handles with ease. A bird chirps from somewhere in the house. A lawn mower whines. Children race past and shout. The cameraman, likely Luiz, keeps saying, "Sylvie."

Sylvie is much smaller than Eleanor imagined, her hair longer and bushier, this time pulled back in a pink headband. No pom-poms. She's at Eleanor's favorite stage, just leaving infancy and bumping against that deliciously sweaty, drooling-puppy state of toddlerhood.

Eleanor cannot decipher what the foster mother is saying over all the background noise, but the woman points excitedly toward the camera lens to encourage Sylvie to look. The child does, but only as she reaches out to touch the lens in wonder. It's obvious Cathy feels some sort of responsibility or pressure to make the girl smile. She's been fostering for fifteen years. She knows what the adoptive parents want to see. She jostles and cajoles, then looks up at the camera as if to say it's impossible. Sylvie will not smile.

"Sylvie, say *Mama*," says Luiz, off-camera. "Say *Mama*."

Suddenly Cathy lifts the baby up in the air and bops her up and down. The keys jangle against Sylvie's wet chin, her red mouth exploring the plastic chain. Eleanor, still on her knees, shuffles right up to the screen, stares, barely able to breathe.

Then Cathy changes her tactic. She moves her face close to the baby's, then buries her mouth in Sylvie's abdomen, giving the child a raspberry kiss. Now, with the keys still in her mouth, Sylvie tucks one knee up to her belly, then the other, and a wide grin opens her face. Sylvie's laughing face fills the screen. Eleanor freezes the frame. A tingle spreads down her arms.

Nothing will stop her from having this child. Nothing.

Chapter 10

The way to accomplish the impossible is to break it down into steps. First you tackle the most doable. This way you get your bearings, you build your confidence. With any luck, by the time you reach the impossible, you're stupid enough to believe you can do it.

When Jonathan was onside with the adoption, the plan had been for Eleanor to oversee the store from upstairs for a month or so while Sylvie got adjusted. During this time, she would interview nannies to find one that was not only *the* most loving and capable nanny since Mary Poppins, but one that formed a quick and tight connection with Sylvie.

Again, that was then. Eleanor can no longer afford a nanny. It's time to arrange the next best thing.

Sunnyside Day Care was recently written up in the *Globe* as the best child-care facility in the downtown core. Located in an historic redbrick house with a wraparound porch, it has walls painted every color of the rainbow. There's a play station, an art station, a food station, a reading nook, and a closet full of rollaway mats for sleepy-time. Through the window, you can see the playground, complete with plastic climber, tricycles, and a grassy island upon which several young boys toss around a ball covered in stars. Bouncy music charges the air with enough fun that little ones are meant to forget about their parents for eight to ten hours, five days a week. The staff appear to be appropriately attentive and nurturing, and the children seem content.

All snacks and meals are locally grown and organic. When a new child joins, she is assigned a Sunny-buddy—an older child whose job it is to make the newcomer feel welcome. Most of the staff have been there since the day they opened their doors. Continuity. That will be especially important for a child like Sylvie.

The owner, Wendy Nicholls, a substantial woman with a friendly red tinge to her skin, pushes a clipboard across her desk to where Eleanor sits perched on a wooden chair. "We have a three-month wait list, but fill it out anyway. You just never know who'll move away, or whose mother decides to quit work and stay home full time. Your daughter could wind up with a spot in the next few weeks."

Your daughter.

Eleanor stifles what will surely appear to be a goofy smile and picks up the pen attached by a long string. The wait list isn't good news. Sunnyside is located within walking distance of the store—Nancy will like that. Being that she'll be raising Sylvie on her own, a farther day care isn't a great option. The form wants the child's name first. Eleanor enjoys printing *Sylvie Sweet*. Allergies, the form wants to know. Eleanor doesn't know this. She writes: *to follow*.

"How many on the list ahead of us?"

"Let's see now." Wendy reaches for a pad nearby and flips it open. "One . . . three . . . no, four. Four kids ahead of your Sylvie. But what often happens is a spot opens up and the parents have made other arrangements, the child gets nicely settled elsewhere and Mom and Dad don't want to disrupt things. So you could just as easily be next in line."

A knock at the door. A smiling woman in a painting smock and clogs leads in a young boy—no more than three— with bouncy yellow curls. His round cheeks are flushed, his eyes glassy. "Sheldon isn't feeling so well, Wendy." She lifts him up and sets him on a chair beside the desk and his legs dangle listlessly over the edge. He starts to slip his thumb into his mouth and the woman—her nametag says *Laurie*— stops him and wipes his hand with a disposable cloth from a package on Wendy's desk. Eleanor approves of the precaution. Laurie motions that it's okay now and the thumb disappears into his mouth. "We're thinking maybe a call to Mom is a good idea."

Wendy places the back of her hand on his forehead and nods. "You've got yourself a bit of a fever, sweetheart. Would you feel better at home with your mom?"

Sheldon nods, a big, springy curl falling over his cheek.

Eleanor continues to fill out the form—occupation, address, and phone number of mother's workplace—while Wendy attempts to contact the little boy's mother. She's not in the office and isn't picking up her cell phone. "Your mommy's out right now, but that's no problem at all." She dials another number. "Let's talk to Daddy, okay?"

Sheldon nods again and mumbles "Daddy" through his wet thumb.

"Oh, hello, Mike. This is Wendy from the day care— everything is fine—I don't want you to worry. But Sheldon isn't feeling all that great right now and we're thinking he'd probably rather be at home with Mom or Dad."

Laurie runs a hand over the boy's head. Father's name, workplace, contact info, Eleanor's form wants to know. She stares at the "Father" box, pen hovering above it.

"Okay, I'll tell him. Sorry to disturb." Wendy hangs up and smiles at Sheldon, giving his knee a loving squeeze. "He's already on his way, honey. Should be here in about ten minutes. Would you like a Freezie to keep you cool while you wait for Daddy?"

Sheldon's eyes widen. He gives a garbled and wet-sounding *yes*. His Velcro'd shoes bang together in excitement for Daddy or frozen treat. Likely both.

Sylvie would have to make do with the treat.

When Laurie leaves the room, Eleanor looks up at Wendy. Her words come out in a near whisper. "What if there's no father and you can't find the mother? Who do you call then?"

Laurie is back. The thumb is replaced with a Freezie.

"No worries at all." Wendy points toward the form. "We'll just call whoever's next in line. It's right there in the next box, see it? 'Next of Kin.' Your parents. Sister, friend. Aunts, uncles. A grandmother. Put down as many as you like."

Eleanor stares at the form. She has no one to offer her daughter but a Great Dane with a penchant for eating ice cream when no one is looking. She can't exactly put that on the form.

There was a fantasy Eleanor had the year she learned she was adopted. The movie *Annie Hall* had been on TV and Eleanor convinced herself Diane Keaton and Woody Allen were her parents. To imagine you sprang from the loins of famous people is common among adoptees, Eleanor would learn later. There's a certain comfort in the belief that in order to give you up, your parents must have been extraordinarily important.

Woody and Diane made perfect sense. They were together from 1972 to 1977, the timing was perfect. In fact, when Diane accepted her Oscar in March of 1978 wearing a shirt and tie, two voluminous skirts over a pair of pants, and her sister's socks, she could very well have been hiding post-pregnancy baby weight. Eleanor was born in '75, but still. Diane is a busy woman. She mightn't have had time to hit the gym.

It explained everything. The crooked nose her adoptive mother called charming. Pale skin that refused to even freckle. A tendency to overdress. *Très* Diane, she convinced herself. From Woody, her diminutive frame maybe? Her poor eyesight? Definitely insecurity.

She made it a point to look up every movie they made together. There was *Play It Again Sam* filmed in '72, *Sleeper* in '73, *Love and Death* in '75, and then *Annie Hall.* The way Eleanor sees it, she was conceived during the pre-production phase of *Love and Death.*

It had to be. Especially when you consider Diane went on to adopt her daughter in '96, her son in 2001. She must have felt at least some guilt for giving up Eleanor . . .

Nancy is right. She's in trouble.

Chapter 11

The next afternoon, a heavily pregnant woman with muted red-gray hair walks in with two much older women, one obviously a relative with the same reddish hair, barely-there cheekbones, tiny ears, and inward tilt to her knees. The other one more solidly built, mocha-skinned with short hair grayed to white. They head straight for the furniture displays.

It is clear, beyond the facial similarities, which one is the pregnant woman's mother. What surprises Eleanor is the pregnant woman's ease with the other woman, the one with the darker skin. It goes beyond mother-in-law, has none of that polite deference. The way she slips her arm through this woman's. She's close with this one. Closer than with her look-alike.

They prowl the cribs. Running their hands over side rails. Leaning inside and pushing down on mattresses, everything but climbing inside and curling up for a trial nap.

The apparent grandmother lowers the rail on the white lacquered Dearest One crib, the highest-priced crib in the store. When the rail doesn't lower right away—this crib has a tiny lever on either side of the frame—the mother-to-be turns away. "Forget it. I read an article about that. Stubborn crib sides. It said they contribute to accidents because the parents delay lowering the mattress as baby grows. Too damned hard to lean over."

"I never lowered the rails once," says the white-haired one. "All three kids, I just leaned in and picked them up. Who needs an extra step?"

Eleanor walks over. "This one is funny. The levers aren't where you'd expect." She shows them the shiny chrome levers and lowers the side with ease. It's a good crib. The same one she has upstairs for Sylvie. Solid hardwood and a nice sleek design. "Costs a bit more up front but it converts into a day-bed for later. You really get your money's worth."

"Is there any discount on it?" The pregnant woman has a hand on her belly. "It's gorgeous but, you know, having a baby is so pricey."

"I'm afraid not. I'm selling it below suggested retail as it is."

She sighs. Moves toward another crib but doesn't seem happy with what she sees. Pretty Baby's most popular model with its recognizable name and appealing price tag. She moves the rail up and down. "This one works better. Plus I like the dark wood." She turns to the white-haired woman. "Try it, Mom."

"I like the glide, sweetie. It's nice and smooth. But don't you think the wood makes it too boyish? You could be having a girl, don't forget."

The pregnant one looks up. "I love it but it's way too much. What do you think, Belle?"

Belle, hugging her purse to her belly, waves away her own opinion. "Oh, it seems pretty enough. It's just the price."

The pregnant woman is adopted. Eleanor is nearly certain.

"This crib is antique pine. Still solid wood but not nearly as bossy as the dark one. And half the price." More than any other customer she's had, Eleanor wants this mother-to-be to make the best choice. "The crib people buy most often when they're unsure about the sex, this is it. It's more neutral. More so than white even, which tends to feel girly once the boy is born. It's weird, before baby comes, how you might think this or that is neutral. Then little Sasha comes home and her green walls feel G.I. Joe instead of natural forest."

The young mother bounces her hands on the crib rail. "Okay. This is the one, then." According to her AMEX, her name is Liza Robbins.

Payment is made, delivery is arranged, and all the while Eleanor is dying to say something. It isn't until the women have left, until they're piling into a cab out front, until Eleanor is certain she'll never see them again, that she gets up the nerve. The doors are slamming shut, but Liza sees Eleanor on the sidewalk and lowers her window.

Eleanor leans in, apologetic and embarrassed. "I'm sorry to pry . . . I have to ask. Are you . . . Is this an adoption, the three of you?"

Liza laughs. "We confuse everyone." She touches the dark-skinned woman's arm. "Yes. This is Jan, my adoptive mother, the woman who raised me—brave thing!"

They all laugh. Then Belle says, "I'm the birth mother. I got pregnant way too young and"—she pauses to swallow, release a deep breath—"ugh, what can I say? I was stupid."

"Don't say that. You were smart. And brave." Liza turns to Eleanor. "I only just found my birth mom two years ago. When my son was born, he had a few health issues. I needed some family history."

"Thank God you did. I'd tried everything to find you," says Belle. She pats her daughter's stomach. "At least I can be there for this one's birth."

Liza adds, "My poor husband. Two mothers-in-law."

"Was it hard?" Eleanor asks. "Finding your mom?"

"It was more scary than hard. What if she refused contact? What if she was no longer alive? That sort of thing. But the procedure, I just contacted the state where I was born and they had open access. I got lucky."

Belle hooks her arm through her daughter's and beams. "So did I, baby." Jan links her other arm. "We all three got lucky."

Eleanor has never told anyone. Not Ginny, not her friends from school. Only Jonathan. She didn't even know herself until she was thirteen. "I was adopted."

"Oh, sweetie . . ." Liza looks at her.

No one outside the adoption community can possibly fathom the enormity of those three words. That wound is primal and forever. Sometimes a piece of lint in your pocket, other times the size of the whole world. This Liza, she may have found her birth mother but still she calls her Belle.

". . . have you and your birth mother been in touch?"

Eleanor rubs her left shoulder. "No. She never . . . And my adoptive parents were against it. Plus, you know. Where to begin. And all the what-ifs."

"Do you know her name?" asks Jan. "Where you were born?"

"Smith . . . and Kansas. I know my birth date. The hospital. That's it, really."

"Look it up online. Plug in all the information on a search site and see. Or go to Kansas, to the records office. It's an open state." The cab starts to move and Liza waves out the window. "You'll have what you need in no time."

Eleanor watches the cab pull into traffic.

It's time to stop waiting for her mother to appear on her doorstep. If Eleanor was never brave enough to start the hunt for herself, she's brave enough to do it for Sylvie. But there's someone she needs to speak to first.

Chapter 12

There's a corner by the entrance of Glen Manor cemetery that is as yet unpopulated. Thick with sugar maples that have all but lost their fiery leaves—the few robust hangers-on, like the last guests to leave a party, continue to twirl and wheel for another day, perhaps another week if the October winds are kind. This area is not as well tended as the rest of the grounds—the caretakers are content to treat it as wilderness until a boom in human expiration dictates further expansion. For now, the forest floor is buried in fallen leaves, all of whom are free to luxuriate as long as they desire.

It suits Angus just fine.

The moment Eleanor unclasps Angus's leash, he lopes straight toward the nearest pile and drops to the ground, wriggling on his back and clawing at the out-of-reach treetops with great, bony toes. He turns his head left and right, and snaps an angry warning at any debris obtuse enough to remain within reach.

"Angus," she pretend-scolds, thrilled to see him behave normally. "Have a little dignity. You're probably rolling in something gangrenous."

The teacups and saucers in her basket make comforting

clinks as she follows the dog to their usual spot. After Eleanor moved out of the house, Marion, her adoptive mother, always had her home for Sunday afternoon tea. They each had their own special cup: Marion's bone china and dotted with tiny pink rosebuds, Eleanor's more austere with its simple band of platinum. Always English breakfast tea with milk and half a sugar. Always Paterson's shortbread. The ritual remains, with the location changed and the conversation decidedly one-sided.

They didn't have much in common, all those years. Marion was good and kind. But her days of chasing a youngster around a park were behind her. She adored Eleanor but had the interests of a retiree—the garden, her knitting, the growing pain in her knees. The one thing they did share, Eleanor wouldn't discover until much later in life: infertility.

She stops in front of matching black granite headstones. *Marion Prue, loving wife of Thomas and mother of Eleanor Jane. Thomas Prue, cherished husband of Marion and father of Eleanor Jane.* Angus knows the drill. He leans down into a deep downward dog stretch and lies down between the stones. Eleanor sets the china on the grass and pulls out a battered tartan thermos, pours tea into the cups. The dog looks up, pants expectantly until Eleanor tosses him a cookie. He usually catches it in his mouth and swallows it whole. This time he watches it land in the grass and stares at it.

Ridiculous that she thinks of herself as abandoned by them. She's thirty-five, for God's sake. Thirty-one when they died. They did all that parents are meant to do. Marion stayed home and raised her. Thomas taught her to read. They attended her dance recitals and swimming lessons. Took her camping in Vermont.

On her birthday every year after she turned fourteen,

Marion woke her up with this: "Your birth mother is think-ing about you today." And Eleanor would imagine Diane Keaton, lounging in an historic Los Angeles home, Spanish in style, surrounded by Mexican art and dogs. Maybe sipping a cup of tea and wondering how Eleanor was doing. Whether her heels had a tendency to blister with new shoes and how many times a week she washes her hair.

One day, Eleanor fantasized, she'd find in her mailbox a letter written in elegant script. Diane couldn't possibly know her adopted name, but somehow the letter would be addressed to Eleanor Prue. There wouldn't be a reply name or address in the upper left corner because very famous people, people too important to keep a baby whose existence is troublesome, have to be careful about security. They have to be guarded. But the letter inside would be anything but cautious. It would gush on and on about regret, longing, and how the important thing was that a private plane was waiting for Eleanor at Logan International Airport. That a man in uniform would escort Eleanor aboard and sitting inside would be her parents: Diane and Woody, so happy they could burst. They would embrace her and shower her with kisses. Most of all, apologize.

It was at this point in the reverie Eleanor would think to bring in Marion and Thomas. They'd get on the plane after Eleanor, and the five of them would be one big, happy sprawling family.

"Mom. Dad," Eleanor says now to the headstones. "I want you to know that what I'm about to do has no bearing on the two of you as parents. You gave me the very best you could and I am forever grateful. It's time I contact my birth mother. The reason isn't important—well, Jonathan turned out to be a piece of shit who walked out on me and now my life is a total—"

A flash of movement to the left of her. A man in a leather jacket bent over a grave.

He shields his eyes from the sun and squints. "Eleanor?"

Noel. She ducks down behind her mother's headstone and gathers up the embarrassment of finery spread out upon the grass. As quietly as she can, she stuffs the cookies into the basket before he sees her juvenile display.

Too late. He's already standing over her. "Tea party?"

"No." She dumps out her tea, drops the cup with a clink into the basket, and slams the lid shut. "Just . . . nothing."

Noel pats his thighs until Angus hauls himself to standing, wagging his tail. Noel holds up a piece of muffin. "May I?"

"No. He detests sweets," she says with an edge.

Noel offers it anyway and Eleanor sits up taller, prepared to savor the dog's rejection of the treat. But Angus throws her under the train. He gobbles up the muffin and pants up at Noel, looking for more.

"Hmm." Eleanor is unwilling to allow Noel any satisfaction. "He must be starving to do that."

"What's his name?"

"Angus," she mumbles, willing her neighbor to leave.

Noel tussles with the dog a bit, and Angus gets down on his elbows and pretends to pounce. It's like a dinosaur trying to skip rope. He takes Noel's arm in his great dripping jowls and feigns swallowing it. "You're a real tough guy, eh?" When Angus catches sight of a squirrel and lopes off, Noel wipes his hand on his jeans.

He motions toward the headstones. "Your parents?"

The wind blows hair in her face. She pushes it away and tightens her scarf.

"They're both gone?"

He seems unable to take the hint. His company is not wanted. She nods.

"How'd it happen?"

"Twin-motor plane in Aruba about four years ago. Bad weather combined with an inexperienced pilot," she says. "Any other questions?"

"Jesus." He flips up his collar, buries his hands in his pockets. His shoulders are wide, she notices now. If he wasn't such a jerk, he'd be quite handsome. He nods toward the teacup in her lap. "That's nice, what you're doing." He shivers and starts to walk away. "Anyway, getting cold. See you back at the ranch."

His politeness catches her off guard. She'd been prepared for a fight. Just before he disappears behind a ridge of evergreens, she calls out, "Noel?"

He turns.

She motions toward the stones where he'd been standing. "Was it someone close?"

He walks off. "Just a nice place for a good think is all."

When he's out of sight, Eleanor scoops up the remainder of her things. He's lying. With Angus in tow, she heads back toward the group of stones Noel had bent over. Most are old, the polished sheen of the granite having worn to a distant ache. She wanders closer to see the tidy ruffle of a single white rose. It lies before a grayish-pink headstone that looks new.

Victoria Bannon
September 30, 1979–November 16, 2009
Beloved wife of Noel Bannon

Chapter 13

There's something wrong with me, she thinks, later that night. The teacups. The shortbread. Four years later. Throwing a graveside party every Sunday.

She goes about the process of unpacking her basket, dumps the cookie crumbs into the sink. Washes the old thermos. The saucers. The cups. Wipes them dry with one of the embroidered towels Marion made herself. She sets each piece carefully on a tray and slides it across the counter to its customary spot by the stove, safe from the counter's edge and Angus's inquisitive snout, then remembers Angus barely enters the kitchen these days.

The tea set has had it. Hairline cracks in the handles. The chip at the edge of her mother's saucer. They're too fragile to survive much more to-ing and fro-ing. It's time to retire them. She opens the cupboard above the stove and pushes a few glasses out of the way. Then she drags over a chair and, with Angus watching, packs away her mother's tea set. Drying her hands on her jeans, she wanders into her bedroom and opens her top drawer. She pulls something out and turns it over and over. A tiny, plastic hospital bracelet.

It was a summer day and Marion had been out. The doctor or the dentist, doesn't really matter. What mattered was Eleanor had a definite time period during which the house would sit empty. She's wondered, since, what she was hoping to find that day. It wasn't as if there hadn't been doctor or dentist visits before. It wasn't as if she'd never been alone. But this day she'd woken up feeling outside of herself, and slipping back in made her entire body feel hoarse and scratchy like a bad throat.

She watched her mother's Jetta round the corner at Hawthorne Boulevard and disappear. Her father, she knew, would be gone all day. He was playing golf at the club, had for weeks been looking forward to drinks with his friends at the nineteenth hole.

Thomas's office had once felt like a haven. A place to retreat to when the thunder grew too loud or her stomach hurt. Many an evening, she curled up on the tufted leather sofa across from his desk and read while he sorted the bills or played a game of solitaire. When she was younger, he would sometimes look up and ask if she'd like to play Go Fish. But now she was thirteen. Too old for baby games.

She tiptoed across the plaid carpet, stepping, as she always did, only on the navy stripes, and opened her father's desk drawer. Creased receipts from hardware stores, a car magazine, a box half full of loose change and a couple of pairs of tarnished cufflinks.

The second drawer proved much more satisfying. Here she found old passports of her father's—the goggled glasses, the slicked-to-one-side hair! She came upon seed packets and money from Italy and Greece. It wasn't until she felt around behind the crumpled cottony bills that she discovered the envelope. Written across the yellowed front, in her mother's cautiously loopy script, was one word.

Eleanor.

Something tapped against the window. She started, then relaxed when she saw the sky had darkened, raindrops were striking the glass.

She pulled folded papers from the envelope. Something fell and she bent down, picked it up. It was a small hospital bracelet, the clear plastic sliced beside the metal clasp from when it was snipped off. *University of Kansas Hospital.* The name: *Baby Girl Smith.*

She might have stared at it a minute. Or it could have been an hour. Time didn't matter. Only the truth mattered.

She was adopted.

With pain shooting through her left shoulder, Eleanor laid the wristband over her skin like a Band-Aid. *Baby Girl.* Her mother—who on earth was her mother, then?—didn't even give her a name.

All at once everything and nothing made sense.

She hadn't yet opened the papers when the back door squeaked. A heavy thud from the mud room, then, "Damned weather. Marion? Eleanor? Game called for lightning."

Eleanor stuffed the sheets back inside the envelope, dropping the bracelet. Her father's footsteps rang in the hallway. She grabbed the plastic band, stuffed the envelope back into the drawer and slammed it shut. No time to get out of the room; he'd be walking in any moment.

Quickly, she pulled down the blind and hopped onto the sofa, lying there with a cushion over her head, hoping her pounding heart wouldn't give her away.

"Ellie?" Her father—was he still her father even?—flicked on the overhead light. "What are you doing?"

"Headache. Must be the weather."

It was the perfect ruse. He rolled his eyes and emptied his pockets into the desk drawer she'd just looked through. She hoped she'd placed the passports back the way they were. "Don't get me started. Three spits of drizzle, God-damned marshal clears the course."

She climbed off the sofa and headed for the privacy of her room with the plastic wristband tucked inside her fist.

The next time she went back to the drawer, the envelope was gone. It would be a whole year before she would get up the nerve to tell them she knew.

Now, she drops into a chair in front of the computer and stares at the screen. Heart hammering in her chest, she types in *searching for birth mother Kansas*. A host of sites come up and she clicks on the first one: "Adoption Search and Connect." A page comes up with options to search by name and location.

Barely able to breathe, Eleanor scrolls down to "United States" and types in the only name she has to go on and possibly the least helpful name on earth: *Smith*.

The screen floods with Smiths: 5,581 of them, to be exact, and they load ten per page.

1. Smith: Leveque: I was adopted at birth out of Richmond, VA, March 28, 1978. My birth name was David Smith and my mother's name was Jacqueline. Born in the evening, huge late-season blizzard. Birth mother came up from another state. Born with blond hair, blue eyes, please help.

2. Smith: Balliol: My name is Heather Lynn Balliol and I am looking for my mother. She was between 23 and 25 when she gave me up at two yrs old in June '69. She was from Houston area and a teacher. Birth father's last name was Cochrane, also from Houston but adoption took place in Vermont. If you want to talk that would be great.

3. Smith: Straitman: Female searching for birth parents, Massachusetts. Adopted from hospital, January 4, 1976, adoptive parents present. Adoptive dad had personality of used car salesman, adoptive mom the hippie type with long graying hair. Birth mother had two other children adopted out and tattoo of a panther on right calf.

4. Smith: Rudolph: At age of two days on November 3, 1953, I was left on the porch of 1649 Lincoln Street in Philadelphia by a young woman with short black hair. I was taken to Kingsbury Hospital and given the name Honor Smith. The hospital sent letters out to women who'd given birth around the 1st but no one . . .

The list goes on and on. Eleanor sits back and stares into space. Finding her birth mother with a last name like Smith is going to be extremely challenging.

The phone rings, the call display flashing a number and *BACK BAY ADOPTION*.

Nancy.

Reluctantly, Eleanor picks up. "Hey, Nancy."

"Hi, Eleanor. Listen. I don't mean to pressure you, but my superior, Lorna, is breathing down my neck. She's coming to the speaker event in four days specifically to meet you, talk to you. How are you doing with your support scenario?"

Eleanor glances at the computer screen: 5,581 Smiths, each one as desperate as she is. "Terrific."

"You have someone in place?"

"Yup. All set."

"Oh, thank God. I was so worried. I know what you've been through and how much you want this. To be perfectly honest, I think I want it as much as you do." The sounds of a drawer opening and pens being pushed around. Then the drawer slams shut and she sighs. "So we'll see you on Thursday. Bye-bye now." Click.

Eleanor hangs up the phone to pick it right back up again and dial. Four rings and a man's voice.

"Galileo Travel, how can I help you?"

Chapter 14

She sets a stack of folded, pressed T-shirts into a small suitcase and stops. Maybe Kansas City isn't as balmy as she thinks. It has to be wrong to gauge the area's probable temperature on what Dorothy wore in *The Wizard of Oz*. Though, with Lorna expecting a name from her in three days, a pair of ruby slippers is exactly what she needs.

Eleanor checks the Weather Channel online and returns to the bedroom to add a pile of vintage cashmere cardigans, a light jacket, two vests, and, at the last minute, two scarves. A pair of gloves would be ridiculous. The temperature isn't supposed to drop below sixty-five.

The trip will take three days. Two for travel and one to visit the Office of Vital Statistics in Topeka, Kansas. A shuttle will take her to the Empress Inn, not far from the airport, but to get to Topeka, she'll have to rent a car. She will leave Boston as Eleanor of Unknown Origin. With any luck, she'll return Eleanor of This or That. Or the Other.

Most important, she'll land at Logan at six o'clock Thursday evening and have one hour to get to Back Bay Adoption, where she will march straight up to Lorna to surrender her mother's name.

The problem is Angus. She took him to the vet for a quick checkup that afternoon and the dog flatly refused to get out of her Volkswagen. The vet, after Eleanor explained the situation, came out to the parking lot to examine him, ultimately agreeing with Eleanor that he is depressed but otherwise healthy. The prescription: lots of love and keep him far, far away from the vet clinic. In other words, do not board him.

She yawns into her hand and glances at the clock. Nearly 1 a.m. Her flight leaves in ten hours. She'd love to sleep, but the problem of Angus needs to be solved. Jonathan is the only solution. He should care for Angus. Besides, it wouldn't be a bad thing for him to be faced with a gigantic, shedding, drooling, depressed reminder of his inability to commit.

Eleanor buttons up her coat and marches down to Mass General.

She waits in a long row of plastic chairs in the ER, surrounded by sick and injured people slumped in seats and wheelchairs, lying on stretchers. Two men are asleep—one a young father whose two kids play on his iPhone, the other older and unshaven and wrapped in a blanket. A teen, being fussed over by his distressed mother, has a bloody towel wrapped around his head.

The Triage nurses must have told Jonathan she's here, but neither of them suggested Eleanor wait in his office like they used to. Instead, they looked at each other, and hesitatingly suggested the patient area. They know what's happened.

She doesn't wait long. Double doors at the end of the hall swing open and there he is in faded hospital greens she's washed, tumbled dry, and ironed hundreds of times for him.

His Littmann stethoscope hangs from his neck; the familiarity of the stylized *L* on the scope's diaphragm almost makes her cry. Such a stupid thing. He strides toward her with his legs wide the way he does, as if he's stepping around something unsavory. When he catches sight of Eleanor he heads toward her, no change in his expression. A spent woman in a wheelchair, bone thin with shoes that appear too heavy for her legs to lift, reaches out to tug on his arm. He bends over and listens to her lengthy complaint, speaks softly to her, then waves over a nurse, who wheels the patient through a doorway.

Now, Jonathan. Planted in front of her, hands pushed into pockets. Something about him is different. She can't place what it is, exactly. She stands and he kisses her cheek. "This is a surprise. Not another fake sprain?"

She has to look away or risk vomiting from nerves. If he would only come back, life would be perfect. She could still search for her mother. But not with a loaded gun at her temple. "No."

He checks his watch, revealing his left hand. His wedding ring. He's still wearing it. "It's so late."

"I know."

"Weird. I was going to come by the store later this morning."

"You were?"

"I just thought, if you're going ahead with things . . ." He stops, tilts his head to one side. "Okay, I'll just spit it out. Remember I signed up for that Saturday class? To build the rocking horse?"

How could she forget? It was a program run through Emerson High School. Three weekday evenings to make your own heirloom-quality wooden rocking horse with leather saddle and a janitor's mophead for a mane. Jonathan signed up as soon as they learned the adoption was approved. She'd imagined Sylvie riding it too many times to fathom.

"The first class was last night," he says.

She waits, confused. "What do you mean?"

"I'm saying I went."

"You're building the horse."

"I am."

"For Sylvie."

"Yes."

Her heart hammers so hard he can probably see it through her coat. "Jonathan, what are you saying?"

"I'm saying I'm building the horse for Sylvie."

Her mind whirls with what this might mean. It's a gallant gesture to show her he's back in? Or it's a self-serving final kiss-off intended to assure the world he's a perfect gentleman? "Wow. I'm shocked."

"Anyway. I wanted to ask you what stain color you prefer. There's a pale one called Yellow Oak, but I like American Walnut. It's dark without being too dark."

Her entire body could curl into a smile. "The American Walnut sounds nice." That didn't sound enthusiastic enough. "Sounds perfect, actually."

"Good." He nods. "That's the one I thought you'd like. You're always so smart with that kind of thing."

A nurse pushes past with an old man on a stretcher, rolling the IV bag on a stand. In their wake a nervous silence floats between them. Eleanor fills it with "I was thinking of giving her a middle name. Once she's here. Marion."

"After your mom."

"Plus . . ."

"Plus what?"

"I kind of need to know what you're doing. Now. With this rocking horse. If you're coming back, she'll keep the name we submitted. Sylvie Sweet. But if not, I may go back to Prue. There are these personalized mobiles this artist makes for the store. I was going to have one done up for her. Even if Sylvie's paperwork needs to be changed, she'll use a mobile for such a short time, I want to know."

"*That's* why you want to know my plans? For a mobile?"

She searches all reason for what is wrong with wanting to know his intentions and comes up blank. "Yes."

"I shaved my beard." He rubs his jawline, which is, of course, smooth now. "First time since you've known me."

He looks younger. Somehow, less married. She hates it. He was desirable enough before with his dark curls, his long legs. But the stubble hid him a bit. Kept him beneath a layer. Now he's vulnerable, open. Now she's going to lose him. "Yes. I mean, I saw. I noticed."

He shakes his head sorrowfully and starts toward the elevators. "This is what I'm talking about, Eleanor. You're gone. You're no longer here for me."

The memory of what was. It comes to her amid the blare of PA messages, the soft bongs of hospital machinery, the distant chatter. A low groan from behind a closed door. It started out just the two of them. The deal wasn't baby. It was Eleanor and Jonathan, Eleanor and Jonathan. She was insane to walk away from that. Before the baby talk, they were great. They could be great with a baby. He just needs to see it.

"Jonathan, wait."

He stops, turns around.

"You're wrong. I am here for you."

"Only if I'm here for her."

She doesn't breathe until the elevator doors slide shut.

Chapter 15

The cab is due to arrive in thirty minutes. Eleanor bumps her yellow suitcase out the door and into the hall with a glance back at Angus, who sits behind her, his ears flattened against his skull. He doesn't take his eyes off her bag. Once again, his enemy has reared its battered leather head. But this week is worse than last. He's down to one human.

Eleanor clips on his leash. "It's good you look sad. Perfect timing."

Ginny has taken care of Angus before. She didn't actually take him home—her youngest once had a dream Angus had two heads—but Ginny fed and walked him and let him sleep in the shop all day while she worked, so Angus was only alone at night. She didn't do it for money or to offer a helping hand. She did it for extra time off work.

Hauling a suitcase and the dog who despises it down the narrow flight of stairs to the street is no easy task. As long as the bag is in Eleanor's hand, Angus won't budge from the top step. Which means she has to make two trips down and nearly trips over Ginny, who is sitting cross-legged on the

Pretty Baby welcome mat. From the look on her face and her all-black attire, it's as if someone died.

It's a terrible time for someone to have died. The cab will be here in—Eleanor checks her watch—twenty-three minutes.

"Hey, Gin." Eleanor puts on a bright face as she unlocks the shop door and ushers Ginny, whose abdomen is already bulging, and Angus, and the despised suitcase inside. Already, Queen thumps through the walls. "You look fantastic. So slender!"

Ginny slumps on the counter stool. "Can you hire a hit man to off yourself? Is that even possible?"

Okay, so no one is dead. Yet. "I suppose. He may insist you pay him up front though."

She motions toward her midsection. "I can't do this. Someone needs to snuff me out."

It happens every time. Ginny's fears multiply with every week of pregnancy. Worries that she'll lose the baby she swore she didn't want consume her throughout the first trimester. During the second trimester, she becomes terrified about birth defects. And closer to her due date, she fears the nurse administering the epidural will sneeze and paralyze her for life. But accidental dural puncture is averted, baby is born healthy, and fear is replaced with exhaustion.

"You can do this, Gin. You've done it three times before."

"No. You don't understand. I can't."

Eleanor turns on the computer behind the cash. Twenty-one minutes until the cab arrives. "Listen, hon. I was wondering—" A gnawing sound behind her makes her turn around. There's Angus, lying on the floor, working diligently to chew off the handle of the suitcase. "Angus!" She drags the bag away from him. He rests his chin on his paws in obedience but doesn't take his gaze off the hated luggage.

Turning back to Ginny, Eleanor smiles. "I need a little favor."

"I went to the doctor, Eleanor. I'm not having a baby."

"What?"

A huge crash of bass as "Bohemian Rhapsody" builds to the chorus. Ginny starts to sob without tears. "I'm having two babies." She grabs her belly. "It's two people I've got in here!"

"Okay, that's a bit of a shock, no question. But lots of women come in carrying twins. It's certainly doable."

"But they don't *already* have three boys under the age of five."

Nineteen minutes left. "You'll do a great job. Listen—"

"Two heartbeats I heard on the ultrasound this morning. You know what that means? It means *two hearts*. And that means two heads to delouse. Which means four more hands—that's twenty fingers! And twenty extra nails I have to clip on top of the sixty I'm already clipping! Do you know what it's going to be like to keep five kids under the age of five still, long enough to trim one hundred nails? And, here's the real trouble . . . those nails? They just keep growing. You think, because you survive the ordeal on a Saturday—an entire Saturday—that you're good for a bit, like with a haircut. But no! By the next Saturday, one kid grabs your wrist and you're bleeding. The nails have already grown in—you understand how quickly it happens? And do you have any idea how many weeks there are in a year? Fifty-two. Every single year! That's . . ."—Ginny, her chest heaving now, two spots of color on her cheeks—"five thousand two hundred clippings per year." She wipes tears from her cheeks and blinks at Eleanor. "And Jamie's toenails are thick." Her voice cracks. "Ted calls them hooves."

"But you'll finally have your girl. For sure out of five kids at least one is a girl, right?"

Out front, a cab pulls to the curb and the driver gets out, stares at the building. He's early.

"No." Ginny pushes matted hair behind her ears. Eleanor doesn't have the heart to point out she has food in her bangs. "That's the thing. I'm having two more boys. I'm going to have *five* boys, Eleanor. Do you know what that is in girl equivalency? It's like having fifteen girls."

Eleanor opens the door and signals to the driver that she's coming. "Ginny, I'm going away for a few days. I need you to watch—"

Ginny pulls her close and sobs onto her cashmere sweater. "What am I going to do? I'll never survive five boys that young. Never. Do you know how many sandwiches I'll be making every morning? And don't get me started on the LEGO."

Eleanor pats her back. It's peanut butter in her hair; the smell is unmistakable now. There's no way she can leave Angus with Ginny. In her state, she might forget the dog exists.

Through the window, Eleanor sees Noel climbing into the Audi. Eleanor pulls back from Ginny. "Quick. What have you got in your lunch?"

With the nail of his index finger pressed into a white rag, he extricates the dust from the decorative trim surrounding the odometer. Once he's swiped all the way around, twice, he shifts the rag to a clean spot and spritzes it with an eco-friendly surface cleaner that smells like grapefruit. Then repeats the procedure around the gas and temperature gauge.

Eleanor sits in the seat beside him and watches. The look on his face is either enthusiastic or maniacal, she can't decide which. Holding up Ginny's crushed box of raisins, she flashes him a smile. "Raisins are surprisingly high in vitamin C. I thought, since it's cold and flu season, you might like—"

"The thing is—and people don't know this—you have to use a gentle cleaner. These chemical-based sprays, they dry out the dashboard. You combine that kind of harsh formulation with the constant glare of the sun and the heat and cold and, man. You've got yourself a recipe for premature desiccation and fading and cracking. Dashboard's never gonna look the same." In and out of the vent slats, along the crevice surrounding the stereo and A/C system goes his rag-covered finger. A slight shift of the hand to find a clean spot on the cloth, then over to the glove box.

Eleanor tightens the scarf around her neck. It's cold this morning. How he's sitting in here in nothing but a Meat Loaf T-shirt defies explanation. From the cab behind them, the driver honks. From the Pretty Baby window, Angus barks. "So, anyway."

"I used to use nothing but warm water. But then I heard there has to be at least some oil in your formulation." He grabs the bottle and shrugs. "This one uses lavender oil. Supposed to keep things well conditioned."

Two businessmen stop in front of Death by Vinyl and peer inside. The cab honks again. The driver will leave and then she's going to miss the second flight in two weeks. She calls out the window that he can take her suitcase, which sits on the sidewalk. With a roll of his eyes, he grabs it and puts it in the trunk. She speaks fast.

"So, I'm going away today and, well, you seemed to take to Angus the other day at the cemetery. You know, the way he ate your muffin and then he wanted to wrestle. It's rare for him these days. He's . . . I don't know. He's been in a depression. Do you think you could watch him while I'm gone? It's just for a few days and he can still sleep at my place."

Noel wipes down the top of the dashboard and frowns. "Look at that lint. I don't think I should use a cotton cloth."

"Anyway. About Angus."

"Who's Angus—your husband?"

Eleanor stares at him, stunned. "My *dog*. Please. I have no one to help me and I have to board a plane in a couple of hours. He's no trouble. If you could feed him and walk him, maybe let him hang with you while you . . ." She was going to say *work*, but there doesn't seem to be much of that going on over there. "Fine-tune your speakers, I'd really appreciate it. My assistant, Ginny, can give you advice, and of course I'll give you my cell."

"Maybe it's a polyester cloth I should use." He looks at her. "You think? What else is lint-free?"

It's ridiculous, but she has no choice. "I've got something you can try." She jumps out of the car and races into the store, returning half a minute later with a box of baby wipes. She drops into the seat and hands it to him, out of breath. "These are lint-free. Guaranteed."

He pulls one out and wipes the dash, skeptical at first. Then he leans closer and grins. "Hey, I think these things work."

"Great. So about the dog."

"Can I keep them?"

"Yes. Will you watch Angus?"

"You're leaving when?"

"Six minutes ago."

He pauses to read the plastic package, worried. "They don't give you very many. I'll be out of these in a couple of weeks."

The driver is out of the car and yelling something in Spanish. "I'll give you an entire carton when I return. It'll last you a year."

"You'll leave instructions?"

"What?"

"For the dog. I'll do it if you leave detailed instructions. How much food. When he goes out. What he likes to do at night. That sort of thing."

Eleanor is so relieved she leans across the center console and gives Noel a hug. "Everything you need is inside my store. I'm home in three days." With a wave goodbye, she jumps into the waiting cab.

Chapter 16

Topeka, Kansas. The Department for Children and Families is nothing much to look at. But sitting on a cement planter out front, staring at the salmon-colored bricks and no-nonsense sign, Eleanor is filled with ridiculous hope. Suddenly every woman shuffling through the revolving door could be her mother. At the very least, her mom spent enough time in the area to give birth. She likely walked along this very street.

Eleanor watches for her own features to pass. Dark blue eyes. Blond hair. Charmingly crooked nose. Wide mouth that should smile more.

For a moment it seems possible that Diane Keaton herself might stroll by. She'd read somewhere that Diane's real surname is Hall, her nickname Annie. That Woody wrote the film specifically for her and that she wore her own clothes, despite the protestations of the wardrobe person on set. Eleanor taps her black and white oxford shoes together. She actually rolled up her jeans today to highlight her pretty lace socks. The polarity of the masculine and the feminine—it made her feel substantial somehow. Diane Keaton–ish, anyway.

She downs the rest of her water, tosses the bottle into a

recycling bin. The office doesn't open until nine. She's been sitting here since ten after eight. The way she sees it, any one of a number of things could happen on this trip. She could find out her birth mother is dead. Or terminally ill. Or that she's impoverished or mentally unstable. Her mother could refuse to see Eleanor—an act that could be more hurtful than the adoption itself and one Eleanor isn't sure she would survive. Her birth mother could be a felon. Worse than any of this, she may never find her mother at all.

The plastic hospital bracelet. She holds it in one palm and stares out into the street. A woman with hair so sculpted and sprayed it resists the morning's breeze strides past carrying four coffees in a cardboard tray. She steps off the curb and checks traffic. It isn't her face, rosy and full-cheeked, that feels familiar; it's something in the way she trots so lightly across the street. Eleanor gets up and follows her down the sidewalk, narrowly missing being flattened by a bicycle courier.

The woman backs through the glass doors of an insurance company, holding it open for Eleanor, who tries not to stare as she smiles her thanks. The woman stabs the elevator button in a way that suggests she works here every day. Eleanor slows. She has no plan, other than to keep this person in sight for as long as possible. Though, really. What is she going to do—follow her up the elevator, into her office and to her desk?

The woman stabs the button again with good-natured impatience. "Thing has been so slow lately." She eyes Eleanor. "Do you work for Kravitz?"

"No! I'm . . ." Eleanor pulls her purse closer. "I think I'm lost, actually. I haven't been here, in Kansas, in a long time."

"Well. Welcome back."

Eleanor smiles. "I was born here. Well, not in Topeka. Kansas City. At the Women's Hospital." She rocks her body side to side hopefully. "Thirty-five years ago . . ."

The woman wiggles one of the smaller coffee cups out of the tray and sips. "I used to live in KCK. Great city. Very cultural these days."

Lived in Kansas City. Eleanor's heart thumps in her throat even though it's nearly impossible that the first person she meets is her mother.

Eleanor's phone rings from inside her purse. "I'm back here to . . ." The ringing bounces against the marble walls, amplifying the sound. "Hang on, sorry." She pulls out her phone, but not before the elevator pings and the doors swish open. "Hello?"

A male voice. Noel's. "Those baby wipes of yours are terrible on windows. Smudged them up bad. I had to Windex them twice and I'm still not sure they're clear."

"I'm kind of busy here, Noel. Can I call you right back?"

"And about your dog. I've fed him two bowls of kibble. I mean, enough to feed a moose, and he's still begging for more. Is this normal?"

The woman steps into the elevator with a polite nod goodbye. Eleanor holds up a finger. Into the phone she says, "What? No! Two bowls back to back?"

"I don't think he even swallowed. You should feed him more. His ribs are sticking out."

Inside the car, the woman hits a button and waits, staring at the numbers above the open doors.

"I do feed him"—she lowers her voice and turns around—"I told you, he's been depressed."

"He's sure not depressed now. He found a tennis ball in the shop. I had to throw it for him all day. Does this dog not sleep?"

All he does is sleep, she wants to say but doesn't. "Listen, I can't talk right now."

"You should've seen him in the park. He was the damned social director—greeting every dog and owner that passed by. He's just so . . . happy."

"I promise you it's not his normal state—"

The doors start to close. Eleanor drops the phone into her purse and lunges to stop them but it's too late. The woman is gone.

"Hello? Eleanor? Hello-o?" Noel's voice comes to her garbled from where the phone has slipped between her wallet and tampon case. Eleanor pulls it out with a sigh. What does it matter anyway? The coiffed woman from KCK was not her mother.

"Yes?"

"Would you mind picking me up some of that BB's Lawnside BBQ sauce? You can't get that stuff up here and I've got this nice rack of beef ribs in the freezer."

Across the street, people are starting to enter the Department of Children and Families. She checks her watch: 9:03. "Noel? I've got to go."

As soon as she reaches the information desk, she thinks she should have called first. She has no desire to stand in front of this uniformed, gum-smacking twenty-two-year-old security guard and explain her predicament. *I have no name. No real information about myself. But, hey, I do have a thirty-five-year-old plastic bracelet!* Eventually, after a few wrong turns and a few confused department receptionists, Eleanor finds herself at the adoption records desk, staring at an employee pretending she's not eating a sandwich.

The woman, with sunken cheeks and cracked lips, wearing a name badge that reads *Brenda*, wraps what's left of her cream cheese bagel in a napkin and tucks it under the counter. Her skin is so thin it clings to her tendons and ligaments, her bones. A few bottles of water could plump it up, bring her to life. She covers her mouth with her fingers while she finishes chewing.

"Sorry. We're short-staffed. I'm all by myself down here most days and I missed dinner last night."

"You have to eat."

Brenda swallows and waves at her face to expedite the process. "What can I do for you?"

"I have a bit of a situation." She waits, nervous, while Brenda reaches for a pen. The one thing she can't take is pity. If, for one second, this woman looks at her with sorrow or embarrassment or concern, Eleanor will spin around and hop a cab back to the airport. "I was born here thirty-five years ago. And, well. My mother, she . . ."

"You were adopted?"

"Yes."

"All you need is twenty dollars and twenty minutes, luv. You got both?"

No sorrow here. Eleanor is relieved. It's business as usual. "Yes, sure." She pulls out a twenty.

"State of Kansas is totally open for adoption records. Lucky for you." Brenda pushes the money into a cash machine. "Now. What have we got? Mother's name? Your birth name?"

Eleanor fumbles to pull the hospital bracelet from her purse. "Baby Girl Smith. August 10, 1975. Women's Hospital. That's all I really know."

Brenda examines the bracelet. "Hard to believe anyone starts out this small, isn't it?"

"I'm just hoping the adoption is on record here somehow. And I can get a bit more information. I really need to find her."

Brenda hands it back to her. "Women's Hospital. Sadly, the name Smith doesn't help us much. More often than not, it's made up." She pulls on a pair of glasses and motions toward the chairs in front of her desk. Eleanor sits. "August tenth, let's see now . . ."

"Nineteen seventy-five." Eleanor refrains from mentioning that Woody and Diane were filming that year.

"A Leo. Nice." She punches the date into her computer. "Good, strong souls, Leos. I married one." She looks up. "You married?"

Eleanor slides her hands beneath her thighs. "I don't really know what I am."

Brenda nods. No judgment, no pity. She returns to the computer screen. "Well, the good news is we've got your mother's name. Or at least the name she gave."

"Wait, what's her name?"

"Ruth Smith. So we've got that as well as your date of birth. But there's absolutely no adoption information from that hospital on that day." She looks at Eleanor from over her papers. "It means the adoption didn't take place here in Kansas state. The birth did, but not the adoption."

"I don't understand. You're saying she took me somewhere else? Packed me onto a plane and took me to someone?"

"That's certainly possible, but more likely the adoption took place close by."

"I don't understand."

"The hospital is just off State Line Road, which divides Kansas City into two states. The west side is Kansas. The east side is Missouri. You, my dear, were born on the Kansas side, but you were probably adopted on the other side of the street. In Missouri. A very common occurrence in Kansas City." She places her cool, dry hand over Eleanor's. "I'm sorry, luv."

"So, what, I go across State Line Road and find the Department of Children and Families in Missouri?"

"I'm afraid it's not that easy. Missouri isn't like Kansas. Adoptions that take place in Missouri are sealed. They won't give you any information about adoptions in Missouri."

"But this must happen all the time, the way the city is cut in half."

"Breaks my heart to have to disappoint people. I'm sorry. Kansas is only one of a handful of states with open records. Most allow access to non-identifying information only. She slides the paper across the counter to Eleanor. "But you do have a few things to go on. Her name: Ruth Smith. And this is your mother's address, however temporary, the day you were born. And here's your birth certificate. Don't leave without this."

Eleanor stares down at the small white piece of paper the woman has placed on the counter. *Baby Girl Smith*. Across the front is stamped in red: VOID.

"Voiding it is just a way to prevent fraud. Identity theft. You know."

Eleanor nods and slips her birth certificate into her purse. Void sounds about right.

"Honey, there are people out there who can help you. They go beyond what the state can do. You know, go back to your public school, your church. They go through cemeteries and archived newspapers."

"Do you have them here?"

Brenda shakes her head. "They're private individuals. Call themselves search angels. They're mostly volunteers, often women who gave up an infant of their own."

"How do I find one?"

"Where'd you say you're from?"

"Boston."

Brenda consults a thick binder and scrawls a name on the back of her business card. She hands it to Eleanor. "Isabelle Santos. She used to live in Boston. I'm not sure if she's still taking clients, but she's one of the best."

Chapter 17

Midday now and cold enough it could snow. The sun is so bright it stings her eyes, and the distant train whistle sounds like a kettle. Eleanor zips up her jacket, flips the collar up to keep out the chilly air. Beneath it, she's layered a thick turtleneck over a blouse. She didn't pack for the weather here. For some reason she expected it to be warmer than home.

The building in front of her, 26 Reeson Road, the address from the records, is actually a large, charcoal-gray Victorian house with original slate roof tiles and a lovingly restored gingerbread porch. On one side, the roof rockets skyward in a fat turret, on the other, a chunky stone chimney.

A backlit sign informs her that Lindquist, Stricker and Blair, Attorneys-at-Law, are based here now, and what once must have been a generous front lawn is now a parking lot filled with Volkswagens and Hyundais, as well as an assortment of expensive black sedans.

Was her mother from a wealthy family? A house this size must have had servants. In Boston, this house would cost a fortune. It's a grand old mansion.

Her phone rings from her pocket. She pulls it out. "Hey, Noel."

"He's gone through that entire bag of dog food. Do you have any more stashed away someplace? Because I don't really have any way to haul back a bag of dog food from the pet store up on Commonwealth, if that's where you get this Science Diet stuff. I'd have to take a cab."

That he has a perfectly nice car parked in front of her store is not worth mentioning. "Angus has finished the entire fifteen-pound bag?"

"If I were you, I'd take him off this high-energy formula. He's active, sure, but if he eats this much every day, he's going to balloon."

Of course it was good he was eating. It's a huge relief that his depression is lifting. But at the same time, Eleanor can't help but feel envious he didn't start eating with her. "There's another bag in the hall closet. But don't overfeed him. Just follow the serving sizes I left in the instructions . . ."

"I haven't seen any of this depression you mentioned . . ."

Eleanor hears shuffling on the sidewalk nearby. A rumpled man, well into his seventies, with a stain on his jacket and trousers nearly worn through in the thighs, traps a cigarette between his lips and pats his pockets.

"Sorry, Noel. I have to run." She slips the phone back into her pocket and approaches the man. "Excuse me. Do you live around here?"

"You got a light?"

"I don't smoke."

"Damn wife hides my fire nowadays. Thinks she's keeping me alive, but I tell you, this way I'd rather be dead."

Eleanor nods emphatically. As if she too is unable to enjoy life because of this shrewish woman.

He motions toward the house. "You work with them lawyers?"

"No. I was just admiring the building."

He nods, his unlit smoke threatening to fall onto the sidewalk, though she has little doubt he'd slide it back into his mouth if it did. "It's a beauty. We all thought these dipshits'd tear the place down, but they did it up real nice."

"You've lived here a long time?"

"Most of my life. Grew up over there in Lanark County but Louise was from the big city and wanted to keep it that way. So I did what a smart man does. Did what my wife said and moved up here."

"This house, do you remember it from, say, the late seventies? Was it a single-family residence?"

"This place?" He chuckles to himself. "Hell, no. This was one of them homes for, you know."

"What?"

"Teenage girls who got themselves into trouble. Missouri, it's dotted with these old places all along the railway. Parents back then'd pack 'em onto a train and send 'em off. 'Don't come back until there's just one of yous again.' Missouri was known for these places. Girls came from everywhere."

Her mother, sent away to give birth to Eleanor in secret.

Eleanor squints into the sun at the house and imagines the faces looking out the window. "Imagine. All those girls."

He slips the smoke out of his mouth and puts it into his shirt pocket, patting it to make sure it's safe. With a tip of his head, he walks away. "Bunch of damned sluts, if you ask me."

Chapter 18

Eleanor stands in front of a red door. The glossy oil paint is fresh, she can smell the solvents evaporating, and when she knocks it has a lingering stickiness to it. The ivy-covered town house, four stories high with original mullioned windows and dentil molding is well worthy of its Beacon Hill accoutrements—the cobblestone streets, the flickering gas lamps, the lacy fronds of trees dropping yellow leaves.

She should have gone from the airport straight to the store to check on Ginny, to pick up Angus. She should at least have called before showing up like this, luggage in tow.

After setting her suitcase beside the door, where the poor woman won't see it and fear Eleanor is moving in, she raps hard on the door. A long silence, followed by the sound of locks being clicked and slid open, then a statuesque figure in the doorway. Isabelle Santos is the perfect mix of elegance and age, with silver-white hair pulled back from a face decorated only with plum lipstick. In her mid- to late sixties, as tall as a man, with cheekbones so sharp they could slice bread, Isabelle is striking. Her long fuchsia silk caftan, delicately embroidered with tiny birds at the cuffs, and black velvet slippers match her understated sophistication to perfection.

Isabelle's black eyes travel from Eleanor's shoes, up her socks and tights to her skirt and turtleneck, blouse, and sweater. Over Eleanor's two scarves—one for fashion, one for warmth—and cape, then through her windblown hair, held back with a jeweled barrette. A slow smile crinkles her face into an expression of pure joy.

"They didn't tell me you'd be a woman. This is refreshing. Bizarre, but refreshing."

Eleanor squints, confused, and allows the woman to usher her inside. If she believed the exterior of the house to be exquisite, the interior nearly makes her gasp. The look is that of old and moneyed Europe, with windows that start at the floor, which is done in oversize tumbled bricks, creamy brown in color and set in a herringbone pattern. The walls are rough-plastered in a hemp tone and curved archways separate enormous rooms. Rough-hewn beams support ceilings that soar upwards of twelve feet. In the center of the living room hangs an iron chandelier that might have been salvaged from a thirteenth-century mansion.

While the envelope of the space is decidedly masculine, the decor is quite the opposite: downy white sofas and chairs groan beneath embankments of decorative pillows. Cushions of linen and silk, burlap and muslin are trimmed with jute and lace and pearls and European family crests.

The plumpy softness is too tempting. Eleanor wants to walk across the room, sink into the love seat, and lose herself in the tickly fill. The fluffiness, the affability, it's like a mother's womb.

"I simply love this day and age. Women can do just about anything. In my day, you became a secretary." Isabelle rushes down the hallway and glances back over her glasses. "Personal assistant, *excuse* me." She opens a door and disappears down a dark set of stairs.

Eleanor isn't sure if she's meant to follow and stays in the doorway. "Brenda in Topeka told me you may not do this kind of thing anymore," she calls down the stairs. "But I'm hoping you'll make an exception. See, I went all the way to Kansas City and found out I wasn't even adopted there."

Isabelle comes back up the stairs with a plunger in her hand. She looks enormously disappointed. "You're not the plumber?"

"No, I'm Eleanor Sweet. I came for—"

"Slipshod plumber is two days late. I was just so excited to get my pipes fixed, I assumed . . ."

"I know I should have called first, but I really need help."

Isabelle hands Eleanor a plunger. "No wasted hands around here, I'm afraid. You're not against a bit of manual labor, are you, Eleanor Sweet?"

Eleanor stands, gloved and embarrassed, holding a plunger over the sink in the main-floor powder room as per Isabelle's instructions. This room is vintage New York City, with its floor-to-ceiling white subway tiles and black and white honeycomb floor, complete with century-old cracks. The sink is chipped in spots and the drain stopper is a shrunken apple core of a thing, but it, like the toilet, is crisp with cleanliness. The window, in spite of its fat and important trim, is tiny and too high to be of much use.

"I don't know what I'm doing," she calls down to Isabelle. "You should call the plumbing company again."

Isabelle's voice is tiny from the bowels of the big house. "They're a conglomerate of imbeciles."

"I'm just not sure this is going to work."

"Ready? Set and go! Plunge away."

They both begin to pump until the pipes in the walls groan, then make a whooshing sound. The water in the toilet beside Eleanor gurgles, and Isabelle calls, "Success, darling."

Eleanor washes her hands and returns to the foyer to wait for Isabelle to emerge from the cellar, and the woman does so wiping her hands on a thick towel.

"I think we should market ourselves immediately. Of course you'll have to do all the legwork. I'm not much for leaving the house these days."

"Actually, that's why I'm here. I need help finding my birth parents. I need a search angel."

Isabelle's face ages ten years. "I'm retired."

"I'm willing to pay if that helps."

"I don't and never did work for money. Now, if you don't mind, I'm very much in the middle of something."

"But you haven't heard me out."

She checks her watch. "I have fifty-three seconds until the soufflé I have in the oven is done. Say anything you want until then."

"I went out to Kansas City, and there's this road. And apparently I was born on the left side and adopted on the right. Wrong. And the thing is, I'm adopting a little girl myself. A baby orphaned in the earthquake out west this year. And I'm doing it all by myself. I got lucky that the agency will let me. But they—and I totally agree—they want me to have some kind of support system. You know, the kind of person you can call in the middle of the night and just bawl your head off to when your baby won't take the bottle or—"

"Eleanor Sweet?"

"Yes."

"Please don't mistake my brevity for lack of concern, but my soufflé is in very real danger of collapsing. If you insist on speaking, you'll have to do so over lunch."

Eleanor follows behind her. "Your house is beautiful."

"I have my late husband to thank for it. Brilliant family lawyer. Never has there been a man who worked as hard or helped as many. I'm lucky to have had him most of my life."

In the kitchen, Isabelle pours red wine into fat juice glasses and sets them on the marble-topped island, then settles herself on a stool across from Eleanor, who watches her from behind a vase stuffed with peonies. On the island, along with a lit candle the shape and size of a can of apple juice, sits the soufflé, all golden brown and steaming from the oven in its orange Le Creuset dish. Tomatoes so fresh they might still be growing lie, red and cubed and juicy in what appears to be a homemade bowl, and a thin bottle stands in the center wearing a monogrammed Santos family crest. On the label, in elegant script, someone has hand-written, *olive oil, garlic, basil, etc.*

On the wall to Eleanor's right is a massive, bleached-wood cupboard with all the pomp and tiers of a wedding cake. The upper shelves are lined with well-used cookbooks in English and French. Tucked between the books is a silver-framed photo of a newborn baby wrapped in blue, his mouth pursed and his fists tucked into his chin. The photo isn't in good shape; it appears creased, torn in one corner.

"Cute baby," says Eleanor.

Isabelle sets down two plates with a bang. Gone is the sweet forcefulness of before. The air itself is sharp, serrated. Eleanor wants to flee; she's done something wrong. She glances at her purse on the floor. Three seconds, she could grab it and be gone. Then again, she needs this woman.

"Kansas City," says Isabelle. "I've had more adoptees approach me with that State Line Road problem than any other place. What I'd like to know is what came first? The city split in two by a state line or the two states deciding it would be a grand idea to go sharesies on a large metropolis."

This is good. Isabelle is onside. Eleanor pulls out the brace-let and, while the woman carves out a deliciously sloppy piece of soufflé, explains that all she has to go on is her birthplace and her mother's possible name of Ruth Smith. "What I don't understand is, if she spent her pregnancy at one of the homes for pregnant girls, didn't they give birth in those places?"

"Birth and death. Often there were 'doctors' in residence or who stopped by, who performed terribly rudimentary abortions or they botched their deliveries. Young girls died. Your mother was smart. And Smith might not be her real name."

Eleanor nods.

"But what might have happened was there were complications. Your mother may have started to give birth in the home and something went wrong. Bleeding, or the baby got stuck. They may have rushed your mother to the nearest hospital. Lucky for you, if so. Many of the administrators of these places didn't act quickly enough."

She thought about her mother, alone and likely underage. Scared for her own life. Or her baby's. "But why wouldn't she have given her real name at the hospital?"

"I'm not saying it isn't her name. It very well could be. But Smith is the most commonly used fake name I've come across." She plays with her wine glass. "There was a good deal of shame surrounding unwed mothers back then. Her parents may've been terrified she'd be found out and it would destroy her life. Or, just as important, theirs." She stands up. "Now, let's eat. I've made a lovely flan for dessert. And I need your help with the dishes. I forbid you to leave until we're all cleaned up."

It isn't until the food and wine are consumed and dishes are dried with a pom-pommed Eiffel Tower tea towel and put into the cupboards that Eleanor musters the nerve to beg. "I can't wait any longer. I'm desperate. Would you be willing to help me?"

"I'm not a young woman, Eleanor Sweet. I've retired recently and after a lifetime of running around, I like to stay put. But I can connect you with someone else."

"Again, I'll pay any amount. I'll borrow against my business—"

Isabelle looks up sharply. "I said I *don't* work for money." The room grows silent but for the soft tick-tick of a clock on the armoire. Isabelle folds the towel and lays it over the oven door pull. "You're wearing a wedding band."

Eleanor fiddles with her ring. "It's complicated. Basically, he panicked once we'd been approved and backed out. He might be coming back—I have no idea. But I do know I have to have Sylvie."

Isabelle has turned. She stares out the sliding glass door into the tiny jewel of a backyard—thick with bare branches that frame stone benches and a large stone fountain emptied out for the coming season. When she turns back, she avoids

Eleanor's eye. Roots through a drawer and hands Eleanor a card. It reads *Martina Kalla, Adoption Search Angel*, with a phone number.

Eleanor takes the card and follows Isabelle to the door, where, she notices now, a stack of empty delivery boxes sits against the wall, all bearing the logo *Benjamin's Market*. On the hall table are unopened bubble envelopes from Amazon with book-shaped contents.

"I wish you luck, Eleanor Sweet," Isabelle says with the door open. "And fewer layers of clothing. It isn't an invisibility cloak you're wearing. Rest assured, we can still see you."

Eleanor feels her cheeks flush. She waits until the door thumps shut before wheeling her suitcase across the stoop and bumping it down the steps.

Chapter 19

Waiting in the apartment foyer when she returns from Isabelle's is the rocking horse, wrapped in a huge yellow bow. Tall and classic, with bridle and thick, ropy mane and tail. Glass eyes. Leather saddle held on by brass grommets and wood polished to a sheen. Inscribed on the haunch: *Sylvie*.

Eleanor carries it into the nursery. Sets it on an angle by the window and rocks it with one finger.

It should mean something, that he attended this class. Sanded the wood, cut the leather, affixed the mane and tail to this beautiful and classic piece. It would be so touching in another scenario. Something a loving father would do. But this way it feels loaded with guilt. A gesture more about the man than the child.

No. She's not giving her daughter a gift from a man too spineless to be part of her life. Eleanor drags the horse into the closet and slams the door.

Jonathan Sweet doesn't get to be both good guy and bad guy at the same time.

There's no sign of Angus in the apartment and Noel isn't picking up his phone. Eleanor has no choice but to head downstairs and see if the dog is waiting in Pretty Baby or Death by Vinyl.

It's near closing time and the shop door is unlocked. No sign of Ginny. One customer roams the aisles. Not even a customer, really. A man with wispy brown strands of hair crisscrossing his scalp and a nervous way of licking his lips before he speaks, who asks Eleanor to turn down the rock music. To which she explains it's coming from next door. Next he asks what age can a child sit in the front seat because his daughter doesn't like him driving his grandson in the front. But the boy's almost nine. It seems ridiculous. Eleanor explains the rule: twelve for cars with air bags. The man doesn't know if his Nissan has any. He assures her he'll go off and check.

Where is Ginny?

The tinkle of the bell announces a FedEx courier, who heads toward the cash in a jangle of keys and pocket change. He sets a dinner-plate-shaped box on the counter and slides it toward Eleanor. "Package for Noel Bannon."

"He's not at this address."

The courier tilts the box toward her. "Says here 'Noel Bannon care of Pretty Baby.'" He takes a look around the store at the pastel-colored wall hangings, the seven brands of breast pumps, the bin of discount newborn sleepers, then the stack of Pretty Baby business cards by the cash register. "Seems the right place."

"Noel's next door. You'll have to take it over there."

"Sorry, ma'am. I can't deliver it anyplace other than what's on the label."

She holds up a finger to ask the courier to wait as she pulls out the ragged business card Noel gave her the other day. The phone rings six times before he picks up.

The fumble of fabric. Then a groggy half-whisper. "Yeah?"

"It's Eleanor. Listen, I have a courier here with a packa—"

"Huh?" More rustling, this time accompanied by a grunt. "Who from? Is it a guy called Andrew something?"

"Wait, you're at home in bed? Why is your music playing in the store?"

"That must be my *Velvet Underground & Nico* reissue. Man, that's fast."

"Noel—"

"It's a first pressing. eBay started at $350 and I took it at $1,295. There was some kind of copyright thing with this cover so right away they reissued with another. Bumped the price way up. I sell that, I can make my rent."

"You open your doors, you can make your rent."

"Oh, that reminds me. A collector is bringing a load of vinyls in to your place tomorrow afternoon. Just have a quick peek and offer him seventy-five dollars if it looks good."

This is too exasperating to warrant a reply. "Do you have Angus with you?"

He yawns like a lion into the receiver. "Do I ever. You know, I taught that dog how to speak—as in bark—on command. Damn thing has been barking ever since. Barked all night. One of my neighbors called the cops."

"Bring him back please, Noel. And come and get your package."

As Eleanor hangs up, Ginny shuffles up from the basement, pulling on her coat. Her hair appears to be in the same ponytail as when Eleanor left and she might not have changed her clothes. Or bathed. Her face is bloated and shiny. She holds up a book on canine behavior, her eyes glassy. Or crazed, it's hard to tell which.

"Hey. I've figured out how to manage all these kids. I'm going to control my litter the way a bitch does, postpartum. There're some great ideas in here. Right down to crate training. The humans have it all wrong. That's why our kids misbehave. For the first time, I think this thing is doable."

"All right." Eleanor pulls the book from her grasp. "You need a day off. Wash your hair, change your shirt, take a nap, and for God's sake put down the dog book before pulling your babies from the amniotic sac with your teeth in the birthing room starts to sound like a good idea."

Chapter 20

The poster on the wall shows the cover of a book—*Chosen*—written by the speaker Nancy mentioned, the woman found as an infant on a street corner in Seoul and adopted out to a middle-class Jewish family in Dallas. The book's image is stunning—a baby's soft shoulder, seen from behind.

Donna Devon herself stands tiny and strong, with wide stance, short black hair, and easy grin, chatting with Nancy next to the podium. Dressed in black T-shirt, tights, and motorcycle boots, she exudes peacefulness and confidence. Strength. This is not a woman who feels unloved. To look at her is to feel weak, incapable in comparison. This is a woman who knows how to live. How to survive.

She's here to give the parents-to-be a glimpse into the adoptee's experience. She is also meant to share what she wishes had been done differently, what she wouldn't change. How it's important not to take it personally if your child is sad about his start in life from time to time.

The room has the humid, yeasty smell of nervous energy, and the floor almost vibrates with the audience's determination to do everything right.

It was short-sighted not to have arrived earlier, Eleanor quickly realizes. She wasted precious minutes soaking Angus's kibble in canned chicken broth, which of course didn't interest him in the least. Now most of the seats in the meeting room are taken. With whispered apologies, Eleanor works her way along a row to an empty chair in the center. Just as she lowers herself into it, a soft hand lands on her arm.

"Sorry. I'm saving that seat for my husband."

Eventually, Eleanor locates a seat in the back row, in the far left corner beside a couple dressed like they just came from running sprints, in matching Saucony shoes, nylon pants, and hooded sweatshirts. The woman, her dark head as sleek as an otter's with its smooth ponytail, twists to one side to allow her to pass.

Miles from Reception lowers the lights and yanks down a projection screen. The high-spirited chatter in the room falls to a respectful hush, but Donna doesn't seem to be in the room.

Eleanor can feel someone's stare and finds the runners focused on her. The man, as bony and gristled as a grapevine, holds out his hand.

"Jim Faust. This is my wife, Bev. What country are you adopting from?"

Eleanor takes his hand and introduces herself. "My daughter's here. Well, California."

"Hyun-Ki is coming from Korea. From National Boys. Yours an infant?"

Eleanor nods and they exchange photos. The Fausts' son is older, they explain, nearly three and recently separated from his younger brother, who was adopted to a couple in the U.K. They'd been after a younger child, but seeing Hyun-Ki crying, alone in his crib, broke their hearts.

"Arrives in January," says Jim. He looks at his wife. "What day is it?"

"Like I don't have it etched into my brain? The ninth. At 11:37. Flight 1833 from Seoul."

Eleanor says, "The cold will be a shock."

Jim laughs. "We've already picked up a snowsuit. Warmest we could find."

Bev turns in her chair to survey the room. "Is your husband coming tonight? I see there are a few chairs stacked; we could pull one over and squeeze it into our row."

It had been Jonathan who, upon hearing they'd been approved, ran out and bought Sylvie every classic children's book he could find. The Beatrix Potter stories, *Goodnight Moon*, Dr. Seuss, Maurice Sendak. He arranged them on her windowsill beside the gliding rocker so he could read to her the night they arrived home. It was important to her adjustment, he'd said, that they establish routines right away.

"He's not here," Eleanor says.

"How'd he manage to sneak past Nancy's 'both spouses attend' rule?" says Jim.

"We're sort of . . . separated at the moment."

"I don't understand. You're going to adopt alone?" asks Bev.

Eleanor nods.

"Oh," says Jim, his expression less chummy now. "Well. I've heard more women are doing that now. Men, too, I would guess."

"The agency doesn't . . . I mean, is this allowed?" Bev asks, one hand on her throat.

"My husband and I split post-approval, so I have to go

through a few more hoops, but yes, from some countries. As Nancy said, 'Not every couple will remain a couple.'"

"I'm sorry," says Bev, leaning across her husband's lap. "I don't see bringing a baby into your life with no father. I understand it can happen, but to do it on purpose?" She shakes her head.

"Bev."

"I get that you want a baby, but there are times, situations where you put the interest of the child ahead of your own needs—"

"Bev. That's enough."

"So sue me. Someone has to speak up for the children. They have no control over where they end up. They're completely in the hands of those who—"

Eleanor stands up. She cannot bear the thought of climbing across this woman's unforgiving lap, so straddles her chair back, knocking it down and falling to her knees in the process. Embarrassed now, on top of being humiliated, her left knee paining, she charges down the hall to the ladies' room, willing herself not to limp.

Checking her lipstick in the mirror is Donna Devon. She looks up, her features softened from the halogen spotlight over her head. Up close, she is extraordinarily beautiful, with skin so smooth it doesn't seem real. She smiles hello when Eleanor stumbles into the room.

Quickly, Eleanor rearranges her face to wipe off Bev Faust's disapproval. "I ordered your book," she says. "I'm so curious how it's been for you as an adoptee, adopting. I'm looking for someone to relate to, I guess."

"I hope you don't relate to all of my stories. At least not the heroin smoothies. Or being chased down Canal Street in New York by the police." Donna touches up her lips and grins devilishly.

"My story is pretty vanilla in comparison."

"Everyone's is."

Eleanor opens the stall door, then turns around. "I'm adopting on my own. My husband is gone. Or . . . might be gone." Her throat tightens up with emotion. "I'm sorry. Not sure why I'm blathering. I'm just . . ." She lets out a sigh so hard she shudders. "I'm all alone."

Donna takes Eleanor's shoulders. "Hey. Having a husband doesn't guarantee anything. I was raised by a couple in Saratoga. My adoptive mom worked two jobs to put me and my adopted sister through private school and pay the mortgage. My adoptive dad? He spent his days at the Cat Call, a strip bar around the corner. Came home every night wrapped in the smell of cheap whisky and nasty perfume. You can do this, you hear me?"

Eleanor nods with far more conviction than she feels. "Thank you."

Donna checks her watch. "We'd better get me in there before Nancy starts without me."

Eleanor follows Donna out. "Can I ask you something? Did your mother raise you two all on her own, then? No help at all?"

"Oh God, no." They march back toward the board room. "My grandmother lived upstairs. It wasn't until I was five that I realized she wasn't my second mother, that she was my grandmother."

A door flies open and Nancy catches sight of Donna. "There you are, Missy. You're on in ten."

Donna squeezes Eleanor's arm and heads to the front

of the room where Miles is adjusting her podium. Nancy approaches Eleanor.

"You look tired. Everything okay?"

I'm perfect. I'm strong and independent and capable of raising a whole army of babies on my own, not just one. "My dog's been keeping me up."

"And Jonathan?"

"It's not looking good."

They both pause as a heavyset woman with spiked hair and dangly earrings walks toward them.

The woman holds out her hand to shake Eleanor's and says in a cigarette-charred voice, "Lorna Gillespie. You must be Eleanor. Come—" She leads them out the door. "Let's chat in the hall."

Let's not, Eleanor thinks, following.

"I'm so sorry to hear about your situation," Lorna says as if speaking to a six-year-old. "I'm sure Nancy told you I have concerns about who you have to assist in a pinch. We all need a little help now and then." She cocks her head and smiles, squinting sympathetically. Eleanor half expects the woman to reach out and button her cardigan, retie her scarf, and send her off to play outside. "Nothing to be ashamed about."

"My mother is going to be my backup."

"Oh?" Nancy looks surprised. "I thought your parents were deceased."

"My birth mother. Her name is Ruth Smith."

"Right. I forgot you were adopted. That's in your file somewhere," says Nancy.

"Wonderful," says Lorna. "There's nothing like having

your mother around when learning to care for a baby. Will she be present at the home visit for Nancy to meet?"

This Martina Kalla had better be quick. "Absolutely."

Chapter 21

Eleanor stares at Martina Kalla's card.

She has two weeks to find her mother. Maybe it would be possible if she'd been born with any surname other than the most common in North America. Or if Isabelle had grabbed an already-packed suitcase from the foyer closet and jumped on the first flight to Kansas City. Even then, fourteen days to find one woman in a country of over three hundred million was beyond ridiculous.

She dials the number and the call goes straight to message: *You have reached Martina Kalla. Thanks for getting in touch. Your call is important to me. Please leave your name and number and we'll find who you're looking for. Namaste.*

Eleanor is careful to enunciate. "Hi, Martina. My name is Eleanor Sweet and I'm looking for my birth mother." She pauses. "Urgently." She leaves her number twice and hangs up.

Angus stares out the front door of Pretty Baby and lets out a woof so airy and hopeless it could be the balloon deflating. He's barked so much since her return, he's almost lost his voice. And now that he's home, he's stopped eating.

Ginny wanders out of the break room, licking the icing off a small vanilla cupcake. She scratches him behind the ear.

"Who's a good boy whose breeders planned an abbreviated life for him? Huh? Who's that good boy?"

"Ginny."

"What? Great Danes live seven years because of breeders. So they can look at these huge beasts and think, 'Whoa. Look what I built.' Let them all be mutts, I say." She swipes icing onto her finger and offers it to Angus. To Eleanor's surprise, Angus licks Ginny's finger clean and sits politely, clearly hoping for more. "I read it in my dog book."

"Can I try feeding him?"

Ginny pops the cupcake into her mouth and says, "I'm eating for three. Get your own."

Eleanor watches Angus lower himself onto the floor. "At first it seemed to be because Jonathan left. But now, I don't know."

"Don't know what?"

"I don't think he likes me."

Ginny wipes crumbs from her mouth and nods. "Yeah. I can see that."

The back door slams against the wall and Noel walks in carrying the milk crate full of records she bought from his customer the day prior. He heaves it up onto the counter.

"Oh good," says Eleanor. "I paid your guy seventy-five dollars from my petty cash. It'd be great if you could reimburse me."

He says nothing. Just rolls his tongue against his inner cheek and grunts. As he removes albums one by one and sets each on the counter, he announces the artist's name. "Let's see here. We have the Irish Rovers, Englebert Humperdinck." He pulls out a handful and fans them out like a giant poker hand. "Backstreet Boys. Mariah Carey. Four Britney Spears albums and a Jessica Simpson." He stares at Eleanor. "The. Spice. Girls. *What* were you thinking?"

"They were all popular in their day. My mother loved Englebert Humperdinck and . . ." She pulls out a David Cassidy album. "And I loved Keith Partridge. Someone will buy them. If you ever allow a customer inside."

"I need you to call him and tell him to come pick up this garbage. I want my money back."

"Really, Eleanor." Ginny holds up a Celine Dion record. "What were you thinking?"

"*Your* money?" Eleanor asks Noel.

"Yes. I can't afford to be shelling out for merchandise that will only damage my reputation. I'm sure you can understand that. I'll leave this stuff with you to take care of?" He pauses to nudge Angus awake and the dog jumps up, dancing and wagging and fussing until the floor shakes. "How's the old goat, huh? How's my boy?"

Angus prances back and forth from Noel to the door, whining hopefully. Noel looks at Eleanor. "You mind if I walk him?"

So that's that. She is so repellent even her dog can't stand her.

"Eleanor?"

"Go ahead! Have a great time!"

Watching Angus bound outside with Noel, tail wagging, tongue lolling out the side of his mouth, Eleanor shakes her head. "Am I so unlikable?"

"That's it." Ginny grabs Eleanor's purse from under the counter. "Come over to my place for dinner. You need to escape yourself. I'd hate you too if I was with you all the time."

Chapter 22

She pulls up in front of Ginny's place and stares out at bare tree branches clawing the evening sky. She's heard nothing from Jonathan since the horse. He's been so quiet, she thinks she's quite possibly offended him by not saying thank you. Seriously, he went to all that trouble of attending the class, making this gorgeous gift for Sylvie, and what did Eleanor do? Nothing.

She pulls out her phone and dials his cell. The call goes to message and his voice booms deep and smooth. *This is Jonathan, sorry I missed your call. Leave a message at the beep.*

Hey. It's Eleanor. The horse is truly stunning and it was so sweet of you to make it. Give me a call; I'd like to thank you. She pauses. *In person.*

She drops the phone into her bag, heart pounding. Why did she have to add "in person?" That was such a mistake. Now he'll think her call is a manipulative ploy to get him back—which it isn't. She picks up the phone again, willing it to ring. When it doesn't, she reaches for the bottle of pinot noir she brought and climbs out of the car.

She shouldn't have left the message. Now her whole night will be ruined.

◈

The atmosphere inside the house is one of chaos. Ginny's dining room mirror hangs slightly askew and one of the linen curtains has torn away from the rod above—Eleanor remembers this story: Greggie tried to climb the drapes after watching *George of the Jungle.* The youngest, William, belted into a high chair with a bent wizard cap on his head, has been howling since Eleanor arrived; and Ginny's oldest, Kyle, has an ear infection and helped himself to the Tylenol bottle not long ago. The boy sits glassy-eyed in his chair, watching Eleanor in silence.

Greggie hums "It's the Hard-Knock Life" from under the table.

As Ginny flies in from the kitchen with a casserole dish full of chicken breasts floating on rice, Ted dumps wine into glasses like he's filling slop buckets. He hands one to Eleanor and motions toward the crying baby with the other. "Lesson number one, dear Eleanor. Sometimes you gotta self-medicate."

"I'd have told you to come over later, once the kids are in bed." Ginny spoons chicken onto everyone's plates. When she looks up, the pouches beneath her eyes shine. "But they never actually go to bed."

"More like they fall over, mid-fight, and pass out cold," Ted says after gulping his wine. "Not that we get to sleep in our own bed." He looks at Kyle. "Why don't Mommy and Daddy sleep in their bed anymore, big boy?"

Kyle doesn't take his eyes off Eleanor. "'Cause I like to sleep like a starfish."

Ted shrugs. "The guest room pullout isn't so bad. Gin and I get some forced snuggling time."

"News flash. Once this belly gets bigger, you're down in the den."

Greggie shouts from under the table, "I wanna sleep in the den, no fair!"

"Daddy's all set, then," Ted says before taking another swig. "He'll sleep in the backseat of the car."

"Anyhow, this way you'll get the real picture." Ginny disappears into the kitchen and returns with a jug of milk. "No delusions of peace or quiet."

"Or juvenile obedience of any kind," Ted adds. "That's Lesson number two."

Ginny sees Kyle feeding chicken to the scrappy Chihuahua mix dancing and yelping on the floor. "Are you feeding Termite, Kyle?"

"No."

"I'm glad they're still up," Eleanor says. "I haven't seen them in a while—right, guys?"

Greggie pokes Eleanor's stockinged toes with a toothpick.

Ted passes Ginny a glass. She holds it to her nose, inhales deeply, and passes it back. "We're having twins, remember?"

He stares at his wife's belly and sinks into his chair. He shakes his head in horror as a green bean flies across the table and hits the wall. "For just one moment, I forgot."

Eleanor peers under the table to the phone in her lap to make sure it's getting a signal. It is.

Ginny leans over William to cut up the chicken on his high-chair tray, which calms him down. "Kyle, don't feed the dog. You know he throws up."

"I wasn't."

"It's Ted's night to cook," Ginny says to Eleanor.

"Chicken and rice. My trademark dish."

"Greggie." Ginny peers beneath the table. "Please come sit on your chair like one of the real humans."

"I am one of the real humans."

She never should have called Jonathan, Eleanor thinks. Someone walks out of your life, you don't go scaring them further away by demanding face-time. Especially a man! He's probably freaked out right now. Cell phones are a terrible invention.

"Okay." Ginny sits up straight, blows a strand of hair off her face. "Daddy made dinner, so everyone check their chicken."

"Very funny, Gin. I'm a great cook."

Eleanor nods with her mouth full. "Delicious." As she slices into another piece, she leans closer to her plate. The chicken actually does look pink. She reaches for her napkin and glances around to make sure no one is looking. Then expels it and hides the evidence in her lap.

The baby pushes a piece of chicken into his mouth.

She has to say something. William could get sick. Eleanor stabs a piece of meat and holds it up to the light. "You know, it might be a teensy bit underdone."

"How long did you cook it?" Ginny snaps at Ted.

"Same as usual."

Ginny scoops William's chicken from the tray and sweeps her finger through his mouth to remove whatever he hasn't swallowed. No surprise, the child begins to scream. "You have to check the center," Ginny calls over the wailing. "How many times have I told you that?"

"I did check. I think I checked . . ."

"'I think I checked' isn't good enough when it comes to chicken, baby. You have to be sure."

"*Sorry.*"

William throws himself onto his tray, sobbing. The wizard hat topples onto the floor. "Wanta have chicken!"

"Kyle, honey, did you eat any?"

"No, I gave it all to Termite."

The baby's sobs grow more intense. "I'm hungry!"

"Why don't I put a few pieces in the microwave for him," says Eleanor. "Make sure they're well done."

Ted reaches down to pick up the fallen hat. "Remember that story about the toddler on Long Island? Didn't that boy die from raw chicken? Salmonella poisoning?"

Kyle starts to cry. "I don't want Willie to die!"

Greggie crawls out from beneath the table. "Is Willie gonna die?" Both boys move to the high chair and wrap their arms around their youngest brother as he howls in fury.

Ted is standing now. "Do you think we should call someone? A doctor?"

Ginny pulls William out of the high chair and sets him on the floor beside his brothers. "Everybody climb on Daddy. Give him something real to worry about."

Tears are gone. All three boys charge their father, yelping with excitement as they climb his legs and poke and tickle Ted while Termite yelps his concern from the floor. Ginny watches, shaking her head, one hand caressing her belly. The mother of darkness is smiling.

The moment is so intimate. Eleanor takes William's chicken into the kitchen and puts it in the microwave. Ginny comes in behind her, carrying the platter of pink chicken. She sets it on the counter and looks at Eleanor.

"You are out of your mind, doing this all by yourself. Out of your freaking mind."

Chapter 23

The video camera Jonathan left behind is too sophisticated. All the buttons with symbols she doesn't recognize. Eleanor twists and pokes and shifts the tiny controls until a green light comes on, then sets the camera on the dresser and hurries over to stand beside the crib.

"Hello, Sylvie," she says, reaching down to stop Angus from devouring his left ankle and point his great sopping snout toward the camera. The dog woofs in defiance. "This is Angus, your dog. He's very friendly. Right, Angus?"

Angus leaves the room, agitated. She hears him drop to the dining room floor in a series of bony clunks. There he lets out yips that sound like a squeaky mattress.

"And I'm Eleanor. Mommy." Why does she feel like a fraud calling herself Mommy? She looks around for what to say next. "This is your new room. Your bed. And . . ." She grabs a few plush animals. "Your toys."

Woof woof.

"Angus, please!" She'll edit that out.

Somewhere in the hallway, a buzzer drones. A neighbor's oven timer most likely, but loud enough to be heard through two closed doors. It's too banal. Might sound depressing on video. Eleanor pauses the filming until it stops.

She holds up a framed photo of her adoptive parents. "These are your grandparents. Papa Thomas and Nana Marion. They're not around anymore, though. So." She sets the photo back on the dresser. "Yeah."

Woof. Woof woof.

"Angus!"

The buzzer drones on again. There's not much else to show so she waves into the camera. "I guess that's it for now. I'm going to see you so soon, honey." Her voice catches at the end. Will she really see Sylvie? Ever?

"You're going to have a long plane ride, then come into a big airport, and then, then there I'll be. We'll be together and you'll have a . . ." She stops. Eleanor and a neurotic canine who hates her do not a real family make. "We'll have so much fun."

Woof woof.

Her phone rings from the kitchen. Eleanor races to see Martina Kalla's number on the screen.

"Hello?"

"Eleanor Sweet?" Martina's voice sounds cool. Capable. Like she could find a granule of sugar in the sand.

"Yes. That's me."

"Hi there, sorry it took so long to get back to you."

Eleanor finds herself bouncing up and down on her toes. "That's fine. No problem at all. Here's my situation. I was born in Kansas City and there's this street—"

"I'm sorry to interrupt, but I'm swamped right now and won't be able to take you on until February. March at the latest. You said 'urgent' in your message, so I wanted to check if you're able to wait that long."

"No." Eleanor drops into a chair and closes her eyes. "I'm not."

Chapter 24

The morning in Boston Common is crisp and sunny. Bright blue sky with clouds so puffy and defined they could have been drawn by preschoolers. Eleanor has layered up even more with leather gloves and a vintage Annie Hall fedora. Something about being able to hide beneath a sturdy brim makes her feel less vulnerable. She lets the grassy slope propel her down to the massive beech tree where eight or nine mothers have set up camp with their babies. It's something the agency arranges to provide a network of friends for parent and child: a meet-and-greet with others whose adoptions are complete. Eleanor had been scheduled to attend this morning with Sylvie, had things gone as planned.

So being here isn't exactly *wrong*.

A flutter in her stomach works its way up her esophagus.

The setups vary from a mother sitting cross-legged with a tightly jacketed baby on her lap and a diaper bag on her blanket, to full-blown camps that include portable playpens, coolers, and bouncy chairs from IKEA. Seeing the babies—with their smiling eyes, skin of every shade, hair that ranges from nonexistent to thin to nappy to thick and spiky—nearly flattens her. A few younger infants are sound asleep in car seats or their mother's arms, others suck from bottles. Two of the older ones sit face to face on a blanket and tussle over a ball.

Likely because it's twelve o'clock on a Tuesday, only one woman has her husband along.

The mothers seem relaxed and familiar with one another. Eleanor recognizes a couple of them from the store. She approaches rather stupidly, prowling around the periphery, then holds up a hand as if to say *I come in peace*.

"Hi. I'm not sure if Nancy mentioned I might be stopping by. I'm Eleanor. My baby was supposed to be here, but isn't just yet. Long story."

And not a lie.

One mother, the jovial brunette who brought along her husband, has a very fussy infant lurching backward in her arms, red-faced, refusing to be burped. "Dee Gilchrist." She pats the corner of her blanket and moves her booted legs out of the way. "Come. So you don't have to sit on the grass in your nice coat."

Her husband spits grape seeds into his palm. "Ian Gilchrist." He tilts his chin toward the baby. "Stay-at-home dad. I'm giving Dee here a little much-needed mother–son time. I'm a peach like that."

Full-time dad. Here is a man wholly present for his adopted baby. No worries about what may or may not happen. What attachment did or did not happen at birth. Ian pulls a bottle of formula from his mini-cooler and excuses himself. He jogs effortlessly toward the change room hut by the wading pool.

"This is Cole, by the way. And don't let his fussing scare you," says Dee. "It's just a bit of colic."

"Not possible to scare me, I've been wanting one for so long."

A black woman in a tidy Burberry jacket hands Eleanor a bottle of water. "We've all been there. I'm Felicia."

The ladies go around the circle and introduce themselves: their names, what part of the city they're from, and the ages and names of their children. One woman—one with twin boys feeding each other Cheerios—asks Eleanor when her daughter will arrive.

"We're still hammering out the date," Eleanor says, before going on to explain the circumstances around Sylvie's adoption. The earthquake. Her mother's death. How, by the grace of God, Sylvie was rescued.

Ian is back with the bottle and hands it to Dee. "Warmed it under the hot-water tap. See if he takes it."

Dee sets Cole on her lap and offers the silicone nipple. It's Kort, from Sweden—Eleanor sells these at the store. The baby refuses the bottle, releases angry cries like little puffs of smoke. His mother struggles to keep him on her lap. "They say colic doesn't last past two months. I pray day and night they're right."

"Try holding him on his stomach like I showed you," Ian says. "Football hold."

Rolling her eyes at the other mothers, Dee gently flips Cole over, rubbing his back with her free hand while he howls.

"So what do you do, Eleanor?" Ian shouts over the din.

"I have a store. Baby store, actually."

Felicia squeals. "That's why you look so familiar. You own Pretty Baby?"

When Eleanor nods, the whole group erupts in excited chatter.

You'll have everything you'll ever need.
Your store is my absolute favorite!

You're going to be so prepared.

Are those convertible toddler beds ever going to go on sale?

Cole's cries grow louder.

"I was in your store once," says a woman in yoga pants. "It was someone else who served me. God, was she pregnant. Third boy under five, she said."

A sympathetic groan erupts from the blanket.

"Imagine?"

"I mean lucky but, wow. Hope she has her mother nearby."

"Nearby? How about living in?"

There's no way Eleanor dares mention the coming twins. She'll never get the conversation on track again. "Someone told me not to schedule the pediatrician appointment the first week. What did you all do? I mean, I want to make sure she's healthy but I don't want her getting poked with a needle as soon as she arrives. I don't want her to associate me with pain."

Cole's face is scrunched up tight and dark red. He tucks his tiny legs close to his body and howls. Ian holds out his hands. "All right, all right. Time to come to the master." It's a role Ian cherishes, that much is clear. He props his son on his enormous shoulder, stands up and massages his back in a firm upward sweep. From Ian comes soothing shushing sounds and he walks Cole around the big tree, pointing up at a squirrel. It doesn't matter what injustices this baby encountered early in life. This man will single-handedly undo them all.

Cole's cries lessen. His body softens; he relinquishes his fight. Before long, he's making quiet whimpers, blinking at the world around him. Ian grins at his audience.

"See? The pay's pretty good, too."

Dee turns to Eleanor. "What about you? Is your husband nervous?"

"I'm actually doing this on my own."

"Wow. I love it," says Dee, her eyes fixed on Eleanor's wedding ring. Eleanor pushes her hands into her pockets. "Like a celebrity."

Felicia, whose baby has fallen asleep in her lap, leans closer. "I heard this one story—this was a surrogate situation. The pregnant birth mother found out the adopting mom was single after her guy walked out. Anyway, birth mom broke the contract. Wouldn't adopt out to the mother alone. The adopting mom took it to court but she lost. A change in circumstance unacceptable to her nullified the deal."

"That's horrible," says Dee. "I'd die."

Felicia looks at Eleanor. "Different situation from yours. Yours was orphaned. Not to be morbid, but did they find both her parents' bodies?"

This Eleanor has never considered. That Sylvie's father could still come forward. "Nothing at all is known about him. Whether he's even in this country. As far as anyone knows, my daughter's birth mom was all on her own. Plus it's been six months since it happened."

Dee pats Eleanor's knee. "Relax. You're fine if no one's come forward by now. We'll have to make a play date for when your girl arrives. What's her name?"

"Sylvie."

"Sylvie, that's so French. I love her already."

Shrinking beneath the brim of her hat, Eleanor feels her heart thump. Sylvie had no father on record. Her mother's sister signed her over as only living kin. The conversation has moved on to preschool waiting lists but Eleanor can no longer focus. She stands up, smoothes her skirt. "I should head back to the store."

But she doesn't.

Eleanor runs up the grassy slope to Beacon Street and marches through the traffic. She jogs along Battersea Road and up the steps to Isabelle's front door. Here, she pulls a scrap piece of paper from her purse and scrawls out a note. She slips it into the mail slot and walks away.

Chapter 25

The rap on the front door is unmistakable. Eleanor lifts her head off the pillow in the dark and looks at the clock: 2:47. Angus's nails chatter against the floor as he dances and yips his pleasure.

He knows the person on the other side.

She stands up, her silky nightgown falling like water down her legs. After the blow of both search angels turning her down, after not hearing from Jonathan, after the story of the thwarted adoption in the park, after Isabelle ignoring her note, she took a full sleeping pill to quiet her mind. It hit her hard.

When she steps forward, she has to steady herself with the nightstand.

Another knock. "Eleanor."

It's him. Her fingers trailing the wall, she pads into the bathroom to rub toothpaste on her tongue, fluff her hair. Then she quiets Angus. Pulls him back from the door. Opens it.

In sweats, his hair in his eyes, his shoes untied. A shy grin on his face. Jonathan.

She opens the door wider and Angus charges his beloved. There is whispering. Affectionate petting. A tail thwacking the wall with joy. When the dog calms, Jonathan looks up at her, his eyes asking if he can come inside. She steps back and allows him.

He kicks off his shoes, drops his keys on the hall table—a sound she didn't know she missed but that now makes it impossible to breathe. In the light from the living room window, she's aware of the sheerness of her nightie.

"God, I miss you." He steps closer.

He walked out. He stiffed you at the agency. One nice gesture, then he ignored your phone call.

Still. He's here. He's home. "I miss you too."

Angus pants, happy, his body weight against Jonathan's thighs as if to keep him here. In the apartment. Where he belongs.

Eleanor reaches for Jonathan's hand and leads him into the bedroom. Knocks Pillow Jonathan to the floor and pulls her husband onto the bed. He nuzzles her hair and she groans. She stares up at him, hair strewn across her face in a way she hopes is sexy.

"You're beautiful." He throws one leg over her and kisses her. He tastes like scotch.

Nothing has ever been so exquisite. She can't even think, can only feel the wet softness of his tongue, his lips. His body against hers, heavy, solid. Safe. She wonders if she's dreaming.

"I've been thinking . . ." he whispers.

She covers his mouth with hers and kisses him harder, not daring to hear what he might say. She sucks on his tongue, teasing him until he moans.

Her hand slides down his shirt and under his waistband. Her fingers find their way to the front of his thigh. She touches his hardness, and for a moment he holds his breath.

"I want you," he says.

She pulls him on top of her and parts her legs, guiding him inside her.

Chapter 26

An hour before opening, Eleanor allows Angus to relieve himself on a street lamp out front, then she heads into the store to make a cup of coffee. The dog shoves his way in as she's partway through the door. She locks up behind her. She's not up to dealing with early morning customers.

With the help of the pill, with the arrival of Jonathan, she slept deeper than she has in weeks. When she finally woke, he was gone. She sat up, blinking. It could have been a dream, if not for Pillow Jonathan tossed on the floor. Then again, it's Saturday. He works the day shift Saturdays. Almost certainly, he went to work. She searched every surface in the apartment for a note.

There was nothing.

She curses herself for not allowing her husband to talk. But his presence, his body, it felt too good. She couldn't risk it.

Still, it means something, his coming. It might even mean everything.

In the shop, Angus steps onto the window display to squeeze himself between baby dresser and glass and lie down.

It's the perfect spot for observation. Offers him countless reasons to woof and growl the entire morning long.

Eleanor removes her outer layer and boots up the computer: *Search Angels*, she types into Google. Thousands of Search Angel sites come up, the second being on Facebook. As she scrolls down the Facebook page, message after message comes up.

"From Ernie Ruiz: looking for my brother Ricky. Born June 1971."

"From Alex Heingarten: birth son given up Dec 11, 2009. Markham-Stouffville Hospital, Ontario, Canada. Birth mother Michele Boisvert, orig from St. Laurent, Quebec."

She scrolls through page after page of pleas for help. All from people looking for a search angel. Of course. Hundreds of thousands of people must be looking for birth relatives. There cannot possibly be enough search angels to help them all.

She checks her phone. Nothing from Jonathan.

Still. He came home. He came home.

Ginny thumps through the door, already deep into her maternity wardrobe of Ted's old police shirt, stretched-out leggings, and UGG boots. She could be six months pregnant. She sees Eleanor and puts down her bag, spins in a circle. "I don't look pregnant, do I?"

"God, no. You look like you've never even met a baby, let alone borne any."

Ginny smiles. "That's what I thought. I'm carrying more compact this time."

As Eleanor turns back to the computer, Angus jumps up in an explosion of barking and window bumping.

Out on the sidewalk, a teenage boy rolls back and forth on a skateboard, squatting down low to leap over sidewalk cracks. The impact when he lands could topple the entire city. In spite of Angus's barking, a few tattoo-soaked girls lean against the Pretty Baby storefront and suck on cigarettes. A little blue-headed girl cheers. They're the same kids as before, Eleanor thinks. The ones who peered through the window, full of hope that Noel would actually open for business. Perfectly reasonable. Why would an adult lease a store, spray the walls in graffiti, drag in a ten-foot Sasquatch, and play the same song over and over if he *didn't* plan to open the doors one day?

A pregnant woman approaches Pretty Baby and steps over a boy sprawled across Eleanor's doormat.

"Sorry," Eleanor says to her customer, who looks unimpressed as she heads for the plush toys.

Before these teenagers get into the habit of depositing themselves in front of her store, Eleanor decides to take action. She marches to the back and returns with an antique bench she painted periwinkle blue—the color of her logo and front door. It's a valuable piece, but not nearly as valuable as the confidence of her customers. These kids need seating. Near *Noel's* door.

With the girls looking on, she bumps the bench through the door and sets it in front of Death by Vinyl, right beneath the window.

Fully aware that the girls are giggling at her, she returns to the shop to find Ginny watching, an amused smile on her face. "You are so naive it almost hurts."

"What? I think it's a brilliant idea. Now they know where to hang out."

One of the smoker girls snuffs out her cigarette and wanders over to the bench. The skateboarder stops his concrete-shattering tricks to follow them over to Noel's. They stand around and observe this foreign object. So quaint. So pretty. The bench might as well have been dropped by aliens, the way they gawk. A tall boy, elbows threatening to pierce his sweatshirt, nudges the bench with the toe of his sneaker. They wait for it to move or fight back.

The bench, of course, does nothing.

"See?" says Eleanor. "They're admiring it."

One of the boys, this one weighty enough that Eleanor feels concern for his skateboard, picks up the bench and drags it out onto the sidewalk in front of Pretty Baby. He kicks it onto its side.

"What's he doing?" Eleanor asks.

Ginny laughs, shakes her head. "I don't think you want to know."

They watch as the boys race up the sidewalk and, one after another, turn, leap onto their boards and shoot back, grinding their wheels across her beautiful bench. Paint chips and splinters scatter and right away the top begins to separate from its base. In seconds, the bench is a splintered pile of periwinkle kindling.

Eleanor bursts out of the store, Ginny in her wake. "Excuse me! I didn't put my bench out here for you to—"

"Out of the way, dude!" The girl with blue hair takes a running jump onto her board and tries to sail over the remains of the bench. Her first attempt results in the board spinning backward and her stumbling toward the mailbox, looking embarrassed. She takes another leap, clearing the bench with the board seemingly taped to her soles, but lands hard on the board's right side—sending her to the ground, and the board shooting like a missile straight into the passenger door of Noel's car.

Curled up on her side, she cradles her wrist, a twisted look of pain on her face.

Though everyone, including Eleanor and Ginny, rushes to the girl, Noel, who has appeared from nowhere, reaches her first. But he runs straight past and drops to his knees at his car door.

"Are you okay?" Eleanor bends over the girl and examines her wrist for swelling, signs of a broken bone. Her friends gather around, all making appropriate sounds of concern.

"I'm fine," she says, twirling her hand, the heel of which is skinned. "It's just surface."

"Still. You need to clean it out. Disinfect," says Eleanor. "I have a first aid kit in my store."

"Chill." The girl laughs and climbs to her feet. "It happens, like, every week."

The kids thunder off down the sidewalk, shoving each other and laughing. Not halfway up the block, one of them tries to leap over a small bike chained to a tree.

"Hi, Noel," Ginny says, grinning and hiding her wedding ring finger behind her back. When he doesn't react, she calls out louder, "HI, NOEL."

He nods his greeting without looking.

"Your speakers sound . . . YOUR SPEAKERS SOUND TERRIFIC."

Something about the way his head is slumped so low, the way he sits almost crumpled into himself, makes Eleanor shoo Ginny back to work. She drops to the curb beside him. Shifts closer. Puts an arm on his back.

"At least you're going to have lots of customers. Once your speakers are all ready to go."

"Speakers are good." He looks up and runs his finger along the dented car door. As Angus barks from the Pretty Baby window display, Noel's eyes redden. "But now I have to deal with this."

She stares at him. Finally, she gets it. This delay isn't about perfect sound systems or keeping a car pristine. Not at all.

Chapter 27

It's called the Puppy Love NoBark 3000 and costs $79.95 at Woofers and Tweeters, over on Commonwealth. The collar is meant to administer a harmless but effective electric shock to the offending animal: vibration-sensor collars being preferable to sound-sensor collars because they reduce false alarms caused by external noise. The nylon collar—which has a black box attached to it—has three correction modes, low, medium, and high, and is meant to amp up the correction if the barking doesn't abate at the previous level.

She has no choice. Customers are too scared to come into the store. And now, if she leaves Angus upstairs like she did before Jonathan walked out and the dog became unglued, the neighbor above has said he'll call Animal Control.

Eleanor steps over Angus, lying beneath the cash register, his hind legs threaded through his front legs to form a large, knobby X. She can't test the shock on the dog—what if the signal actually hurts him? Singes his neck?

She adjusts the collar in the way the instructions suggest, holds the black box so the metal prods touch her own neck and clips it on herself. She'll try it out. Say something loud enough to create a vibration and see if she can tolerate it.

No one's around.

Though, a dog does have the advantage of at least a thin layer of fur between shock and skin. It would be far safer to test it out while wearing a turtleneck. Or at least having slipped a Kleenex beneath the metal.

"Don't wear that during your home visit." Ginny lowers her sunglasses as she comes in. "Bondage slave collars don't give off that maternal vibe adoption agencies hope for."

"It's not—"

The jolt hits Eleanor's skin like a bad carpet shock on a dry winter day. Tears prick her eyes and she exclaims aloud, only to be zapped harder. Angus sets front legs atop the counter and starts baying deafeningly toward the ceiling, as Ginny watches, confused.

Eleanor scrambles to unclick the collar and whips it to the ground. Leaning over, she blinks back tears. "Oh my God. That hurt *so* much."

Ginny picks it up and examines it. "Wait a sec. Do they make these for kids?"

"I can't do it to him."

They both turn to watch Angus as he backs up, taking with him the display of diaper creams set up as point-of-purchase temptations by the cash. In a bid to disguise his lack of elegance, he proceeds to sit atop the fallen items and howl.

Then the bell above the door chimes and in walks Isabelle.

She pauses a moment to take in the dog, the mess, and the collar on the ground, then sets her Chanel bag on the counter with an expensive clink. "I didn't think it was legal in this country to keep horses as pets." She braces herself, eyes clamped shut, as Angus charges her, heaving his weight into her legs. "Dear God, please tell me I'm not dead."

"He's friendly, Isabelle. He wants you to pet him."

"I'll indulge in no such thing." She sidles away from Angus and glares at Eleanor. "You're in terrible shape, Eleanor Sweet."

"Excuse me?"

"I've never even been approached by someone with the name Smith who was actually named Smith. It is, as you can imagine, the single most common name used by women looking to give birth and vanish. And Kansas City. It's as close to being an impossible case as I've ever seen."

"So, you're saying it's not worth trying?"

"I'm saying you're going to have a terrible time finding a search angel to help you. We are human—we do consider the odds of success in taking on any new cases. Some people are simply unfindable. Surely you can see that."

Eleanor is terrified to speak lest she frighten the woman away. She hadn't considered this. That her case is undesirable. "I guess. I hadn't thought—"

"You can't just go to anybody."

"Right. Okay . . ."

Isabelle pulls a plane ticket from her purse and slaps it on the counter. "I am going to Missouri in the morning. I have many reservations about it. Lately, I do not like planes or travel or other people for that matter. Every nerve in my soon-to-be corpse is shouting at me, but there you have it. I'm going to find this mother of yours if it kills me. And it may very well do so." She takes her purse and heads to the door, turning back to add, "And next time you compose a note intended to tempt another to travel hither and yon on your behalf, take the time to make sure you haven't done so on the flap of a tampon box." With that, Isabelle is gone.

"Seriously?" asks Ginny, staring at her boss. "A tampon box?"

Eleanor leans over to pick up the shock collar. "What? It got her here, didn't it?"

Chapter 28

C an you read the inscription in the picture?" Isabelle shouts into the phone. In the background, from the comfort of her kitchen, Eleanor can hear the wind and rain pounding against Isabelle's jacket. "Can you make out the name?"

It's the eleventh cemetery Isabelle has visited this week. This is her favorite part of a search, she'd said. The stillness. The stories. She told Eleanor that sometimes she plays games with herself. Looks at the names of family members, especially the husbands and wives. Looks at who died first. Imagines the circumstance, whether sudden or ongoing. The surviving spouse's feelings. Agony or relief?

The first place Isabelle went after getting off the plane on Tuesday was Women's Hospital, where Eleanor was born. The usual procedure for obtaining birth records this old is to submit your request to the Medical Records department and wait three or four weeks to hear whether or not the desired record is still on file. But Isabelle's years of sleuthing have earned her special status. A young man named Dwight Mason, thin and serious in his wire-framed glasses, agreed to drive out to offsite record storage some fifteen miles away, in the sleepy suburb of Lansing, while Isabelle waited in the motel room. The file was over thirty years old. The chances of it being found, the chances of it even existing anymore, were slim.

But without it, the search couldn't get started. They needed to find out if Ruth Smith was or wasn't Eleanor's mother's name before any more work could be done. The answer, Isabelle told Eleanor, came Thursday morning at 8:37 when the phone in her motel room woke her.

"I think I've found what you're looking for," Dwight Mason said at the other end of the line.

Now, Eleanor stares down at the photo Isabelle has just texted her. The stony grave marker, soaked with rain. The inscription: *Woolsey*. Beneath that, *Estelle Jane*. She presses the phone to her ear and can hear the roar of wind. "Is this my mother? Her real name?"

"Her grandmother, I believe," Isabelle shouts over the weather. "Can you read what it says below?"

Eleanor looks again. "Just *Beloved Wife of . . .*" She peers closer. "Below that it gets blurry."

"I'll try to take another." There's a pause, some crackling, then Isabelle is back. "Too rainy just now. I can't do it without soaking my phone."

At the kitchen table, Eleanor reaches for Angus, pulls his head onto her lap. "What does it say?"

"Says *1905–1979. Beloved wife of Herbert John Woolsey.* She's too old to be your mother. Could be your mother's mother or grandmother."

Her great-grandmother. "What else does it say?"

"It says, *Loving mother to Brian.*" Isabelle pauses. "*And Janet.*"

"So Janet could be my mother?"

"More likely your grandmother. Most women gave birth young back then."

Eleanor looks at the photo again. "I've only ever thought of myself as adopted. Never as having been . . . born. Makes no sense, I know."

"That's common. Don't go thinking you're so special, buttercup."

"What about my mom?"

"We don't have her name confirmed yet."

"But Woolsey. How did you learn this?"

"A friend of mine got hold of your hospital records. Apparently your mother came into ER because you were breach. Very lucky she did so because the girls' home had a terrible record for live births from breach deliveries. The hospital was full. They didn't want to admit your mother and were calling her a cab to go back to the home for girls. But your mom was scared enough, I guess, to call a family member. A woman named Estelle Woolsey. It shows in your file she paid for your birth, as well as a private room for your mom to recover in. My guess is Estelle wasn't your mother's mother. Her mother put her in the girls' home. My guess it was an aunt or a grandmother. You know what this means, don't you?"

"No."

Isabelle pauses a moment. "Our search has narrowed dramatically."

Chapter 29

The light pouring through Isabelle's curtains stretches across the wall like fingers. While Angus stares through the window looking for excuses to woof and growl, Eleanor sits on the floor beside the coffee table and twists the corner of her sweater around a finger.

"Get yourself up onto the sofa," Isabelle says as she pours two cups of coffee from a silver urn. "Like one of the grown-ups."

The yearbook lies on the table, navy leather faded to powder blue at the edges, gold embossing barely legible: *Trent Falls High School, 1973–74.*

Eleanor shakes her head. "I need to be on the ground for this."

"You're like my old spaniel. Anyplace higher than sea level and he threw up his boiled liver. Speaking of which, why does that animal of yours insist on making so much noise?"

"Can we open the book now?"

She points toward the window, massive twists of beige linen hanging over like bangs in need of a good trim. "What do you think of these curtains? Too fussy? I can never decide."

"Isabelle!"

"Okay." She shifts forward in her seat. "It shouldn't come as any surprise that I was right about Janet being your mother's mother and Estelle being your mother's grandmother. Who better to save a pregnant girl from the shame of her overly conventional parents than her adoring and, judging from the fact that she upgraded the two of you to a private room, wealthy grandma? You likely owe Great-Granny your life."

"Thank you, Estelle."

"All right, then. Ready to see your mother?"

"I've waited thirty-five years. I couldn't be more ready."

Isabelle sets the yearbook on her lap and opens it to where a neon green Post-it marks a page. She turns the yearbook around and sets it on Eleanor's lap. The page is filled with tiny black and white headshots. Isabelle points to one at the bottom right corner.

A girl. Longish blond hair. Shadows under the eyes, wide downturned mouth on a narrow face. The resemblance to Eleanor is unmistakable. She's staring at a young version of herself. But the expression in this girl's eyes—it's as if she has control of the entire world and she knows it. As if she's certain that every day after this one will unfold however she tells it to and she's amused by the very thought of it.

Eleanor continues to stare, desperate to know this girl— what makes her laugh, what makes her cry, what amuses her, bores her, makes her want to scream. But the more she examines her, the more convinced Eleanor is that her mother is unknowable.

"Her name is Ruth. Ruth Woolsey."

Eleanor stands, walks across the room to Angus and reaches for the comfort of his velvety ears.

Isabelle says nothing. She gets up, opens a cabinet and fills a shot glass with Johnnie Walker Blue. Hands it to Eleanor. "All in one gulp. Come on."

Eleanor swallows, holds the glass out for Isabelle to refill. Swallows again. It isn't until the burning stops and the blurred feeling starts that she speaks. "Ruth. Her name really is Ruth."

"It really is. The Smith part was fictitious."

"Are there any more pictures of her?"

Isabelle shows her two more photos, one a photography club group shot and the other a random one of campus life: Ruth perched on a brick wall, eating a sandwich by herself. She doesn't appear lonely or self-conscious. She's just fine on her own.

"Do we know where she is now?"

Isabelle flips to the Homecoming Royalty. The queen and king. Ruth, trying not to smile too wide in a cheap-looking tiara. And a boy named Daniel Leland.

"My father?"

She drains her coffee cup and reaches for her purse. "Many adoptions stem from teen pregnancies, so Daniel Leland is exactly where I plan to start."

"Back to Kansas City?"

"Our Homecoming king lives on the Cape now."

Eleanor gets up and trots after Isabelle, who is already through the front door. "Wait, you're just going to show up? No calling first or whatever?"

Isabelle tilts her chin skyward and the light catches the tiny blond hairs on her skin. "See this face? It's impossible to ignore." She swings her purse over her shoulder and folds her arms. "Now, Eleanor Sweet. Are you coming or not? I despise driving my antediluvian car."

❧

The floor of Isabelle's old Mercedes rumbles like a subway train under their feet as they stare at the ramshackle cottage. The peeling picket fence has fallen into the garden and one section of the house's faded green siding has been ripped off by a storm. And what appears to have been an enclosed back-room has burned away and been left to tough out the elements. Out front, a rusted claw-foot tub boasts only sickly, yellow-legged geraniums covered with dead leaves.

"There's no going back from something like that," Isabelle mumbles.

"Hmm?"

"I once rented a little house in Vermont. There was a bathtub out front that the owners had left sitting there, having replaced it with a Home Depot special. My sister suggested I plant in it." She shakes her head, deep in thought. "But I said no. Once you plant nasturtiums in an abandoned bathroom fixture, there's no going back. There's no undoing who you've become."

His rump on the seat and front feet on the floor, Angus pushes his great head between the two seats and starts to pant.

"My adoptive mother planted in a rain barrel. And her garden won awards every year."

"That doesn't make it right, darling." Isabelle applies plum lipstick and winces at the malodorous puff cloud that is Angus's breath. "All right. Let's find you a less-foul-smelling family member than this creature."

They pick their way along a cracked cement path and onto the porch while Angus woofs his discontent from the backseat of the car. It's hard not to peer through the living room window before they knock. There, in a tweedy recliner, wearing gym shorts and a stretched-out T-shirt with stains on the belly, is an overweight man with the chubby, hairless legs of a toddler. Light from the TV flickers across his face as he eats from a bag of Cheetos.

Eleanor's concern must show because Isabelle winks. "We don't know he's your father. It's just a place to start." She pulls a bottle of merlot from her bag. "Always best to arrive on a stranger's stoop with a gift in your hand." Eleanor raps once on the screen door. The Cheetos disappear behind the chair and the man who may or may not be her father gets up.

The screen door squeaks open to a chin stubbled with white and pale blue eyes spidered with red veins. Right away the eyes shift hopefully to the bottle. "Yeah?"

"Are you Daniel Leland?" Isabelle's voice is all business.

"Who wants to know?"

"I'm Isabelle Santos. I'm looking for a woman named Ruth Woolsey. You went to high sch—"

"What the hell you need Ruth for?"

"Do you know anything about her?"

"Can't be trusted is what I know."

Isabelle puts her hand on Eleanor's arm as if to say, *It's all right.* "When was the last time you saw her?"

"Senior year. Back when she told me she was pregnant with my best friend's baby. Bitch is still with him. Married now, over somewhere in Upstate New York. Albany area, I think."

He's not my father. Eleanor is both saddened and relieved.

"What's his name?"

"Ricky Pantera."

He holds out his palm. Isabelle fills it with the bottle.

"Ricky Pantera, Richard Pantera, Rick Pantera . . ." Back in the car, Isabelle pulls out her iPhone.

Eleanor waits, barely daring to breathe, while the phone searches the New York State Yellow Pages.

The screen fills up and there it is.

"Richard S. Pantera. 701 N. Broadland Street, Hampton Manor, NY 12144."

Isabelle watches Eleanor, holds up her phone to show the number. "We could call her right now. Up to you."

Eleanor turns to watch as a wasp zigzags toward her open window, slips inside to inspect her shoulder. She waves it away. Somewhere nearby, the sound of a leaf blower drones. "Not here. I think I'd rather be home."

"All right. I'll be there tomorrow night at eight. Just have ready a couple of lemons and a zester."

"Excuse me?"

Isabelle starts the engine. "Rule number one. Never question the search angel."

Chapter 30

Ruth Woolsey's existence, her address, her husband's name (maybe that of Eleanor's father?), it doesn't have the impact on her she'd thought. She feels no joy the next morning. More like terror. Eleanor hasn't eaten since before they visited Daniel Leland's house yesterday. What if Ruth doesn't want to be found? What if she gave up her baby and walked away determined to live her life as if it never happened? It could easily be the case. Eleanor doesn't know if she would survive that pain.

Besides these possibilities, there's also the possibility that Isabelle is wrong. That they call this Ruth Woolsey and she says they've got the wrong person. Or that she's no longer alive.

Eleanor adjusts the front window display—a black crib with the side rail lowered to allow for a rumpled gray linen duvet to spill out in an artful imitation of real life—and adjusts the sun and moon mobile hanging overhead. Angus, mercifully, is asleep in the window after spending the afternoon yelping at Faith, Death by Vinyl's sleepless upstairs neighbor, as she moved out of her apartment.

The only customer in the store is an elderly woman in pressed navy pants and cardigan. She glances up at Eleanor

and raises a crooked finger. The older ones often get confused. Taking care of baby used to be so simple. A bassinet
and a glass bottle. A rattle. Pacifier. A few nice outfits for
when the neighbors came to call. It's these customers Eleanor
takes special care of. She imagines them going home, wrapping their gift (chosen with painstaking deliberation), writing out the card in wavering script, then waiting for the baby
shower, where they will be guided to a chair at the edge of the
room, just on the outside of the excitement that comes from
young women who believe they're the first ones in history
ever to have given birth.

Eleanor doesn't want these senior relatives—most often
women—to show up with an unwanted gift that provokes a
false exclamation of joy, followed by the item being tucked
away in the back of the hall closet.

"Do you carry Dr. Spock?"

Spock. His methods, in Eleanor's opinion, spawned
the baby boomers' reactive and overly permissive attitude
and, eventually, the resultant pamperedness of today's teens.
Parenting through love, she understands. Parenting through
indulgence—or neglect—is nothing short of dangerous.

"We're all out, but there are a few great ones here, one
by Dr. David Austin. This one by K.C. Bowery—it's a good
one for strengthening the bond between infant and child.
Research has proven that a mother's reactions to baby's—"

"It's all so overwhelming these days, isn't it? I don't know
how you young women do it. So much to think about now."

"There's also this one about baby sign language written
by—"

"Sign language . . . for babies?" The lines in the woman's
chin deepen. "I'm not sure I understand."

"They think it eliminates tantrums. Babies can be taught simple signs for, say, *eat, more, cookie, bottle, hug*. That kind of thing. They say speech lags behind cognitive development, but hand–eye coordination doesn't. So baby learns a few signs and suddenly she can tell you what's wrong. Can you imagine how much less frustrating that would be for new mothers? To know why their baby is crying?"

The woman wiggles gnarled fingers by her ears. "Signing? Like for the deaf?"

"That's right."

The creases in her face grow complicated. "I really don't know . . ." She glances at her watch, then toward the door.

Eleanor looks around, determined to keep this woman in the store. She needs the sale. She doesn't want to walk her past the exit, make it too easy to leave. "Have you thought about music? Researchers say listening to classical music builds an infant's brain." When her customer appears confused again, Eleanor adds, "And calms the mother during times she's all alone. Sometimes I suggest as a gift something useful like an infant gym, then we slip a nice CD by Bach into the box with a ribbon. Makes for a wonderfully layered presentation."

Music. Now this makes sense to the woman. She moves over to the CD section and lets her fingers worry through the Genius Baby collection, stopping to examine this one or that. So much rides on her choice.

Close to the dividing wall that separates her store from Noel's, Eleanor notices a trickle of water coming from ceiling tiles that appear to be soaked. The water starts to drip on the floor, slow, steady, then pour out in one thin stream, then another. And another. Eleanor excuses herself and races to the storage closet for a roll of paper towels to mop up the floor. Another trickle, this one fatter than the rest, sprouts from the front of the store. And another. Four, five, six leaks now.

"Ginny!" With this, Angus wakes up and lopes down the aisle, woofing at the ceiling and slipping on the wet floor.

Ginny pokes her head out of the break room. "What the . . . ?"

"Just grab pots, bowls, teacups. Anything!"

Ginny vanishes into the back closet and reappears with an armload of plastic bathtubs and empty diaper pails, which she arranges beneath the closest dribbles and streams. She might as well not have bothered, as the water now buckets down in too many places to control and ceiling tiles are dropping in soggy clumps onto a rack of Italian sleepers. Angus is energized by the action, and takes a sopping pillow between his teeth to shake the life out of it. Or maybe into it. Ginny and Eleanor rush to push strollers, Baby Bjorns, and fabric bouncy chairs out of the way as more of the sky falls. The three pails are no longer enough; the entire rear right corner of the store is under deluge.

The customer, who'd been bent down examining a Baby Bach CD, stands tall now and looks around, astonished, then reaches into her purse and pulls out a collapsible umbrella. She gives it a shake and, once it has bloomed in full, holds it over her head and marches out of the store.

Eleanor is now soaked. She pulls off blazer and silk scarf, the blouse, vest, and boots, until she's down to camisole and khakis, which she rolls up to her knees.

She marches past Ginny, who has bits of wet pink insulation dotting her head and shoulders. "I'm going to check upstairs and next door."

✺

Her apartment was dry and quiet, but it's as if a tsunami has hit Death by Vinyl. A few of Noel's shelves are knocked over, likely from the huge metal fan that has fallen from the ceiling. Records and magazines and T-shirts lie in a chunky swamp on the floor. Noel sloshes through the water, which is still pouring from above, his pants soaked to the ankles, his boots blackened with wet. Beside him, face down in the lake: Sasquatch. His go away sign has drifted away.

"Oh no," she says, surveying the devastation.

"Bohemian Rhapsody" plays on but the sound has gone drunken and squishy. All that painstaking work on speakers that are now waterlogged.

His countertops are dripping with pooled water and Eleanor rushes to lift files and flyers and masses of mail, reaching down to retrieve what's fallen into the pond. As she sorts it in her arms, she notices piles of unopened envelopes. Three notices from Boston Water and Sewer, countless letters from TD North and a credit bureau. Four, maybe five, from Chickadee Investments—the company Birdie owned with her husband, now run by their grown children. They owned nearly the entire block, including Eleanor's building. One of the envelopes is marked in red "Third Notice."

It doesn't look as if he's paid a single bill.

She looks up to catch him staring at her shoulders. Suddenly she feels naked. He lunges down to her feet and picks up a dripping-wet picture frame. He stares down at it, immobilized. A jagged crack criss-crosses his wife's face.

Eleanor takes it out of his hands and unlatches the back

of the frame to remove the photo. "This will dry." She looks around for a safe place and leans it up high on a shelf behind the cash. "It'll be fine if you don't touch it."

He nods, his face completely devoid of expression.

"Should we get to work? See what we can save around here?"

Noel points at red and blue plastic milk crates running the length of the store on a long wooden shelving unit. They're still dry. "Start with these?"

"Sure. Just set everything on higher ground."

Lift.

Stack.

Splash.

Repeat.

Water continues to gush from above and Eleanor helps him move dry crates from the epicenter of the storm. They stack them at the store's perimeter, alongside a mound of concert T-shirts, record players, and DVDs. At the back of the store, the old floorboards are higher, creating a safe zone for a rolling rack of posters, the milk crate full of Britney and Posh Spice.

"Must be one of the apartments above you. It's not nearly as bad in my place."

He stops. "Wait. You're flooded too?"

"Why do you think I arrived half naked and soaked?" Without waiting for an answer, she asks, "Any access to the second floor from here?"

He motions toward a poster-covered partial wall at the rear. "Birdie had a staircase built."

The black iron circular staircase wraps tightly around a center pole and Eleanor, being wet, holds onto it for dear life as she climbs in bare feet to the second floor. At the top, she pushes open a flimsy door and scans the hall, which smells like water.

There's no answer when she knocks at the back unit. No answer at the front either, but Eleanor hears splashing from inside. She turns the knob and the door swings open.

The apartment is empty, all dingy white walls speckled with nail holes and dark-stained floors faded where furniture used to be. Orange batik fabric hangs from the living room, giving the room a weird, coppery glow. With the painted flowers on one wall, the vibe is distinctly hippie-ish. And the floor is covered in water.

Water gurgles out from the galley kitchen, where the tap is on full and the sink is overflowing. She splashes across the room to turn off the tap, then races to the bathroom to do the same for sink and bathtub. All the drains are stoppered.

Which means Auntie Faith followed Ginny's advice. She went drastic. And then some.

Chapter 31

She's read the message some five or ten times, each time a different way.

Hey. El. Any chance we can chat or meet?

It's everything she's been hoping for. Forget rocking horses and drunken sex, this time he wants to talk. He's finally come to his senses and wants her back. He came home, got in her—their—bed and said he missed her. He slept with her. So he took a few days to think—so what? Now he's back for real. He's realized the greatest reward can only come from risk, from holding your breath and jumping in.

She could float, she feels so light.

It couldn't be that he would just walk away. Getting Sylvie was way too joyous a life event. A child is what they both want. He couldn't be willing to give that up. And it isn't as if adoption is some crazy, untried life choice. It's been happening since the beginning of time. It happened to her!

The e-mail came in at the end of the workday, just as Eleanor climbed the stairs to change out of her sodden clothes. Come to think of it, the ping sounded different than usual. Louder. Or more clear. She knew before looking that it was from him.

Upstairs, she pads into the bedroom and strips. She'll see him. No question she'll see him.

Hey. El. Any chance we can chat or meet?

Of course, it could be something bad he wants to tell her. He's met someone else and wants a divorce. Worse—he's met someone else and she's pregnant.

Eleanor turns on the shower and waits for the water to heat up, then steps into the tub and lets the steaming hot spray pelt her back.

She answered him too quickly. Not ten minutes later, she said, with as much nonchalance as she could fake: *Hi. Sure, I guess we could meet or whatever. Sometime.* (She wasn't going to say "chat." He might suggest a phone call.) *How about tonight?*

Tonight is the night she and Isabelle are planning to call Ruth. Eleanor has waited thirty-five years to hear her birth mother's voice. She can wait one more day. More important is Sylvie and rebuilding her family. Ruth comes into Eleanor's life and maybe it fixes some things. Jonathan comes back, it fixes everything.

Nothing—*nothing*—will stop Eleanor from seeing Jonathan tonight. If he agrees.

Her phone pings from atop the toilet. She dries her hands on the shower curtain and grabs it.

Jonathan: *Sounds good. Piatto Vecchio at eight?*

Piatto Vecchio was their place. Charming, and she could arrive a few minutes late and walk all sexy across the room while he watches from the table. He'd remember what they had, their connection. He'd see her as his wife, his lover, and not just as the soon-to-be mother of a baby that scared him out of her life.

Baby. That was a good point. Piatto Vecchio might remind him of the night she told him about Sylvie. The beginning of the end that, with any luck, was not the end. In fact, probably best to avoid Italian food altogether. Seafood might be better.

She texts back, *Blue Water Grill?*

He replies, *Great, see u in an hour.*

She plunges her face into the shower jet and screams for joy.

Once she's dried off and doused herself in a scent he once said he adores, she scans her closet for an outfit. Not so many layers tonight. Tonight she'll show a bit of skin if it kills her. She pulls out a light blue Calvin Klein with a structured sixties feel. Fitted bodice and an A-line skirt. It'll set off her eyes and make her waist look tiny. The perfect vibe to get her husband back. With a pair of nice pumps, her calves would look shapely, toned. Jonathan always loved her calves.

She slips the dress on and stares in the mirror.

What if the note doesn't mean he wants her back? What if it means nothing of the sort. Maybe the guy simply wants to make things official. Talk lawyers and separation agreements and moving trucks.

She could throw up from not knowing.

In the meantime, there is Isabelle. She texts her:

Something came up tonight. May be good. Rain check— tomorrow?

"Ma'am?" Cal, the only available contractor Noel could find online, stares at her with a chisel in one hand. He waves it toward the wall, which he has already opened up to expose the brick underneath. The ceilings on both sides saved him time, as Noel's was already exposed and Eleanor's exposed itself. "You got a sec to see something?"

She should never have poked her head into the store. Now she'll wind up getting caught up in flood talk when she should be heading to the restaurant to meet Jonathan. Cal leads her over to the wall, where his assistant scrubs cracked mortar from between the bricks. Cal tugs out a thick chunk of cement, as well as a few surrounding bricks, to reveal Noel on the other side.

"Wow." Noel stares at her. "You look fancy."

Eleanor looks at Cal. "Can we discuss this tomorrow? I'm really in a—"

"What we have here," he says as if she hasn't spoken, "is a case of ancient masonry. Holes go clear through." He points to gaps all over the wall, all of which offer tiny glimpses of Noel's graffitied walls and posters. "You people ever have any problems with noise?"

"HEY, NOEL," Ginny says through the wall. She fluffs her hair and grins.

"Yes," says Eleanor. "All the time. But I just thought . . ."

"See now, you squish all these holes into one and you'd have yourself a hole some five feet in diameter."

"I'm actually late for—"

"YOUR GRAFFITI LOOKS GREAT. I'VE NEVER REALLY SEEN IT BEFORE."

Eleanor looks at Ginny and hisses, "He's not hearing impaired!"

"It's true," Noel says. "I can hear just fine."

Ginny peers closer at the hair covering his ears and

frowns. Backs away. It's possible she liked him better deaf.

"But the drywall," says Noel. "Both sides were drywalled floor to ceiling."

"Drywall doesn't offer much of a sound barrier. If either of you did any cooking in these places, you'd likely have smells coming through the wall too. Good thing yous both get along. Some neighbors fight like the devil over sound coming through the walls."

Eleanor looks down and pretends to pick lint from her dress.

"What about ceilings," Noel says. "Think we had the same problem there?"

"No brickwork in your ceiling or you might not've survived the flood." Cal waits for Eleanor or Noel to join him in laughter, then grows serious. "You had zero insulation up above. Ever have any complaints from your upstairs neighbor?"

"Said it was noisy once or twice. Didn't seem like she was upset enough to do something this crazy." Noel looks at Eleanor. "I saw her go into your store, kind of a granola type in those crazy skirts and mukluk boots. She ever complain to you?"

Eleanor feels her cheeks heat up. "I don't remember anyone by that description."

Chapter 32

She struts across the restaurant in her little blue dress, confident in the knowledge that the crossover neckline knows instinctively which parts to hug tight and which parts to treat as total strangers. Turns out planning to arrive ten minutes late was a wasted scheme, as Jonathan's seat faces away from the door. Her eyes caress the back of his head, his thinning black waves, shiny as ever, grazing his collar in a way they never did before. She forces herself to look away. Not good to show up reeking of desperation.

"Hey. Wow." He stands up to kiss her hello. She thinks he's aiming for her lips, but the kiss lands on her cheek. Nerves, she decides. "I forgot how gorgeous you are when you dress up."

She can't speak right away. That sweet almond soap smell from the hospital. Almost astringent. It's Jonathan. Her eyes move to his left hand. He's still wearing his ring.

"You change your hair?"

She touches her side ponytail. It took a half-dozen spritzes of hair spray and several bobby pins to keep the shorter pieces tucked in. "I just threw it in a clip, no big deal."

"People at work have been talking about this place. I've been meaning to come check it out."

Not good that he's talking first person singular. "They had that great review in the *Globe*. I didn't actually see it. But I heard about it," she says.

She can see his shoe now. It sticks out from beneath the tablecloth. It's new. Dark brown leather, very long and pointed in the toe. He used to buy shoes for function only. Mainly for ER comfort. Now, it seems, he buys for elegance. Another bad sign.

"I actually came straight from the hospital. Told them my dad had fallen." His knee bounces up and down the way it does when he's anxious. "Lied just to see you."

Eleanor tries to hide the thrill that inches up her core. He's never backed out of his schedule. Not in the entire ten years he's been working. *Stop it*, she chides herself. *Stop keeping score.*

"How are your parents?"

"The usual. Dad still with the cigars. Mom still spraying the place with her lime-basil deodorizers that smell worse than the cigars. How's Angus doing?"

The small talk is surreal. Torture. Nothing matters but why they are here. "He's fine. I'm fine."

"Good. And the store?"

She shuts out the vision of the flood damage, the holey wall, the lack of sales, Ginny's pregnancy. "Never better. The ER?"

"Same old. We had this borderline patient back in this morning. Miscarried three nights ago and came back in today with bleeding. Demanded to be released so she could OD on Tylenol. Which she did this aft. Came back by ambulance, screaming and carrying on. Unbelievable." He shifts and the shoe vanishes from view.

The last subject she wants to get stuck on is the atrocities of the ER. Jonathan could settle into that for an hour, if only to escape the tension.

"Then we had the typical slew of after-school cases. Parents who think the school's Band-Aids aren't big enough, the Polysporin isn't effective enough. They're desperate to be able to march back into the school in the morning and inform the staff that little Greyson, in fact, needed eleven stitches, seven of which were internal, and could they promise to call the moment he falls from the playscape next time and refrain from making life and death decisions for children who aren't their own."

"Yeah. I bet."

"Something about Tuesdays, I swear. Mondays, kids are still sluggish with denial the weekend is over. But by Tuesday, they've accepted it. Friday's nowhere in sight and they're pissed. Worst day of the week, in my opinion." He raises the wine bottle and she nods. He fills both glasses and sips from his.

"Maybe you could adjust your schedule."

"Six to seven p.m. That's the witching hour for the nine-to-fivers." The knee starts bouncing again. "They've spent all day wanting to spit in their boss's coffee cup, because if they said they didn't feel well and wanted to go home, he'd make a face. And that lack of control—you'd be surprised how that amps up the most minor symptoms."

"Sure . . ."

A silence wraps itself around the table. Jonathan chews on his lip worriedly. Then brightens. "Then there was the swallower. Comes in last night and announces she's just downed two nails and a Bic ballpoint pen. Not only that but I see from her chart she was in three weeks back with some more nails and a plastic butter knife and they sent her home. Of course the bowels were ruptured and now she's septic. Only a matter of time, right?"

Stop this, she wants to shout. *Let's get to something that matters.* "I suppose so."

"I got her into the OR. That shit has to come out. Saddest thing. Twenty-eight and it's going to kill her if we can't lock her up. And we can't."

She fakes a shiver. "I wasn't sure what to wear to this place. How fancy it was."

"They say the red snapper's outrageous here."

Eleanor doesn't eat fish. Their entire relationship she's never eaten fish. How hard is it to remember your wife doesn't eat fish?

"The other night, I was glad you came over." She almost said *came home*. But it seemed presumptuous.

"Me too." They say nothing for a moment. His hand retracts. "The sex was always good."

Was? "Still is."

A waiter approaches to take their orders. After refilling their wineglasses, Jonathan sets his chin on his fists, focuses on her. "I'm aware how unforgivable it was. What I did."

She lifts a shoulder in an effort to reward his self-censure.

"Just all of a sudden like that. I just . . . work was crazy, I heard those stories. I freaked out."

"It's okay." *You're here. It's all I care about.*

"No. You're my wife. You deserve better."

A warmth starts in her breast and works its way up her

neck. She tries to swallow. "I know your job's insane. Or . . ."
—she half smiles—"I can sort of imagine. My day at work
is more: 'Do you want the stroller in silver or red?' And
'Cloth diapers?' 'Yes, they're a great idea if you have full-
time help.'"

"Mine is: 'Should I pull the Swiss Army knife out of your
liver via your ear or your asshole?'" He sips from his wine.
"You're lucky to have a job that centers on a happy event. The
birth of a baby." Eleanor's failure to conceive hangs over the
table like a little raincloud she wishes she could blow away.
"Sorry," he says, making it worse.

She blinks to show him he's forgiven. Everything is forgiven. *When are you moving back in?* she is dying to ask. *How
soon can the smell of your Pert Plus drift up from your pillowcase,
your scrubs fill the laundry basket, your keys clank on the front hall
table?* She gulps down her entire glass of wine and feels her
head swim.

"I miss you."

"Me too. I miss us." He looks up, tilts his head, his brows
pressed lower as if he might cry. "And I've been giving you
mixed signals. It's not fair."

"You were just . . . you were going through something."

"You're an exceptional woman. I've always known that,
but now even more. You're brave. You're strong."

She waits, fingering her wedding band.

"I'm behind you in this. I want you to know that."

"Behind me," she repeats stupidly, her heart thumping a
warning. "What does that mean?"

"I get it. I do. You chose the baby over me, over us. I
respect that. I could never do what you're doing, taking on a
baby by yourself, but I get it."

For a moment she thinks she's misunderstood. That the wine has muddied her thinking. But no, he said it. "So . . . this dinner." She waves at the wine. "Tonight. The other night. The rocking horse. You don't want to get back together? That's not what's going on?"

He grips the armrests and tenses. As if, more than anything on earth, he'd like to bolt. "Uh . . ."

She dumps wine into her glass. Fills it to the top. Swigs.

"I really wanted to apologize in person for the way I handled things. Tell you I think you're just incredible. I wanted you to know that if you need anything, even money . . ."

Her empty glass bangs on the table. The candlelight, the other diners, the fireplace, all swirl around her as she reaches for her purse and stands up. "I'm incredible. So incredible that you're leaving me."

"Are you drunk?" He reaches across the table and takes her arm, which she tugs from his grasp. "Sit down."

"Don't touch me."

"El."

"And don't El me." She hugs her bag to her chest like a bulletproof vest. She wishes she had a sweater, a coat. A sack. She'd wrap herself in anything right now. "You're such a sweetheart of a man, aren't you. Lucky, lucky me."

The couple at the next table try not to stare. She can see Jonathan getting nervous about what she might do. There is no predicting this outcome. He hisses, "Lower your voice. And sit down. You're causing a scene."

"That's the thing about breaking up, Jonathan. It's like trying to get pregnant. You can't always control the outcome."

⪻

Eleanor sits in her car and tries to massage what feels like a bullet hole in her left shoulder. She has no idea how she got out of the restaurant. She found the car, the steering wheel in her hands is proof of that. Someone asked if she was okay, back by the front doors. Someone else—maybe the hostess, maybe a diner—followed her out, stood watching as she fumbled with her keys in the rain.

Her phone rings and she picks it up, hoping it's him. Apologizing. Begging her to return.

"Yes?"

"I'm standing, in a bone-chilling fog no less, on the sidewalk with the riffraff, in front of a purple door that refuses to open. Please explain."

Isabelle.

"I texted you earlier," Eleanor says. "I told you I needed a rain check."

"Rule number two. The search angel doesn't read texts and she doesn't take rain checks."

"It's just that my ex got in touch and I thought maybe he wanted to get back—"

"Do you know what I'm doing right now, Eleanor Sweet?"

"Yes, you said, standing with the riffraff . . ."

"I'm playing the world's tiniest violin between index finger and thumb. Be here within ten minutes or I shall return to the splendor of my twelve-foot ceilings, my heated limestone floors, *and* the leisurely retirement I richly deserve."

Chapter 33

Isabelle sits at Eleanor's linoleum table and fingers a red leather address book so weathered the edges have turned seashell pink. "I'm not accustomed to being locked out of any establishment, least of all one as shabby as this. Living above a store—are you certain it's legal?"

Eleanor sets two mugs on the counter, one of them Jonathan's green Starbucks mug. After careful consideration, she stomps on the pedal of the trash can and drops the mug into the garbage with a muffled smash.

Isabelle clutches her chest. "Was that a gunshot?"

"I'm so stupid." Eleanor reaches for a Dunkin' Donuts mug and pours steeped tea into both. She brings them to the table and sets them beside the milk carton, sugar bowl, and spoons. "I actually thought he wanted to reconcile."

"The water is safe, I presume."

"I mean, I actually thought he wanted to come back."

"Who?"

"Jonathan. That's where I was. At Blue Water Grill making a fool of myself."

Isabelle stares at her. "Eleanor Sweet, I did not risk life and limb coming here to discuss your war-torn love life. Do you realize how quickly the traffic moves along Beacon? Where are all those people heading at this hour?"

Battersea Road meets Beacon. The intersection is two blocks from Isabelle's house. Eleanor thinks back to the delivery cartons in Isabelle's foyer. The books that arrive by mail. "You coming to my store the other day. Coming here. Is that rare for you? Getting out of the house like that?"

Isabelle pushes the address book across the table toward Eleanor. "Let's just keep our focus, shall we?"

Eleanor obeys. She stares at the little book. It has no doubt squatted atop many, many tables, waiting for connections to be made. Some healing. Some not. The anticipation the book has witnessed—the moment before that initial phone call is made. The second thoughts. The dreams made. The dreams crushed. "You don't think it's too late to call?"

Isabelle glances at the clock. Eight forty. "Anyone who's turned in for the night at this hour doesn't deserve our notice. If your mother is in bed, she's dead to us. We'll find you another one."

Beside them, Angus yawns, revealing rows of ominous white stalactites and stalagmites and a long tongue stained with a black birthmark on one side. The yawn ends with a high-pitched yowl.

"Must the animal sit so close?"

"He likes to be part of things."

"I'd like not to be part of him, thank you very much."

Eleanor runs her fingers over the cover of the little red book. She put Sylvie's arrival at risk, ditching Isabelle to meet with Jonathan. What if Isabelle had walked? Dropped out of the search? Things would be looking a lot worse right now.

"It isn't going to go as you're likely imagining," Isabelle says, shifting her chair away from Angus. "I don't like to approach directly. It's a huge piece of information for the searched-for relative, and rather than to blurt it out, I prefer to just give a hint of news and see if the person wants to move forward with the discovery. Some people are flatly against contact. As much as it hurts, we have to be prepared for that."

Eleanor's fingers find the velvety comfort of Angus's ears. She doesn't take her eyes off him. He doesn't take his eyes off Isabelle.

"Why does he look at me like that?"

"He's curious."

"But he's been fed?"

"What if my mother isn't interested?"

"He doesn't have a pen we can lock him in? A stall?"

"What about my mother?"

Isabelle sighs. "If she isn't interested, you won't take it as final. She may think about it and change her mind. Which would be perfectly reasonable." She touches Eleanor's chin and tilts her face up until their eyes meet. "Are you ready?"

Eleanor can't answer.

Isabelle opens her book and reaches for the phone. Dials the number Eleanor has already memorized.

The phone is on speaker. One ring. Two, three. On the fifth ring, the line clicks and a machine, a man's voice, says: *You've reached Ruth and Richard. Leave us a message and we'll get right back to you.*

Isabelle clears her throat before speaking. "This message is for Ruth Woolsey. My name is Isabelle Santos and I have some information about a family member of hers." She gives Eleanor's cell number.

"Why not a family member of his?"

"We don't know for sure that he's your father." She reaches for an overloaded canvas bag and sets it with a bang on the table.

"What's this?"

Out of the sac comes blue plastic Tupperware ranging from the size of a tangerine to that of a cooked chicken. "Ingredients for lemon squares. So you don't drive me to drink while we wait." She stands and ties a rumpled linen apron around her hips, then roots through the kitchen drawers, pulling out a package of plastic spoons and making a face. "Where on earth do you keep your whisk?"

"Is that one of those little brushes?"

Isabelle closes her eyes in frustration. "I always suspected it, but now I know for sure." She tosses the plastic cutlery back in the drawer. "Being outside of Beacon Hill is exactly like camping."

After watching Eleanor mix butter, sugar, and eggs into a shortbread paste and set it inside the oven, Isabelle leaves her to whip up four egg whites with—the horror—a large fork meant to toss salads. Eleanor beats the eggs, looking from Isabelle to the bowl and back again.

"Who is he?"

"Who is who?"

"The baby boy. The photo in your kitchen."

"That child is none of your business."

Eleanor opens the oven door to check the shortbread. Just starting to turn golden at the edges. She eyes Isabelle as she turns back to the bowl and folds the sugar into the mix. "He's programmed to love you no matter what. You know that, right?"

Isabelle snatches the bowl from her and starts to beat the mixture. She stirs harder. Faster. Soon tiny golden teardrops splatter out of the bowl and onto the counter. Then longer threads of lemon topping fly, attaching themselves to the cupboard doors, Isabelle's elegant apron, the floor at their feet.

"I'm sorry," Eleanor says, reaching for the bowl. "I shouldn't have pried."

Isabelle refuses to relinquish the bowl. With it tucked beneath her breast, she opens the oven and, with a bare hand, reaches for the metal pan. She shrieks and drops it to the floor, along with the mixing bowl. A strip of singed red flesh runs along her fingers and thumb. Before their eyes, the flesh starts to bubble.

Eleanor rushes her to the sink and runs cold water, pushes Isabelle's hand into the stream. "Keep it there!"

"Just fill a Ziploc bag with ice." Isabelle leans over the counter, pale. "I need to sit."

Eleanor does as told and helps Isabelle to the table, where they wrap a tea towel around the little bag of ice and press it to her hand. Angus wanders over to the mess of broken shortbread and wet lemon topping and sniffs at it, even deigning to taste small bits of crust. Isabelle stares at the dog. After a few minutes, she speaks.

"The boy in the photograph is my son. I left him in the hospital the day he was born. While he slept in the nursery, I got out of bed. Pulled on my clothes. Lit a cigarette and walked to the nearest bus stop."

Outside a horn honks. Angus pads into the other room, leaving behind a trail of lemon-shortbread paw prints.

"You don't have to talk about it, Isabelle."

"I was eight months pregnant when my boyfriend left

me. Sixteen and extraordinarily stupid. Our plan—however injudicious—was to marry once the baby was born. Dean was going to drop out of school and work at a motorcycle repair shop run by his best friend's brother. His salary, however meager, would pay the rent and keep our baby in diaper cream and strained apricots. The plan never would have worked, not least of all because Dean was lazier than tar and delusional enough to believe he was born to be a rock star. He told me in my thirty-sixth week of pregnancy that he was moving to Australia to be lead singer in an Aerosmith cover band. He said that me not terminating the pregnancy had been a mistake. That I was free—lucky girl that I am—to do with the baby whatever I wished. I am thoroughly ashamed of what I did."

"How could you be ashamed? You were a child yourself. You left your baby in a safe place where he would be safe. That was brave. Not stupid."

"Bravery didn't enter into it for a second. I was furious and immature. I didn't leave my baby in that hospital for his own good. I did it to wound Dean, who never bothered to find out what happened." The timer buzzes and Isabelle gets up to silence it and turn off the oven. When she turns around, her cheeks shine with tears. "I gave away my son out of spite." Eleanor starts toward her and Isabelle holds up a hand. "I am not now, nor ever was I, a creature to be pitied."

The clock ticking from the wall. Angus groaning and stretching out on the floor by the fridge. The constant hiss of the radiators heating up. "Do you know where your son is now?"

"I do. He's at 341 Cherry Blossom Court, Sandwich, Massachusetts. He has a sensible wife and two towheaded children who leave their bicycles on the lawn no matter how many times they're told to put them in the garage. He keeps his driveway impeccably shoveled and when the snow is particularly bad, he shovels the driveway of an elderly neighbor. No one can say he isn't a good person."

"So you've seen him."

"Oh, I've seen him. Only from afar, though. I've never actually approached him or introduced myself."

"Don't you think it's time for that now?"

"I do not."

"Why?"

"Because the time has passed."

From the center of the table, Isabelle's cell phone rings. She composes herself and wipes her cheeks before holding it up to show Eleanor. Area code 317.

"Your decision, Eleanor Sweet. You answer it or I will."

Another ring.

Eleanor takes the phone, taps it to accept the call, and presses it to her ear. She whispers, "Hello?"

Chapter 34

Now, lined up at Security at Logan International Airport, Eleanor realizes she can stop looking for Woody Allen. Diane Keaton is not her mother, and unless Ruth Woolsey had a fling with Woody Allen in the mid-seventies, he's not her father.

She thought she saw Woody Allen once in New York City. She was on a twelfth-grade class trip, and between the Central Park Zoo and dinner in Times Square, the students were allotted two hours of freedom. Most kids went shopping. Or to Central Park to look at the autumn leaves. Not Eleanor. She was determined to find her famous father. And to catch his attention, she was going to dress like Annie Hall in one of the most iconic Woody Allen moments ever: the lobster scene. It was during this sequence that Alvy Singer fell in love with Annie.

She knew, as did the rest of the world, that Woody's bucket hat and rumpled khaki jacket were a common sighting in the city, particularly around East 55th and 3rd on Monday nights when he played clarinet at Michael's Pub. So when he bumped into her on the street, clutching his little leather briefcase, he would be struck by something vaguely familiar. At the very least, she figured, he'd give her a second glance.

Eleanor spent three days planning. Her hair would be in a loose bun, she would dress in white pants and matching blouse—untucked! collar flipped up!—with a creamy vest and white neck scarf. To top it off: a tweed blazer.

Even as a teenager she felt better wrapped up.

The Soon-Yi Previn scandal (something Eleanor, as his birth child, was willing to overlook) was fresh, so there was no sharing her plans with the other kids. Eleanor slipped away and planted herself in front of Michael's. After a few hours, from across the street, she spotted a diminutive man in a khaki jacket and canvas rain hat, his face long and his glasses black. He kept his face down in a way that was befitting of the very famous.

Eleanor, her white scarf flying behind her, her hair falling out of the too-loose bun, trotted behind him for four blocks. When he disappeared into a market, she carefully arranged herself against a lamp post so they'd be face to face when he came out. In a few minutes he emerged, carrying a bouquet of orange sunflowers. He looked up and gave her a half smile. Hesitated a moment, then headed back the way he came.

Eleanor walked the other way. It wasn't Woody. This man's nose was different—much smaller and more structured. And the teeth were too big. But she didn't need to see his face. She knew the moment she saw the flowers. No way would Woody pick out such a flashy bouquet.

Now the airport security officer, his shirt buttons straining, waits with a plastic tray. "You got the thick soles and the high heels. The boots have to come off or you go next door for a pat-down."

The woman by the X-ray machine appears ominous with her linebacker hands and chin criss-crossed with frown lines. On the other hand, it had taken some effort to tuck her jeans into knee socks, then riding boots, before the cab arrived to pick her up. "Up to you, ma'am." Eleanor had been up before 4 a.m. trying to decide what to wear to meet her birth parents. Was it best to appear businesslike in a pale gray suit and sensible shoes, or elegant in her navy shift and matching pumps? She wants them to be assured she is taking this meeting seriously. But doesn't want to make them uncomfortable if they're all sitting around in sweats. Eventually, she settled on what made her feel both comfortable and insulated: dark jeans tucked into riding boots, and a crisp blue shirt over a long-sleeved white T-shirt, topped by a vintage cardigan with ruffled edges.

Ruth's voice had been a surprise. Deep and throaty, not unlike Angus growling in his sleep. Maybe her voice was wrecked from years of smoking. Maybe she was just born with splintered vocal cords. It was clear that her mother was every bit as nervous as Eleanor. She kept saying, "My word, it's really you? This is really you?"

Eleanor had dreamed of this moment all her life. She'd imagined it this way and that way, but never with the workaday undertone of the actual conversation.

Isabelle, with the call on speaker, had explained the situation. That she was sitting across from Eleanor Sweet, the child Ruth gave up thirty-five years ago. Ruth had gone silent a full minute. Eleanor thought the call had been dropped. Or, worse, her mother had hung up.

Finally, Ruth whispered, "I don't believe it. All these years, it's really you."

Eleanor's turn. "It is. It's me . . . and this is you."

"Oh, this is unbelievable. Unbelieva— Richard?" She covers the phone a moment and calls out to Richard again. Then she's back. "You won't believe this, sweetie, but I married your biological father. Richard?" More scuffling. "Oh, this is ridiculous. When can I get my hands on you for a big hug?"

The man at Security stares at Eleanor and smacks his gum. "Some folks just don't like to be in their stocking feet. My wife hates it. Makes her feel like a kindergartner, she says."

"Eleanor Sweet!" Isabelle is already seated at the gate, waving. "I've been waiting forever."

A businessman in line behind Eleanor sets his brogues in her shoe tray. There. Decision made. She looks at the security guard. "I'll take the pat-down."

"They've informed me there's no business class on this flight," Isabelle says as Eleanor drops into the seat next to her. "None at all. I thought I'd misheard the woman. I asked if the plane has wings or will I be required to flap my arms to keep the machine in the air."

"I don't think these little commuter airlines have business class. The flight is short. They assume you can rough it for an hour and a half."

"If I'd wanted to rough it, I'd have strapped a saddle onto that plow horse you keep on your kitchen floor. Do you know they tried to charge me extra for the weight of my bag?"

"We're only gone overnight. How much could you possibly—?"

"I pointed to the hefty person behind me and demanded they compare our weights, bags included. Said if my total exceeded hers, I'd gladly pay." She huffs out a sigh and nods toward a large woman with piercings that ridge her entire left ear and tattoos creeping up her neck. Beside her is her equally massive boyfriend, studs dotted along the lapel of his leather jacket. "They let me through."

"Jesus, Isabelle. You're going to get us killed."

"Nonsense. I've booked the bulkhead for us. It may be a short flight, but I refuse to spend it dying of deep-vein thrombosis."

"Bulkhead's fine with me."

"You'll take the window. And you'll shut the blind before takeoff. I prefer to pretend I'm in the back of a cab, rather than forty thousand feet above any sort of common sense."

"I insist on reimbursing you for your flight," Eleanor says. "You have to agree to that."

Isabelle leans back in her chair, crosses her arms over the purse in her lap, and closes her eyes. "Shut up, Eleanor Sweet. And wake me when they have my plane ready."

The flight is delayed almost two hours because the pilots are late for work. Something about a traffic jam on the I-95. Drinks and snacks are suddenly free, but the passengers are warned that the toilets aren't functioning because the engines haven't been turned on yet. As a result, Isabelle orders herself a cup of coffee, but refuses to drink it. "I'm far too old to subject myself to staring down at another person's shortsightedness."

"Do what I just did in the bathroom," Eleanor says, biting into a muffin. "Don't look down."

"I'm not a cave woman." Isabelle hauls her oversize leather bag onto her lap and washes down a Gravol with the tiniest sip of coffee, then proceeds to dig through her Gucci purse. "Damn these hippie sacks. You cannot find a thing when you need it." She pulls out a fluffy sleep-mask and sets to work untangling the elastic band.

"What's his name?"

"Whose name?"

"You know."

"Ethan Bradley Santos and I think about him every day."

Isabelle tugs the sleep-mask over her eyes and leans back. She lets her bag slide down her leg. It catches on the tray and, fully blinded, she gives it a shove, knocking her entire coffee cup onto Eleanor's lap.

"Hey, I'm soaked!"

Isabelle balls her jacket up into a pillow and tucks it between her head and the shaded window. "Keep it down, darling. I've taken a pill."

Chapter 35

"It's like something out of a movie."

They stand on the sidewalk and stare at creamy gold brick, luscious white trim, and a cedar-shingled roof. The house is flanked by old trees long past the height of their autumn color. Masses of spent hydrangea, pinkish green dried to brown, line the base of a stone porch, the steps of which are scattered with leaves. In the air, far warmer than at home, the smoky tang of burning leaves. At one side of the property, a wheelbarrow full of clippings beside a partially denuded cedar suggests someone was distracted by the football game on TV.

From an ancient, sprawling chestnut tree hangs an old rope swing. The way it sways in the breeze is almost taunting. *You weren't good enough*, it seems to whisper.

"I wonder if they'll adopt me." Isabelle starts up the steps. When Eleanor doesn't follow her, she turns around. "Two for one, what do you think?"

"I think I want to throw up."

"If this is a bid to get your clutches on my Gravol, you can give it up right now. I have two pills left—one for the terrible sleep I'll have sharing a hotel room with you, and the other to

207

knock me out when we step back onto that cattle-mover with bar service tomorrow morning. Now, get your delicate system up here and let's get this done."

Eleanor climbs the steps, aware of her own rumpledness next to Isabelle's fresh-pressed perfection. They had both set out at the same time, traveled on the same flight. Why does Eleanor look like something pulled out of a trash can?

"Can we just leave? Go back? I don't think I can do this."

"Nonsense. Now take off that scarf. You look like you've been rear-ended and are too miserly to buy a proper neck brace." She starts to untie the linen scarf.

"No, no, no!" Eleanor's hands go to her throat to stop her. "I need it."

But Isabelle already has it off. She rolls it up and stuffs it in her bag. "There. How does that feel?"

"Naked." Eleanor looks at the toes of her boots. At home they looked so much newer. "What if she doesn't like me?"

"Won't happen. She's been wondering about you for even longer than you've been wondering about her. She's likely worried you won't like *her*. Think about it. You have every right to be angry."

"You're coming in, right? You're staying?"

Isabelle tucks a stray piece of hair behind Eleanor's ear. "I am, darling. Now, take two steps back. You smell like stale urine."

"Urine? That's your coffee!"

"Stale coffee smells remarkably like urine."

"Is it too late to fire you?"

"Rule number three. The search angel cannot be fired. But she can quit at any time. Rule number four is that they're to open the door with a snifter of brandy in each hand, both for the search angel." She rings the bell and shakes her head. "Rule number four doesn't seem to take."

Distraction. Isabelle knows exactly what she's doing.

The front door flies open. Standing before them is a beautiful woman of about fifty. With her long, wavy, ash-blond hair, wide mouth, and teacup-handle ears, this is, without question, a sophisticated version of the girl from the yearbook. The way she smiles, exposing her lower teeth, the way she holds her hand (devoid of brandy snifter) with her fingers lined up like a Chinese fan—Eleanor can see these in herself.

Ruth steps onto the porch. "I don't believe it. I don't even believe what I'm seeing. You look exactly like me." She takes Eleanor's hands. "May I give you a hug?"

Eleanor nods. Right away she is wrapped in her mother. She tries to feel something. Anything other than numbness and wonder. Ruth's shoulders start to shake. "Sorry. Heavens . . . just to have you here."

Her mother's back is muscled and strong through her blouse. Her athletic build Eleanor did not inherit. The hug continues and Eleanor finds herself staring at Isabelle, who motions that she's sipping from an invisible snifter and nods toward the house. Eleanor smiles. Then closes her eyes and shuts Isabelle out. All thoughts of finding Ruth for Sylvie are momentarily pushed aside. This is her mother, flesh and blood and Chanel No. 5.

Ruth pulls back. "You're simply gorgeous. So delicate with that perfect bone structure."

A small child, also blond, comes barreling out of the house and attaches himself to Ruth's leg. Stupidly, Eleanor feels jealous. She's waited thirty-five years for this moment. Can't it last longer than twenty seconds?

With his finger looking for his nostril, the boy gazes up at Eleanor. "She doesn't look like a baby."

Ruth laughs, pulling away and wiping wet eyes. "This, dear Eleanor, is your nephew Robbie. Robbie, this is your Auntie Eleanor, all grown up."

"Why did you give her away, Nana?"

Robbie's question hangs in the air between them. From the yard, the porch swing creaks. A small plane buzzes overhead. Leaves blow across the porch at their feet. No one moves, speaks. If Eleanor had any strength in her legs, she'd run.

"Our flight was delayed due to good weather," Isabelle says quickly. "The pilots, who showed up with suntans, were likely off on a beach somewhere drinking mojitos."

Robbie runs back into the house, chanting, "Mosquito juice, mosquito juice!"

And the tension has passed.

"Never a dull moment around here." Ruth squeezes Eleanor's arm in hers and winks. "Come. Everyone is dying to meet you. We're a big family."

I'm from a big family, she'll tell people. She'll tell Jonathan. *And you should see them. They're straight out of the movies.*

Inside, the hallway is empty but jovial voices come from the back of the house—a man telling a story, a woman shrieking in laughter. It's a lively home.

Her life at the Prues' didn't sound like this. Marion and Thomas were good and kind, but old enough to be her grandparents. Saturday afternoons like this one were filled with the scratch of Eleanor's pencil as she did homework on the dining room table, or the soft scrape of Thomas turning a page in his book.

Ruth stops. "I want a moment with you. Just you. Before

the others invade. We never had this at the hospital. They whisked you away before I could even see you." Her strong hands squeeze her daughter's as she studies Eleanor's face. "You're like a more feminine version of your sisters."

Clearly Eleanor did not inherit her infertility from Ruth. "I have sisters?"

A bald man, tall and wide-shouldered, nicely weathered, in jeans and a buffalo-plaid shirt, heads down the hall with a side-to-side swagger. His hand reaches for hers from miles away. "This must be our girl."

Eleanor looks at Ruth, who nods. "This is Richard. My husband. And your father." Eleanor's face is mashed into Richard's flannel sleeve.

"I married your mom not two years after you were born." He steps back but leaves an arm draped over her shoulder. "Because of you, I've always thought. Pulled my whole life together, princess. Went back to high school. Started working on an engineering degree, later opened up the business. A real wake-up call, you were."

"He did good, your old dad," Ruth says.

He would have been such a wonderful father. Strong and energetic. Young enough to run alongside her bike as she learned how to ride. As it was, she taught herself. Eleanor looks around. This would have been her life.

"That's great," she hears herself say.

"You want to hear great," says Ruth. "The twins—your sisters, full sisters—were born two years after you. Ronnie and Roxie are thirty-three."

Ronnie, Roxie, Ruth, Richard, Robbie. The entire family with the *R*s. Ruth continues. "Identical twins—you should know that it runs in the family in case you ever . . . wait." She stops, her face brightening. "Thirty-five, you must have kids of your own?"

Eleanor shakes her head. "No, Well, yes. Hopefully . . ."

The clomping of footsteps from what appears to be an open kitchen and family room drowns out Eleanor's voice. The twins, clearly, with their long blond hair and bangs, matching peach-toned lipstick, and wide, denimed hips, rush forward with toothy grins. They're shorter, but share the lower-half smiles with Ruth and Eleanor, and something else around the eyebrows—a definitive slope toward the nose—that Eleanor has. No sexy arch there. More of a hasty slash, and much darker than their hair.

"Lordy, lordy," says the one with the slightly longer face. "Mom told us—we had no idea. Holy crap, this is wild. We have a big sister. Ronnie has been lording her six-minutes-older status over me all my life." Her grin is genuine and could not get any wider. "I'm Rox. So completely incredible to meet you." A quick hug.

"I'm Ronnie. And you're a total bitch for usurping me . . ." Another hug and everyone bursts into soft laughter. "Robbie's mine. You'll meet my husband later."

"And how come you got the long legs?" Rox says. "So not fair."

Isabelle stands by the front door. She watches Eleanor's face with a controlled urgency, acknowledging the fact that her parents going on without her, marrying each other after giving her up, going on to have more kids—all of whom are her full siblings—*is* something to get upset about, yes. But Eleanor was not to freak out.

"And you're all together still. I never pictured that." Eleanor forces a smile. "It's amazing."

With a slow blink, Isabelle nods her approval.

Eleanor's throat is nearly closed tight with envy. With hurt. These girls weren't left behind. They grew up cherished, wanted. Why didn't Ruth come looking for Eleanor if the whole gang was intact? Even just for visitation?

"Honey, you're shaking," says Ruth, taking her hands. "You want a drink to calm your nerves?"

Eleanor nods.

Ruth leads Isabelle and Eleanor back into a massive great room with huge pine beams overhead and a floor-to-ceiling stone fireplace. The fridge is covered in photographs and Robbie's crayon drawings of bullets hitting army men and exploding rocket ships and roaring *T. rexes*. On the marble island are plates of tiny spring rolls and dips and veggies and miniature pita, homemade cookies and iced brownies dusted with icing sugar. In the oven, a turkey sizzles.

It smells like a home.

"Why don't you ladies get comfortable, and I'll get you both a glass of wine," says Richard. "You okay with white?" When they both nod, he opens the fridge and fills two glasses from a box.

Eleanor accepts hers, wanders over to where a wooden train set is arranged on the rug by the fire, and watches Robbie push a yellow engine through a covered bridge. "Grandpa, will you play with me?"

Richard calls out from where he's checking the roast. "In a sec, big man. Just let Grandpa check the dinner."

"I want somebody to play with me *now*."

Ronnie and Roxie drape themselves over the same stuffed armchair as if they're still tangled in the womb. Ruth drops onto the sofa and pats the seat beside her. "Come, Eleanor.

Sit with me. We have decades of catching up to do. Tell me what's going on in your life."

Eleanor sits. Behind her mother are framed family photos that could very well be on Eleanor's windowsill at home. An arty black and white of the entire family in a studio. A color shot of all of the *R*s frolicking in the surf, everyone dressed in rolled-up jeans and white T-shirts, skin the color of summer and blond hair blowing in the wind. Grinning and feeling the ocean lap at their toes. A picture of the entire clan at the base of a Christmas tree. In every shot, the family appears as joyous as if they were faking it in a stock photo. Only, this family is real.

She should have been in these shots. Christmas after Christmas, thirty-four times over, they didn't reach out to her. Did Ruth or Richard ever, while wrapping presents for the twins, wonder about Eleanor? What she was doing Christmas morning?

She looks at Ruth. "Did you tell Rox and Ronnie about me?"

"Of course! You see them sitting here, don't you?"

"No, I mean when they were young. Did they grow up knowing?"

"Oh goodness, no. I guess I worried I'd scar them or who knows what. Or worried what they'd think of me." She looks at the twins, who smile back. "I didn't tell them until just after your phone call."

"It's fine, Mom," says Ronnie. "We're glad we know now is all."

"So, Eleanor. Spill," says Roxie, leaning over her sister's legs as if they're her own. "We want to hear all about your life."

Ruth smiles up at Isabelle, who cradles her wineglass at the entry to the hall. "Won't you come sit, Isabelle? We owe so much of our joy to you."

Isabelle shakes her head, her eyes a bit glassy. "Thank you, but if you would you kindly direct me to the powder room?" Ruth sends her down the hall and to the left, then all eyes turn to Eleanor, who gulps from her glass.

"Actually, I'm about to adopt a baby girl. All by myself."

As the room fills up with *ooh*s and *aah*s and pats of approval, Ruth touches Eleanor's wedding band. "But there's someone in your life?"

"That is a bit of a story . . ."

Isabelle has been gone too long. Once her story has been told, and Robbie has commandeered everyone's attention with his train set, Eleanor wanders into the kitchen to refill her glass from the box on the island. Once sure no one is watching, she hoists the carton onto her hip and slips down the hall to rap on the bathroom door.

"Isabelle? Are you okay?"

From inside: "Eleanor Sweet, if there is one thing I forbid my clients to do, it's harass the search angel when they should be bonding with their newfound birth families. Now get back to that perfect family of yours."

Eleanor rattles the knob. "Let me in."

"I will do no such thing."

"How's your wineglass?"

"Aside from being thoroughly horrified at having been filled with wine from a cardboard casket, it is empty. Thank you for asking."

"Then unlock the door. I've brought you a refill."

Isabelle opens the door. Eleanor pushes her way in and locks up behind her. "Don't just stand there. Help me with this box."

Isabelle supports the carton while Eleanor positions the

spout over the glass and presses the button. Chardonnay splashes into the glass. "You have got to be the rudest birth daughter I've encountered. In here saucing up the search angel when you should be out there sharing your lifetime of anguish with those who deserted you."

"Your eyes are red. Have you been crying?"

"I haven't been able to produce tears in twenty-seven years. What you are seeing is evidence of a poor air-filtration system in that pterodactyl we rode in on the back of."

"Is it your son? That's why you're hiding?"

"Is nothing in my life sacred? I suppose you'll want my white blood count next."

"I just think there's more that you're not telling me."

Isabelle sits on the closed lid of the toilet and swirls the wine in her glass, staring down at it. Laughter explodes from the other room. "His new family named him Walter William Runion. Walt."

"When was the last time you saw him?"

She sighs deeply, looks up at the ceiling. "June twenty-fifth of this year. He came out of the house wearing a Dallas Cowboys sweatshirt and a pair of navy shorts to mow the lawn. His two little boys banged on the living room window and gave him the thumbs-up. The whole process took forty minutes and I am proud to say he was meticulous in his detailed edging where grass meets walkway." Her eyes drift out to a sparrow perched on the sill. "No one could ever call that man anything less than meticulous."

"Where were you when he was mowing the lawn?"

"In the car. Watching through the window. And if you'd like to pry further, why don't you ask me how many times I've seen him that were not through some sort of glass."

Eleanor says nothing.

"Once. The moment they pulled him out of me and whisked him out of the room."

The thought of Ruth caring enough to watch her from afar gives Eleanor a thrill. She longed for it all her life. "He has no idea?"

Isabelle shakes her head.

"It's not too late, Isabelle. I can't tell you what this contact means to me. And if she'd been the one to initiate . . ." Eleanor pauses to release a breath. "You could do it for your son. You could call him. I'd even come with you to see him if you want support. It's not too late."

Isabelle's hand shakes enough that the wine quivers in the glass. When she speaks, her voice is sharper than intended. "Don't tell me what I can or cannot do, Eleanor Sweet. One found family does not make you an expert. I cannot approach Ethan now or ever."

"Sure you can—"

"Ethan is dead."

As Eleanor stands frozen, struggling to process this, Isabelle tops up her glass and breezes out the door. Eleanor follows her into the great room to set the wine box on the island while Isabelle arranges herself beside little Robbie in front of the fire.

"Now. Let's establish the rules straight away." Isabelle plasters a smile on her face. "I get to be the red engine or I throw a tantrum. Are we clear?"

Robbie beams and, with his socked foot, pushes the red engine toward her.

Chapter 36

Isabelle stands in the cramped entryway of their hotel room and stares accusingly at the light switch. "It's the single most deadly source of aerobic bacteria in a hotel room after the TV remote. Streptococcus. Staphylococcus. And, the worst offender imaginable, fecal coliform."

Eleanor watches from the foot of one of the beds. "How bad could the TV remote be?"

"What"—Isabelle's head snaps around—"do you think people reach for immediately following sex?"

She refused to speak a word about Ethan in the cab ride from Ruth and Richard's place. Every time Eleanor tried to talk, Isabelle pointed out the window at an old church or a tree that hadn't yet dropped its leaves and commented on the pretty view.

"There was a study," Isabelle says now. "All measurements were taken in colony-forming units of bacteria per cubic centimeter squared. CFUs. TV remotes, bathroom sinks, door handles, all the usual suspects were highlighted. The telephone had twenty-one CFUs. TV remotes had seventy. The main light switch? Almost 125 CFUs. And if you'd care to know the fecal bacteria count . . . ?"

"I don't care to know. Not in the slightest."

"Over 115. And just so you can compare, guess what level hospitals aim for?"

"Do you think room service would send up a bowl of cereal? Or do I have to order more than that?"

"Five or less." Isabelle is already elbow deep in her suitcase, digging through perfectly folded dress shirts and jeans. She holds up a flat red package of antibacterial hand wipes. "Your immune system will thank me for bringing these."

"Isabelle, forget the light switch."

It's too late; she's already detailing the brass switch plate, as well as the wall surface surrounding it.

"Can we talk? Please? It's not healthy, to avoid discussing it."

Isabelle scrubs harder, then pulls out another wipe and decontaminates doorknobs, sink handles, the towel racks, phone, and, finally, the grandfather of CFU offenders, the TV remote. As she scrubs, the television turns on, then off again. Then on. To the children's movies available, then to the porn selections—complete with assurances that movie titles will not appear on their hotel bill.

Eleanor sits on her bed and watches Isabelle use a corner of the cloth to clean between the tiny rubber buttons. "This isn't about hotel bacteria," she says. But Isabelle just scrubs harder and the TV turns to the local news. The volume vanishes for a moment, then grows increasingly louder to the point that the ghostly weatherman is shouting that temperatures will fall to almost forty degrees overnight. "Isabelle. Talk to me."

She stops. Turns off the TV. Tosses the remote onto the foot of her bed. "I was better off in my town house on Battersea Road. That's all I have to say."

Down the hall, children's voices shriek as they thunder along the carpeted corridor, then bang on a door nearby. A man's voice, teasing, "I'm gonna get you!" makes them shriek with delight. The voices grow quiet and a door thumps shut.

"This day is not about me, Eleanor Sweet. And I forbid you to make it so."

"Isabelle . . ."

"You've waited a lifetime to meet your mother. How do you feel after this afternoon? That's what we should discuss."

Ruth was fantastic. Eleanor had explained to her, to all of them, the situation with Sylvie. Adopting her without Jonathan. Ruth squeezed Eleanor's knee and actually volunteered to drive the four hours into Boston to be there for the home visit. Insisted she be appointed as Eleanor's support system—and not just for Nancy's approval. For real. Said she'd be there for Eleanor and Sylvie no matter what. No matter when.

If the home meeting goes well this week, everything will be in place.

"How did he die?"

Isabelle reaches for a fresh wipe and turns to the bedside lamp. Starts to scrub the switch and stops. Her elbows drop to her sides. "It was a heart attack." She sits back on the bed and draws her knees to her chest. "No one saw it coming; he was in good shape and had much to look forward to, and all the silly things people tell themselves to feel better. Heart trouble doesn't run in my family. No idea about his father's. I'd love to be dramatic and say I'd just decided to come out of the shadows and introduce myself and then it happened, but I'd decided no such thing."

"When did it happen?"

"July fourteenth. Ethan played hockey with a bunch of

friends once a week. Finished the game and collapsed getting into the car. One of his teammates ran back to the arena for the defibrillator, while another called 911. It was too late for either."

"Oh God, I'm so sorry."

"I read it in the paper like a perfect stranger. Even after his death, I was too cowardly to approach his family." Isabelle stares at her toes. "That was it for me. I couldn't continue to bring other people together after failing so colossally with my own son. So I stopped searching. Then I found myself making excuses not to leave the house. It might rain. It might snow. Days passed where I didn't step outside. Eventually I decided it made more sense to have whatever I needed sent to the house."

"So you actually stopped going out."

"What gave me the right? If Ethan wasn't going to have a life, neither was I."

Eleanor is silent a moment, allowing this to sink in. Isabelle had become a recluse. Yet she had left the house to help her. "Can I ask you something?"

Isabelle huffs her indignance. "Nothing seems to have stopped you yet!"

"Why me? Why did you come out of exile for my case?"

"Because I know how it feels to be left by the man you love at the very worst time imaginable and I didn't want you to lose a baby, like I did, as a result."

Eleanor closes her eyes for a moment. She owes this woman everything. "Isabelle . . ."

"Don't Isabelle me and don't get sentimental. I have every right to wallow. My only child died not knowing how much his birth mother loved him."

A small spider crawls up the wall above Isabelle's headboard. It zigs to the right, resumes its upward journey, then zags to the left. Eleanor stares at the indecisive creature as if it's personally responsible for the tragedy of Isabelle's son never knowing her.

She can tell Isabelle that he knew she loved him. Those words can come out of her mouth. But the truth is he probably didn't. Eleanor of all people knows how badly she needed affirmation of her own birth mother's affection. She slides off the bed and leans over Isabelle, wraps her arms around this woman who has helped so many people out of their loneliness and guilt, only to be destroyed by her own.

Chapter 37

S he felt the change before she saw it. The air in the apartment actually seemed thinner. As if there were less oxygen. It was hard to take in a deep breath—her lungs were unable to fill up. Even the door swung open too easily when she hauled her suitcase inside.

He had moved his things out while she was away.

She dropped her keys on the hall table and wandered into the kitchen. His wood-handled knives were gone, the ones he bought two summers ago at a sidewalk sale in Brookline. The living room was more dramatic. Two-thirds of the bookshelves were empty. The black love seat was gone, as were the two turquoise leather cubes they used as a coffee table. Now, the candles that were perched upon them sit directly on the floor.

Empty patches of wall where his posters used to hang. A lamp here, a bowl there. The vintage Coke crate full of *Popular Science* magazines.

In the bedroom, his drawers were all empty except for an $89.99 Nordstrom price tag—knowing Jonathan he probably spent this on one T-shirt—a few buttons, and a pair of concert ticket stubs from when they saw Billy Joel in New York City a few years back.

The closet was all but empty on his side, nothing but wire hangers that chattered when she flung open the door. On the floor, an old pair of runners he long ago replaced. A sealed package of Odor-Eaters. She reached for the insoles and hurled them into the trash can. Leaving her with his garbage, the message in that, made her throat burn.

Angus. It hit her now that the dog didn't greet her at the door, begging for his evening walk. Noel had said he'd leave him in the apartment for her return. Surely Jonathan didn't take the dog too.

"Angus?" Eleanor rushed through the apartment again. "Angus?"

There. In the dining room. Four black feet, as big and knobby as those of an elephant calf, poked out from beneath the dining room table. Thwack thwack went the tip of his tail against a chair leg. She got down on the floor and draped herself over him.

Thwack thwack—but otherwise no movement from the Great Dane.

"But you love to hate squirrels. Let's go."

No movement.

An hour later, to stop her pacing, to give herself something to do other than stare at the holes Jonathan left behind, Eleanor filled the bathroom sink with icy cold water and splashed it on her face until her hair, her shirt, her forearms were soaked. Dripping, shivering, she reached for her toothbrush and looked around for the paste. Without question, she had put a fresh tube on the counter the morning she left.

Which meant he took it.

After finding a crumpled old tube of paste in the bathroom cabinet, she tried, unsuccessfully, to squeeze out the tiniest amount of paste onto the bristles. Furious now—how much more damage could he inflict upon her life?—she grabbed a pair of scissors from the kitchen, sliced the toothpaste tube up the middle, and splayed it open like a worm from tenth-grade biology class. It wasn't until blood dripped into the sink that she realized she'd cut her finger on the tube's edge.

Calmly, she wrapped the wound in toilet paper and sat on the bed. Here, she dialed Jonathan's cell phone and waited for him to pick up.

A television on in the background. Then his voice. "Hello?"

Eleanor slammed the receiver down onto the nightstand three times.

That was one week ago.

She should have checked the forecast, Eleanor thinks. She could have gotten up earlier to warm the place before the home visit. Nancy's been inside for half an hour and still hasn't taken off her jacket. Ruth, who arrived much earlier, has pulled her chair up close to the radiators.

The weather outside has turned frigid and the radiators lining the living room window hiss and tick with effort to warm the place up in the morning. The apartment grew cold enough overnight that Angus came out from beneath the dining room table to sleep on the throw rug in the living room. Eleanor carries a tea tray into the living room, remembering too late that the leather cubes are gone. The tray will have to go on the floor.

"Coffee tables are so dangerous." She hands each woman

a cup of tea. "Sharp corners. I was thinking of getting a leather ottoman."

"I love that look," says Ruth, as Nancy nods her approval.

From the floor, Noel's song whines and sputters like a broken buzz saw. He's trying to fix his now-damaged speakers and, with construction having temporarily opened up the wall between the stores, the music is louder than ever.

From the slipper chair, Nancy wraps her hands around her teacup. "So, Ruth, will Sylvie be your first grandchild?"

"Our first granddaughter. My daughter Ronnie has a three-year-old son, Robbie." She grins at Eleanor. "Quite the personality that one. He's very excited to meet his new cousin."

Nancy writes something in a small pad, then cocks her head. "Ruth, Ronnie, Robbie. All *R*s."

Eleanor watches her mother, the way she keeps massaging her fingertips to calm herself down. It irritates her that Ruth is nervous. She and Richard were the ones who inadvertently set up a little club of *R* names that Eleanor will always be excluded from.

"And my husband is Richard, and Roz is my second daughter." Quickly, Ruth looks at Eleanor. "Third!"

This doesn't look good. Quickly, Eleanor says, "Can you believe how the weather changed? Went from autumn to winter overnight?"

"I didn't pack a warm enough coat. Wasn't thinking." Ruth glances at Eleanor as if asking for forgiveness. "As usual."

"So when did the two of you find each other? And who found whom?" Nancy leans over her knees, seemingly undisturbed by the exchange. "I'm so busy arranging for these adoptions, I rarely get to see people come together later."

Eleanor debated, when she took Angus out earlier,

whether Nancy should be told the truth. That she and Ruth have only just reconnected. Or perhaps *reconnected* isn't the right word. Does connecting count when you're being pulled out of someone's uterus and bustled off into another room? *Connected for the first time* is more accurate. It might be safer to pretend they've lived a normal life as mother and daughter. Or, if not normal, that they were reunited—*united*—some time ago. That they aren't nearly complete strangers.

Nancy is not here hoping to find more change in Eleanor's life. She wants to see some nice, boring consistency. Which doesn't exactly come with having found your birth mother seven days ago.

Still. Eleanor watches Ruth squeezing her palms now. She doesn't have it in her to give the woman such a victory. Not after the "third daughter" slip. "I contacted Ruth through a search angel recently. Until then, I didn't even know if she was alive." She smiles. "I'm glad she is."

Ruth cocks her head. "I'm so proud of my daughter for reaching out. It's a difficult thing to do."

"I wanted *my* daughter to have grandparents, a real family. That made it easy. And now I've found the *R*s."

Ruth busies herself with her knees now.

Nancy looks at Eleanor with concern. "And then there's our little *E* and *S* wing of the family."

Before Eleanor can respond, there's a long jagged screech from Noel's speakers below, followed by the rat-a-tat-tat sound of a nail gun. Angus jumps up and barks, unsure where to aim his efforts.

"Angus!" Eleanor says sharply, rushing to settle him before he gives Nancy the impression he's a threat.

"You can't say it isn't lively around here," says Ruth.

"I won't argue that. So, Ruth, obviously Eleanor has told me about Jonathan leaving. How do you feel about the situation—your daughter adopting on her own?"

Ruth looks at her daughter. "Eleanor is strong. I couldn't be more proud of her. Her store. Her life. She can handle this without him or any other man. I'm behind her one hundred percent. Anything she needs, anytime she needs it."

A satisfied smile creases Nancy's face. She sets her teacup on the tray and stands. "I think I've got all I need." From her briefcase she pulls out a piece of paper and hands it to Eleanor. "We prefer that she travel here with Luiz, because the travel itself is a stressor and she knows him. We were making an exception for you and . . . anyway. You'll pick her up at Logan."

Eleanor stares down at the note, which reads:

American Airlines Flight 943 Palm Springs—Boston Arrives November 24th 10:30 a.m.

Eleanor looks up at Nancy. "Sylvie's mine?"
"All yours."

She didn't expect the front doors to be open after work that evening. It's after six o'clock; you'd think all the parents would have picked up their kids by now. Inside, the big house that is Sunnyside Day Care echoes with her own footsteps. No sounds of chairs scraping or children chattering to muffle her arrival. Eleanor stops, listens for audible signs of life. When she hears the swish of shuffling papers, she follows it to a photocopy room near the back of the building.

"The doors were unlocked," she says to a ponytailed young woman in green glasses and an oversized sweater. "I hope it's okay I came right in."

"Oh!" The girl starts, slapping a file folder to her chest. "You scared me!"

"Is Wendy around? I just need to add something to my application."

"She's gone home." She waves for Eleanor to follow her. "I'm Bree. Come. The applications are on her desk; we'll dig yours up." She heads into the next room and picks through a tidy stack of papers.

"Eleanor Sweet. My daughter's name is Sylvie."

"Sylvie. Yup. Here it is." Bree motions to the pens in a melted-looking clay mug obviously made by tiny hands. "Grab a pen and have at it."

Eleanor scans the sheet and stops at the line "Next of Kin."

On the line, which is now blank, she writes *Ruth Pantera*.

Chapter 38

While Cal's assistant rolls a fresh coat of white paint over the now-repaired-and-soundproofed wall to the sound of Vivaldi's gloriously soothing cello music, Eleanor goes through the morning mail. Among the usual collection of bills and flyers is a note from her insurance agent. The entire renovation will be covered, through Noel's insurance company.

A huge relief with Sylvie coming.

The last piece of mail is a square envelope with the name *Pantera* in the upper left corner. She tears it open to find a thick white invitation.

Miss Roxanne Lynne Pantera
and
Mr. Peter Matheson McGrath
request the honor of your presence
at their marriage
on November 20th
Liberty Suites Ballroom
Cambridge, Massachusetts

Roxie had mentioned being engaged, but not that the wedding was so soon. She'd barely spoken about it the other day and her fiancé hadn't been there—he is a philosophy professor at Harvard. Eleanor had assumed the ceremony was in the spring.

But . . . she's included. She's part of the family. Finally, she'll be in a family photo. It'll go on the mantel. She'll get a copy and put it on her windowsill. When Sylvie arrives, she'll show her. "This is me at your aunt's wedding." Eleanor hugs herself.

Not only that, but it will be Eleanor's inadvertent coming-out party. She has no idea how large the Liberty Suites Ballroom is, but there have to be a couple of hundred extended family members, neighbors, friends. She'll meet others. Aunts, uncles, cousins, old friends of the family.

It's a dream come true.

The invitation is addressed to *Eleanor Sweet plus one*. She slips the invitation into the drawer and puts her family—and where Jonathan will be November twentieth—out of her mind.

Ginny wanders up from the back, a Baby Bjorn strapped across her chest. She looks around the store. "Almost feels smaller in here now. I'd gotten sort of used to seeing through to the record store."

"Maybe it's Noel you miss seeing," Eleanor says.

Ginny shrugs and turns to examine the carrier in the mirror. "I find him weirdly unappealing now."

Eleanor hides her smile.

"Hey, do these things come with twin pouches?"

"You strap the fussiest one into the carrier. That's what the women tell me."

"Want to know my biggest fear? What if I can't tell them apart?"

"They're never that alike, are they?"

"In the OB's office, I heard one mother say she dressed her twins differently from birth and that was the only way she knew. Then one day she went out for eggs and her husband changed them. Guy didn't know which was which. She panicked. What if she never figured it out? Then she remembered one had a scratch on his wrist. From then on she kept a dot of nail polish on that kid's toe."

The bell above the door tinkles and a very familiar, very pregnant woman walks in and stares at the missing ceiling tiles. The painter dipping his roller into a tray of paint. She turns to Eleanor. "This can't be good."

"We had a bit of a flood," Eleanor explains. "We weren't hit nearly as hard as the place next door."

The woman motions toward Noel's wall and Eleanor realizes who she is. It's Ali McGraw, sister to Auntie Faith from above Death by Vinyl. "Oh my God. When did this happen?"

The day your sister moved out, Eleanor doesn't say. "Last week sometime."

Ali glances at the exposed pipes overhead. She knows her sister is responsible. "Oh God. Oh God."

"Are you back for the bassinet?"

"Yes. And a few other . . ." She pauses to survey the destruction again. The dusty Rubbermaid cans filled with crumbled drywall and crown molding. The drop sheets laid out along the floor. The racks of baby wear crowded to the center of the store. "Has it cost you a fortune?"

"No, no. The neighbor's insurance company has been great. Here, come with me." Eleanor emerges from behind the counter and guides her to the back corner—an area untouched by water damage. The massive bassinet she'd looked at before—the Badger Basket, dark cherry, round with eyelet canopy—is still waiting. Eleanor scoops out the stuffed animals that Ginny tossed in for safekeeping the night the rains came down, and adjusted the duvet. "It's still here. All is well. Did you drive?"

She nods. "An SUV, it'll fit. It's just that I can't really do any lifting . . . I'm so sorry about this mess. What can I do? Tell me there's something I can do."

"You can take this thing out of the store today. As you can see I have very little space."

The bassinet is easy to wheel to the front of the store, but with its width, with the way the door doesn't fully open, it's nearly impossible to wiggle through the doorway alone. It arrived unassembled, Eleanor realizes now. Jonathan helped her build it in the shop. Ali McGraw is of no use, not with the size of her belly; she can't get her hands far enough around the crib to pull while Eleanor pushes.

"I think you're stuck."

"I think you're right."

Ali bends down and squints at the cherry dowels. "It's possible one of these just cracked."

"It's not cracked. It's just a bit bent."

"I don't know. It looks like a crack."

Eleanor sighs louder than intended. "Can you pull it from your end?"

The woman gives a feeble tug. "If it wasn't on such an angle."

Worried her customer might go into labor or, worse, get fed up and walk away from the sale, Eleanor climbs over the bassinet and tries to pull from the outside. She only succeeds in jamming the bassinet in at a worse angle than before. Finally, she pokes her head into Death by Vinyl and waves to Noel.

He grins. "Good news. I've fixed the speakers. Listen." He hits a button on the remote control and the warbled sound grows louder, but sounds no better." His face falls. "Damn."

"Could we borrow you for just a sec?"

"We don't want to disturb you," Ali McGraw shouts from behind Eleanor. "If it's too much bother, I can come another day. The baby'll probably be late anyway."

Noel stands on the sidewalk, scratching his stubbled chin. Next door he's left his music on, or what's left of it. A loud hissing thump comes through the wall. Eleanor doesn't feel it in her best interest to point out the obvious: that he needs new speakers.

"How'd you get it jammed so tight like that?"

"If you could just help us give it enough of a jiggle," Eleanor says.

The three customers inside Pretty Baby are waiting to exit. "Can we just squeeze past?"

"Might be a while," Noel says.

"Go out the back door," Eleanor says to her customers. "The alley leads to a walkway to the street." When they look doubtful, she adds, "It's perfectly safe!"

From Death by Vinyl, the music turns into a flat buzz. Ali closes her eyes in horror.

"Thing's on an angle," Noel says. "That's what went wrong, Eleanor. If you'd kept it straight."

"I realize that!" Eleanor snaps. A young couple now stand outside, waiting to get in. "Can we just wiggle it straight again?"

He takes hold of the rails and they both go at the right side. The bassinet budges, but not much. "We just wedged it the opposite way," Noel says, squatting lower. "Try it one more time, but less muscle."

A loud buzz drowns out what remained of "Bohemian Rhapsody."

"Those speakers sound fixable," Eleanor says.

Ali McGraw smiles so wide it must hurt. "Oh, he can fix them." She laughs almost maniacally. "I can tell you right now he'll fix them."

They jerk the rails up and to the left now and finally the bassinet starts to move. Noel cries out in pain as his arm lodges between crib side and door frame. "Push it back. Push back!" They bump it back and then forward again until the bassinet is on the sidewalk. Noel rolls up his sleeve to reveal a long jagged gash. "You didn't tell me the posts were cracked."

"I said it. Eleanor, did I not say it?" Ali McGraw takes Noel's forearm. "Look at him. The poor man is bleeding."

"I'm fine." A drop of blood hits the sidewalk.

Ginny walks up with a steaming cup of what smells like mint tea. She motions for the waiting customers to head out the door now and examines the cut. "You're going to need stitches."

"We should take him to Emerg," says Ali. "I'll drive."

"I'm married to an ER doctor," Eleanor says. Noel looks at her quickly and she adds, "Or I was. Noel doesn't need Emerg. Ginny please bring us the first aid kit."

Ginny returns with a near-flattened tube of Polysporin and a frilly pink receiving blanket covered in baby polar bears. "I took it home the other night and my kids emptied it. This is all I could come up with."

"That blanket's from Italy!"

"It's clean. I'm fine."

"Here, let me." Ali takes the Polysporin and squeezes it

onto his wound. "So you sell old records? I hear they're making a huge comeback. All the hipsters are buying them."

"I won't sell to hipsters." He winces as Eleanor tugs his sleeve up higher. "Ow!"

"Stop squirming," she says. "It's not that bad."

"What's your most expensive record?" asks Ali.

Noel stops glaring at Eleanor long enough to say, "Definitely the Beatles' butcher-cover album. They pressed a couple of thousand covers before someone decided that showing the band covered with the blood and bodies of dismembered baby dolls maybe wasn't so great for their image. Dead babies don't tend to sell." He notices her belly and adds, "Sorry. Inappropriate imagery."

Ali fans away his worries. "How much for it?"

"Got it listed at eleven thousand dollars."

The woman pulls a credit card out of her wallet, writes something on the back of an envelope, and places it in his good hand. "Here's my Visa number and delivery address. Will you courier it to my house?"

"Are you serious?"

Ali glances at the pile of sodden vintage *Rolling Stone* magazines and rust-stained T-shirts, clearly unsellable, beside his door. "I *have* to have it for my collection. Get it to me a.s.a.p., promise?" She waddles toward a Cadillac Escalade up the block.

Eleanor calls out, "Wait—what about the bassinet?"

"I can't put my baby in that thing. It's cracked."

Chapter 39

I don't understand why you're so upset." Ginny tries to sidle past Angus, bumping him with her ballooning midsection as she follows Eleanor into the living room. She maneuvers herself onto the floor and pulls disposable chopsticks, then container after container of Chinese food, from a paper bag. Eleanor counts eight containers on the table.

"Seriously, Gin? This is enough food for six people."

Ginny sighs. "I'm counting four and that's without the dog." She opens a carton of spring rolls and offers one to Angus, who practically swallows it whole. "The only time I don't feel sick is when I'm eating."

Eleanor watches Angus gobble another spring roll and shakes her head. "I even switched hand lotions, in case I was tainting his meals with the scent of orange blossom or something. It makes no sense."

"Makes perfect sense. It's Canine Psychology 101. The dog's depressed because his pack split up. Did he listen to Jonathan over you?"

Eleanor thinks about this a moment. "Actually, yes.

Obeyed Jonathan the first time he asked. I have to beg, plead. Eventually I give up."

Ginny pops a whole chicken ball into her mouth and says, "You should be reading my dog book. Angus is like a kid. He needs an alpha. A pack leader. Doesn't know what's what with nothing but a wishy-washy littermate in charge."

"So why won't he eat for me?"

"I told you, he wants a pack. With me here, he feels more complete. Plus I'm not wimpy."

"Neither am I!"

Ginny stares at her. "Whatever gets you through the night. So spill. Why are we upset about a DVD of Sylvie?"

Eleanor flops down onto the couch and pulls her bare feet up onto the cushion. "You know how they sent me a 'Mama' DVD the other week? The 'Dada' version just arrived."

"Shit."

"Yes. I'm dying to see it—it's Sylvie, of course—but I can't watch it alone."

"Ah. Okay, hang on." Ginny opens up a few more containers and scrapes a mountain of food onto her plate. "You got anything good to drink?"

Eleanor gets up and heads to the kitchen, returning with a glass of mango juice for Ginny and red wine for herself. Ginny waves over the wine.

"Forget it. You don't get to have any."

Ginny takes the glass and holds it under her nose. Inhales deeply. "I'm allowed a daily whiff. No rules against that." She settles a pillow behind her back and nods toward the TV. "I'm ready. Bring on the agony."

Eleanor taps the remote at the TV and Sylvie's face appears. This video was likely made before the first she received. Sylvie's hair is loose this time. Wild and natural and gorgeous, but shorter. And Sylvie's front teeth haven't come in. Again, Cathy holds her. Sylvie keeps reaching up with splayed fingers to touch her foster mother's daisy earrings. Eleanor looks closer. Sylvie is wearing the red jumper from the store. She had mailed it as soon as she and Jonathan were approved.

Seeing Sylvie in something from home makes this all less surreal.

Cathy, holding Sylvie under the arms as she stands on her lap, says, "Say *Dada. Dada*." It's not as noisy in this video. Easier to hear what's being said.

Sylvie says nothing, just stares wide-eyed at the camera.

Now Cathy bounces her up and down and shows her how to wave, which Sylvie doesn't imitate. A tiny finger goes in her mouth and a string of drool hits her collar.

"Say *Dada*, Sylvie. *Dada* . . ."

Sylvie grunts, points a wet finger at the camera.

"*Dada*," Cathy repeats.

More determined now, Sylvie stands up taller and holds out both arms.

"*Dada*." Cathy looks worried.

"Just freaking say it already, kid! You're killing me!" Ginny blurts out.

Eleanor shoots her a look. "We don't want her to say *Dada*! She didn't say *Mama*!"

"But we know she's going to say it and you're going to cry!"

On cue, Sylvie tilts her chin up and whispers, "*Da-da*."

"Yes, wonderful!" her foster mother squeals, bouncing her in delight. She says something to the cameraman and the video clip abruptly ends.

Ginny turns to look at Eleanor, who pinches her hand to force herself not to cry. Once she has control over her emotions, she reaches for a carton of steamed veggies and swallows a mouthful. "There. Done. I lived."

"It doesn't mean anything that she didn't say *Mama*. You do know that."

"Of course I know that. It's developmental, etcetera, etcetera."

"But still, it's killing you."

"Of course it's killing me. I am human."

"Oh no. Don't even think about doing what you're thinking about doing."

Eleanor puts down the carton and ejects the DVD. Snaps it back into its case and sets it high up on a bookshelf. "I am absolutely not taking this to him."

"Good girl. Jonathan walked away. To get him back via emotional manipulation would not serve you well."

"Exactly. Now pass me the chicken fried rice."

Chapter 40

It's almost 11 p.m. by the time Ginny leaves. Eleanor, in an attempt to avoid watching the video again, pulls on boots, jeans, two big sweaters, and her Annie Hall hat, and coaxes the reluctant Angus out for a walk in the cold night air.

Once outside in the crisp night air, the dog perks up and actually strains against his leash in an effort to get going. She tugs him back as she locks the door to the building. "Hang on, Angus." As they pass Death by Vinyl, she glances inside. It's dark. The Sasquatch is barely recognizable as such over by the counter. He could be an oafish man in a hairy coat, albeit alarmingly large. She sees light streaming in from the back of the store and leans closer to the window. The alley door is propped open by a crateful of records. Either Noel is being robbed or he's out back putting out the trash.

Marion used to give Eleanor this advice: when considering whether or not you should do something, ask yourself "would an idiot do it?" If the answer is yes, reconsider. Aware that only the very biggest of idiots would do this, she makes for the dark passageway that leads from the buildings to the back alley.

Angus is so excited he practically drags her. The alley is a cornucopia of smells usually off limits. It's where the garbage lives. There is glorious rotted meat, cheese that has liquefied in the sun, cast-off clothing, fouled kitty litter and—forget the banality of canine urine—there is the single most interesting bodily fluid of all. Human urine. Add to the mix the possibility of chasing from the Dumpster a raccoon or an urban coyote, and you have a veritable Disneyland for an apartment-dwelling dog.

He pulls so hard against his leash, his breath comes in broken, croupy coughs. "Angus!" Eleanor tugs him back. A series of crashes and bangs from the back only make Angus pull harder. "Settle down."

They emerge from between the buildings to find Noel outside rearranging trash cans. He's arranged his, hers, and the closest neighbors' cans from biggest to smallest right beside the Dumpster. Dressed in a Dead Kennedys T-shirt and pajama bottoms, he looks up to see them and runs his hand through his hair as if he's been working all evening to solve the world's renewable energy crisis.

"Hey."

Angus rushes him and inspects his pajamas for leftover dinner, evidence of him having petted another dog, whatever, and Eleanor is pulled along behind. She stares at the bins. "How am I going to know which is mine?"

"That's the beauty part. It doesn't matter."

"Plus, it's all the way over here. It's not by my back door."

"No. This way we've opened the space behind our stores and the stench of garbage is farther away from our doors—which some of us like to prop open."

"And in the weather—an umbrella in one hand, the trash

in the other. And then there's the snow. I see your point, but really, I don't think this is going to work so well . . ."

"I'm actually thinking of installing a screen door. It gets so hot inside now that the rads come on. And, really, why do we care which bin belongs to whom? Trash is trash. Next I'm going to figure out how we can get the Dumpster moved across the alley to sit between those two garages over there. What do you think?"

If she didn't know him, she'd swear he was high, the speed at which the words tumbled out of his mouth, his overly amped arm movements.

He positions himself where the Dumpster could be and explains why it would be easier for the trucks to empty it. As he moves from one graffitied garage door to the next, going on and on about efficiency and odors and rats, as Angus sits at the end of his leash, wagging his tail as if in full agreement, Eleanor stares at Noel's boots. They were clean this afternoon. Now they're covered in mud.

There is no mud in the alley.

Suddenly the significance of the day hits her. His wife died November sixteenth. One year ago today.

He's been to the cemetery.

She lowers herself onto the asphalt and pulls the panting Angus close, rubbing his shoulder. "Noel?"

He stops talking. "You know what I've discovered, since I started living alone?"

"What."

"That the best time of day is the evening. Just after work, when you get home and turn on a lamp or two, maybe light a candle. You grab something like celery and peanut butter from the fridge because no one's watching. You pour yourself a glass of wine and turn on a movie. I mean, it was fun to be together and do that. But when you're together it's the 'us' you're aware of. When you're alone, you get to know the evening itself. Its quirks. Its glow."

He sets his hands on his hips, blinking. "Yeah. You're kind of sorry when it ends."

"Yes!"

"I mean, you're going to see it again, same time the next day, but still. You're sad to leave it behind and go to sleep."

Eleanor's face slides into a smile. "Exactly."

They stare at each other, silent but knowing. He shifts his weight to one side and opens his mouth as if to say something. Then a neighbor's car door slams and Angus barks, and the moment has passed. Noel turns back to the Dumpster and sets his hands on it, tries to shake it as if he might be able to drag it across the alley by himself. Eleanor unclips Angus and lets him race around with his nose to the ground.

She shades her eyes from the light. "Noel?"

He turns.

"Are you doing anything November twentieth?"

Chapter 41

His wife and children aren't difficult to find. Ethan's death was so recent, he's still in the current phone book—address and all.

She debated what to do. Even doing nothing at all. But Isabelle, who has helped so many, who helped Eleanor herself, doesn't deserve to live the rest of her life alone in that gigantic Beacon Hill town house. A house that big needs to be filled with people. Family.

Eleanor doesn't want to call and leave a message. She doesn't even know Ethan's widow's name. She tells Ginny she'll be out for the morning, fills up her Volkswagen Beetle with gas, and drives out to Sandwich. Parks across the street from 341 Cherry Blossom Court, beside the communal mailboxes, between two rhododendron hedges, and waits.

Most of the homes in this subdivision have a salty Cape Cod feel to them. All are different shades of gray clapboard with white trim and a peaked roof. The neighborhood is fairly new, judging from the landscaping. All the shrubs are undersized and spaced quite far apart. It'll be a few years yet before they grow up and out and start to spill into each other.

It's a rare driveway that doesn't have a basketball net, and a bike path at the end of the courtyard leads to an open green space. An ideal place to raise children.

When Eleanor set out, she had no idea what she'd do. Scurry up to the front door when no one is home and leave a note or wait until Mrs. Runion is home and speak to her in person. She sips her now-cold coffee and debates. On the one hand, it would be more dignified, more personal to introduce herself and give the woman the message in person. On the other, she has no way of knowing how Ethan felt about being adopted or if he even knew at all. If he did, he may have had no interest in meeting his birth mother, and who is Eleanor to put his grieving widow under that kind of pressure?

It's two forty in the afternoon; the kids are likely in school. A navy minivan sits in the driveway. Eleanor leans back in her seat and waits. Just as she hoped, at about 3:05, the front door opens and a woman with short brown hair steps out, locks the door behind her. She's thin, broad-shouldered. Looks like she could be quite athletic. She's not dressed for the weather either, in her T-shirt and sweat-pants. With nothing in her hands but wallet and keys, she's not planning to be gone long. Probably back up Acacia to the public school just over the hill.

Eleanor will have to act fast.

She watches the woman climb into the van. As the vehicle speeds past, Eleanor ducks. It isn't until she hears the vehicle stop at the corner and pull into traffic that she sits up and reaches for a pen. On a blank card, she writes:

Mrs. Runion,
I am deeply sorry for your loss. I have some information about

your late husband's family that may help you. Please call me at
518–555–1726.

    Warmest wishes,
    Eleanor Sweet

She runs across the street and places the sealed envelope in the mailbox and gets back in the car. With any luck, she'll hear from Ethan's wife soon.

As she pulls away from the curb, she decides it was the right thing to do, leaving the note rather than shocking Mrs. Runion in person.

Of course, she's learned from the best.

Chapter 42

Isabelle's closet is dark. In such a house, one bare bulb hanging from a wire—it's incongruous. Wrong. It should be a grand chandelier illuminating her wardrobe.

"When you're going to a wedding like this," Isabelle says, pulling out a long navy shift, making a face and putting it back. "Formal, in Cambridge, and you're meeting people for the first time, you don't want to wear anything that people will remember. You want them to say, 'It was lovely meeting Eleanor.' Not 'I didn't quite understand the pattern of Eleanor's skirt.' Besides that, I insist you wear at least three fewer layers of armor than you would otherwise. Left to your own will, you're likely to pile a caftan atop a dress atop several pairs of trousers."

"Layers aren't armor. They're fashion."

"That's not your reason and you know it. Somehow you've gotten it into your head that you can prevent people from hurting you by wearing as many skins as an onion. Well, I'm here to tell you that none of us gets through it unscathed. And all the scarves in the world won't stop it from happening to you. How about this?" She holds up a full-length peach gown with capped sleeves and a sweetheart neckline.

"No. This one's too long for me. You'll trip on it even if we give you the highest pumps. Speaking of which—what shoe size are you?"

"Seven and a half."

"I'm eight. It's close enough."

Eleanor stands. Trails her fingers along the hanging items. Isabelle's suits are arranged lovingly, artfully, by muted color, much like a rainbow of overripe produce. Past-its-sell-date eggplant seeps into hoary blueberry which bleeds into rotted pepper. Cashmere sweaters lie folded and stacked on a ladder of glass shelves. Her dress shirts—all white and pressed to perfection—drape from wooden hangers, spaced two inches apart. One hanger, the last, is bare. The fitted white shirt she wears now, most likely.

It's been a day and a half and no word from Ethan's wife. Eleanor has wondered whether the note was frightening in any way. Surely the woman didn't think she had any sort of bad news to impart. Eleanor had said specifically that the information could help her.

"On another topic, I don't normally permit clients' great slobbering buffalo to salivate on my Aubusson rug," Isabelle says, sliding a pressed linen hand towel beneath Angus's chin. "Is he eating yet?"

"Yes. Now we feed him in the store. He's a bit less depressed down there."

"Quite frankly I don't know how you got on all these years without making a complete cock-up of your life. Who, possessing any intelligence whatsoever, buys a dog the size of a UPS truck when they live in a shabby walk-up apartment?"

Eleanor suppresses a smile. Isabelle would have made a terrific mother. She pulls out a red dress—strapless and to the knee—and holds it up. "How about this?"

"Honestly." Isabelle snatches it up and hangs it on another rail. "You don't want to give anyone a reason to judge you. A trendy shoe, a plunging neckline, a too-broad shoulder— these are all things that open you up to scrutiny."

"You met them. They don't seem so prone to judgment."

"But Great-Aunt Betsy from Minnesota may be prone to that and more." Isabelle sets hands on hips and looks Eleanor up and down. "I'm thinking plain dark dress and low, ladylike pumps."

"Whatever."

Isabelle stares at her, appalled by her naïveté. "You're being introduced as the child they never admitted to. 'Whatever' does not apply in *any* form to this event." She pulls out a sleeveless black dress. "Try this one."

From her purse on Isabelle's bed, Eleanor's phone pings. It's a text.

"Have you had a stroke, Eleanor Sweet? Take off your seventeen layers and try on the dress."

With glances back to assure herself Isabelle is not looking, Eleanor pulls off her blazer and scarf, cardigan and skirt, and slips on the dress over wooly tights. Steps into the shoes. The fit around the bust and shoulders is good. She turns around, pleased by the way it swirls around her thighs. "It's fine."

"It's atrocious. Take it off."

"What?"

"It's miles too short. Makes you look cheap with those noodly woolen legs of yours."

Reluctantly, Eleanor pulls it off and waits for the next gar-ment—a steel-gray tank-style dress that goes all the way to the floor. She tugs it on over her curves and busies herself with the hemline. Eventually, she stands and looks in the mirror.

"No way. Too much shoulder. I need something with more coverage."

"You're wearing it." Isabelle hands her a pair of sky-high black patent pumps. "With these it'll be long enough to look elegant without being so long that it trails across the restroom tiles at the Liberty."

Eleanor slips them on and turns around. "There. I look spectacular. Can I go check my phone now?"

Isabelle grunts. "I'd ease up on the self-congratulations, Cinderella. You don't look that good."

Eleanor walks past her to pull her phone from her purse. The text is from a number Eleanor doesn't recognize.

Hi, this is Tiffany Runion. I'm very interested to hear. Please call me at the number below. Thanks. xo Tiff

Chapter 43

Adorably unloved. That's how Noel looks tonight, Eleanor thinks as he reaches for his dropped napkin. From the front he's great. Well, his tie could use a good tweak to tighten the knot. But from behind, his suit jacket is wrinkled across the shoulders and his hair is splayed out. It's as if he showered, got dressed, and gave up. Fell back onto his bed and went to sleep. Then left the house with no one to point out the rear view. It makes her sad.

Rustic twig chandeliers wrapped in fairy lights hang from a fabric-draped ceiling. Silver balloons drift lazily upward like bubbles. With wooden tables and chairs slipcovered in white, and centerpieces made of calla lilies, the total effect is simple and elegant.

The band plays a decent rendition of Michael Jackson's "Beat It." Guests gather in groups, drinks in hand, while their children bounce and jump on the dance floor, a group of three tween girls forcing little Robbie to dance in their midst. He doesn't seem to mind one bit.

Everywhere people laugh. Smile. Congratulate.

And Eleanor cannot wait to leave.

She glances over to where Ruth and Richard have appeared, chatting and sipping champagne by the doors. Before the service, they'd greeted her at the front steps of the church. But instead of asking her to join them in the front rows, Ruth called over one of the ushers—a hulking, long-haired blond who never actually spoke—and asked him to find an extra-special seat for Eleanor and her date, Joel. He sat them in the ninth row, far end, by the restroom.

Ruth found her after the ceremony and pulled her aside. Explained that they hadn't told anyone about her yet. No one knew outside of the immediate family. It's Roxie's wedding, she explained. Probably not the best time to drop such a bomb. Might detract from Roxie's big day, and Ruth didn't think that was a good idea.

Eleanor agreed, even as she crumbled inside.

After the service, once the crowd piled into cars and everyone headed for the banquet hall, the Pantera family stayed behind to pose for pictures. Eleanor stood in the entryway and watched as the photographer's assistant filed them all into the church library. As Eleanor stood there waiting for an invitation, the photographer's assistant said, "Sorry, this is just for family," and shut the door.

No one opened it again. No one came out looking for her.

Noel waves toward the fairy lights with his dinner roll. "Nice party. Your twin sister, you said?"

"Not my twin. Roxie and Ronnie are twins. They're my little—" She stops herself. The word *sisters* seems to get stuck on her tongue. Which is ridiculous. She accepts what Ruth said—this isn't the occasion to go public. Of course that included the photo session. She smiles at Noel. "I like this song."

"'Sunday Morning' is the only Maroon 5 song that is remotely acceptable. Only because of the nod to Paul Simon," says Noel.

"I actually thought this song *was* by Paul Simon."

He throws his head back and laughs. "You say that like your lack of taste in music should surprise me."

"Really." She nudges his leg. "Should a guy who sells music be such a snob?"

"If he isn't, he's in the wrong business. Hey, I got that one speaker up and running again. The one that got soaked the worst."

"Does this mean we're back to our old standby— 'Bohemian Rhapsody'?"

"Oh yeah. By tomorrow morning, no worries."

"Good." She rips apart her dinner roll and pops a piece into her mouth. "At least that I can count on."

He leans back and observes the room. "So what's with the lousy seating? You didn't want to be at the head table with the rest of them?"

"It's very last minute, me even being here," Eleanor explains. "They can't just reorganize all the seating when a long-lost relative shows up."

"Long-lost?"

Oops. "I'll explain later."

He hadn't answered her right away, when Eleanor asked him to be her plus-one. The high from his trash planning out in the alley vanished, he mumbled something about staples and disappeared inside his store. It wasn't until the next afternoon she got her answer. She was on her way out for lunch and noticed a Post-it on the Pretty Baby side of the wall. All the note said was *I'm free the 20th.*

"I'm so glad you're here." Roxie bends over from behind and hugs Eleanor in a froth of satin and veil and hair curled into shiny blond ribbons. She straightens and pulls her new husband closer. "Peter, this is my big sister, Eleanor."

He hugs her tight, thumping Eleanor's shoulder like she's the team quarterback. "Mind if we call you Ellie?"

Eleanor stands. "I can take it."

After introducing herself to Noel and reaching out to tighten his tie, Roxie says to Eleanor, "So? When does my little niece arrive?"

It's Noel who answers. "In four days. American Airlines Flight 943. Arrives 10:30 a.m."

"You were listening," says Eleanor. "I'm impressed."

"You said it three times in the car on the way over. Hey, do we know if she's into The Ramones? Because I've got a very tiny T-shirt . . ."

"How's my girl?" Ruth appears, her gray-blond hair swept up in a sparkly clip. Richard hovers behind her. She kisses Eleanor's cheek. "I can't tell you how happy it makes me to see you here."

My girl. Eleanor blushes. It's crazy how she feels about Ruth. No matter how much weirdness has gone on today, she can't get enough of her. "Me too."

Richard shakes Noel's hand and introduces himself. "You taking good care of our sweetheart?"

"We still haven't decided if she's tolerating me or I'm tolerating her," says Noel. "I'm thinking of installing a scoreboard out front of the stores."

Ruth loops her arm through Eleanor's and pulls her aside. "I've barely been able to focus on the wedding since you came out. I think about you, I dream of you. I'm just so happy to have you in my life. Our lives."

This. *This* is what Eleanor needs to hear. "I am too. And for Sylvie. She'll actually have grandparents and aunts and uncles. And a cousin."

"Listen. I've been thinking about something. And, please, don't feel obligated. But I'd, well, I'd just be over the moon if you'd consider calling me Mom."

Eleanor stares at her and inhales as if able to get a deep breath for the first time in her life.

"Mom, Mama, Mother, anything of the sort will do." She pulls back and takes Eleanor's hands. "What do you think?"

The lead singer says something about slowing down the tempo and the band launches into Billy Joel's "Piano Man." Couples gravitate to the dance floor and pull each other close.

"Eleanor?"

"Okay." She squeezes Ruth's fingers and closes her eyes. "Yes. Mom."

"That's it. I can die happy. I don't care if it happens tonight, even!" Ruth looks up and waves to a boxy woman in a pink dress and too much lipstick. "That, my dear, is cousin Shelagh. She once tried to drown me in her parents' pool, the witch. To hear her tell the story is hilarious." Ruth moves off to say hello.

Eleanor waits for her to bring Shelagh back, to hear her tell the story, but the women glide toward Roxie, who is two tables away now, mugging for a video camera.

Eleanor sits, glancing back regularly to see if Ruth will return. She doesn't.

"Your mother's stunning."

"Thanks."

"You look a lot like her."

Eleanor could hug him. Never in her life has she heard those words uttered—that she resembles anyone. Until Ruth. She stares down at her lap. She could confide in Noel. It's not as if *she* needs to keep the adoption a secret. She'll tell him. But not tonight. "Thank you."

"You know, an evening with you is even better," he says, resting his forearms on his knees and leaning closer.

"Better than what?"

"Than that stupid-ass evening you described with peanut butter and a candle. I think you made the whole thing up."

They both laugh. She feels something on her wrist and realizes it's his hand wrapping itself around hers. He leans back quickly when his fingertips touch her wedding band.

She'd debated taking it off earlier. There was no reason to wear it now.

Across the dance floor, Ruth excuses herself from cousin Shelagh and makes her way to the restroom. Eleanor chides herself for being so needy. Ruth will return. She asked Eleanor to call her "Mom" for God's sake.

"Hey." Noel holds up a small, blue-lace-trimmed hankie streaked with mascara. "Is this yours?"

Eleanor takes it from him and stands. "I'll be right back."

She knows the handkerchief is not Ruth's. Roxie had been clutching something in her hand, dabbing her eyes as she spoke. The hankie is clearly hers. But Eleanor can't help herself. The desire to have more of Ruth is overwhelming.

In the muffled hush of the ladies' room, Ruth's voice rings clear. Two women about her age have her attention. One in a nondescript dress Isabelle would approve of, the other so athletic she looks like a man playing dress-up in his wife's pumps and silk. They offer congratulations and good wishes while Ruth applies lipstick and fluffs her hair.

Eleanor's heart pounds with all the intensity of being certain she's doing the wrong thing. Pasting a smile on her face, she approaches.

"They haven't been seeing each other long, but from the start it was like kismet. They're inseparable." Ruth looks up to see Eleanor in the mirror. "Eleanor, dear." She spins around. "That man of yours seems a sweetheart."

Eleanor approaches, holding out the handkerchief. "I think you left this at the table."

"Hmm." Ruth examines the dried mascara. "It's Roxie's something blue." She grins to her friends. "My youngest wears far too much eye makeup. Therese, May, this is Eleanor Sweet. Owns the most famous baby store in the country."

"Well, maybe on my block," Eleanor says, feeling stung, but not sure if she should be. "I own Pretty Baby."

"Oh, in Boston. I read about your store in a magazine once," says the cross-dresser.

"*Good Housekeeping.*" The sensibly shod woman folds her arms across her chest in businesslike approval. "I saw that. My daughter wanted to fly in from Sarasota for her baby but I told her it was ludicrous. The flight alone was eight hundred dollars, then there's hotel and what have you."

"You're a friend of Roxie's?" asks the other.

"Well, no . . ." Eleanor looks to Ruth for help. *Say it*, she pleads silently. *Say I'm your daughter, even though you said we wouldn't today. Point out that we look alike. That you asked me twenty minutes ago to call you Mom.*

"Eleanor is a close family friend. We go way, way back, don't we, dear?"

The champagne rises up and scalds her throat. If she'd eaten anything at all today, she'd be lunging for the toilet. She needs to escape. "Nice to meet you both," she manages before walking into a stall and closing the door behind her. She drops down to the toilet seat and leans over her knees.

Eleanor wanders back to the table and slides into her seat. The music, the dancing, the lights, it's all a blur. The thing is this: to explain—in a public restroom no less—all that went on thirty-five years ago at a girls' home on the wrong side of State Line Road, Roxie's wedding is no place for that. Ruth explained that earlier at the church. This event is not about Eleanor or the decision Ruth and Richard felt they had to make back then. It's about Roxie. When Ruth reveals what happened to her outer circle of family and friends, it should be in a more intimate setting.

That's that.

Noel cuts into a piece of roast beef and pops it into his mouth. "The band knew Belle & Sebastian's 'Dear Catastrophe Waitress,' can you believe it? They're pretty decent guys. Said they're going to send me a CD of their original music. I told them I'd sell it in the store. Really glad I came tonight." He winks at her. "Roast is a little dry, though."

Something about him having an opinion about the quality of his meal makes her snap. "Try opening first."

He stops chewing. "What?"

"Before you go getting the band's hopes up. Try opening your doors for a full day and actually selling something."

"I have sold something. You were there. That customer of yours bought a very expensive album."

"Yeah, out of pity."

"What are you talking about?" A tuxedoed man on the other side of the table asks Eleanor to pass the pepper. Noel gets to it first and passes it across. He leans back and watches Eleanor. "What's going on?"

"Nothing. I'm just on edge."

The band launches into Eric Clapton's "Wonderful Tonight." Roxie and Peter get on the dance floor. As do all the kids, about a dozen other couples, and Ronnie and her husband.

Eleanor stands. "Let's dance."

"But the waiter just went to get me extra Yorkshire pudding . . ."

She tugs him to his feet. "Come on. We have to dance now."

Out on the floor, she guides Noel ever closer to Ruth. She overreacted, back in the restroom. She doesn't want Ruth to think she doesn't understand. Slowly they spin in circles until finally Eleanor catches Ruth's eye. Her mother winks at her and Eleanor relaxes. There. Proof. Everything is fine.

Noel pulls her close. His warm hand on her back reminds her what it is to be held by a man, and she allows herself to lean into him.

"Thanks," he whispers in her ear.

"Hmm?"

"Thanks for bringing me here. You have a nice family. It's nice to be in a room full of happy people."

Yes, we are happy, she thinks. A happy family.

Chapter 44

Her alarm doesn't go off.

This clock radio has been reliable an entire decade until the morning she really needs it. The morning Sylvie arrives. Of course this would be the one time she sleeps in—the days since the wedding have been full of noisy repairs, too much barking, and sleepless nights of anticipation. It was bound to catch up with her.

She flies out of bed to pull on a pair of jeans and a baggy sweater. There's no time to wash even. It's 9:49 and Sylvie's plane lands at 10:30. Angus looks at her, wagging his tail and panting expectantly by the door. There's no time to take him down, wait for him to do his business, and bring him back up, so bringing him in the car it is. Even if it does mean stuffing him into the front seat so he doesn't drool on Sylvie the entire way home. He races out leash-free to water the tree out front as she unlocks the Beetle.

"Angus, let's go!"

Once he's finally bundled in, the car seat and diaper bag loaded, and Eleanor buckled, she turns the key in the ignition—to be met with a limp sputter.

Again, she turns the key and waits while, this time, the engine groans and actually makes a choking sound. It's 10:03 and the car won't start. Sylvie's plane lands in twenty-seven minutes. Angus sits unconcerned with his rump on the passenger seat, feet on the floor, and head over the dashboard, hot breath fogging up the window.

She turns the key again. This time, nothing at all.

No cabs in sight. Not one.

Panicked, she looks around to see Noel has come outside to clean the store windows.

She climbs across to open the passenger door. "Noel?" When he doesn't react, she calls louder, "Noel!" This time he turns around and squints at her, Windex bottle dangling from one finger. "My car's dead."

He turns away, squirts the window, and starts polishing. "You have Triple A?"

"No . . ." She struggles to unbuckle and climbs out of the car. "I just . . . I was wondering if you could give us a ride real quick."

He stands upon a splintered chunk of Eleanor's antique bench to spray the upper half of the window. Then winds paper towel around one hand and wipes. Sprays again. Wipes. Works a tiny bit of the towel into the corners, then leans close to assess the window from the side view. Scrubs at the odd smear. "No can do."

"I can't be late."

"I don't drive that car. I will never drive that car."

"I'm desperate. You have to help me."

"Sorry."

"Please."

He scrubs the same spot on the window now, over and over. "Can't do it."

Eleanor crosses the sidewalk. "Noel, I get that it's hers but you can't bring her back by refusing to drive it. It doesn't change the fact that she's gone."

He stops scrubbing. Stares at the glass. "I said no, okay? You can take a bus. You can call a cab."

"What good does it do to make it a shrine to her?" Her voice grows more shrill with each passing second. "How is that going to help?"

He turns. Stares at the Audi for a moment, then swipes at his eyes with a wrist because his hands are full. Runs his hands through his hair. "I can't talk about it."

"Noel, I'm desperate. I have to get to Logan in twenty-two minutes—"

"Logan?"

"Today's the day, remember? November twenty-fourth, 10:30. American Airlines."

"Sylvie," he says.

"Sylvie."

It takes him a moment to react. Then, with a tilt of his head, he pats his pockets, pulls out a set of keys, and heads toward the always gleaming black Audi. "I can't promise it'll start."

It does. As the engine warms up—it's likely been some time since the car has been turned on—Noel roots through the glove box and pulls out a CD. First thing he does, before buckling up even, is slide it into the CD player.

It sounds like all dialogue. Like an audio book. First crickets, then two *Twilight*-type teenagers discuss whether they're all alone, then a familiar-sounding voice launches into none other than "Bohemian Rhapsody."

Eleanor looks at him. Noel nods, flips on a pair of dusty aviators, and roars into traffic. The entire way to the Callahan Tunnel, they listen to William Shatner walk through "Bohemian Rhapsody." She supposes she had it coming.

Once they leave daylight behind and descend into the quiet hum of the tunnel, he speaks. "It was my fault."

"What was your fault?"

"I insisted that morning that we switch vehicles. I had a little Smart car and was planning to drive up to Marblehead to pick up this guy's dead father's record collection. He had a ton of cool rock—from Elvis to The Doors to Hendrix. Victoria was going to take my car to her mom's down near Quincy. I hadn't even left the house yet when I got the call. It was an SUV, the driver was texting. It was instant."

Eleanor puts her hand on his arm. "Oh God. I'm sorry."

"The records could've fit. I could've made them fit. I was just being lazy. The Audi has the bigger trunk."

"Noel. You can't blame yourself for something like that. It's shitty and wrong and terrible. But it's not your fault."

He doesn't answer. Just points at the clock, 10:22, and hits the gas.

After a further fifteen minutes of no conversation, three episodes of Angus barking at other dogs, and a near collision with a city bus that would have proved fatal to Eleanor's time-line, the Audi lurches to a stop in front of the American Airlines gate and Noel cuts the engine. He looks at her.

"You're seven minutes late. I'll wait here. Go!"

Eleanor grabs the diaper bag and jumps out of the car. She slams the door and starts to run, then races back to the window, which he lowers. "I know what this meant to you. I know how hard it was. Just . . . thank you."

"What kind of parent stands here and makes small talk?" He waves her away. "Get going!"

Standing in front of the domestic flights arrivals gate, Eleanor is aware she looks like not only an unfit mother, but an unfit citizen. She needs a shower. Her sweater won't stay on her shoulders, and her sneakers are untied. Not that Sylvie will care. The important thing is she arrived on time. Though, as she stands here alone, a welcoming committee of one, the moment feels a bit ordinary and sad. Not much of a pack, Ginny would say.

Passengers from the flight begin to trickle out, looking dazed and rumpled from the cross-country flight. A white-haired man in a floral shirt, carrying a bag of duty-free liquor, a newspaper, and a laptop, looks surprised to find himself in an airport. He smiles and makes for an older man—a shrunken, more hairless version of himself—and gives him a hearty hug. They talk, laugh. Walk out toward the parking garage.

A businessman in square glasses comes out next, fresh and full of purpose. Heads straight for the taxi stand. Three girls in their early twenties are met by someone's brother or boyfriend.

A black woman in a long dress and braids leads a gaggle of young children through the crowd. They hang onto her jacket and scuttle along to keep pace.

Eleanor sets the diaper bag on the floor and stands up taller as if this might bolster her presence. A few more people, most of them tired-looking and in pairs, find waiting loved ones or leave on their own.

Suddenly, her knees are bumped from behind and Angus

dances around her, his tongue lolling and his leash dragging. She looks around to find Noel has fixed his iPhone on her. "It's November twenty-fourth and Eleanor Sweet is here at Logan waiting for a most special arrival." He pauses, swings the car seat from the crook of his arm onto the floor. Attached to the handle is a bundle of pink helium balloons he must have picked up just now at the gift shop. To her, Noel says, "Angus and I decided you need a videographer to chronicle the moment."

She reaches down to scrub Angus's sides and hide the tears brimming in her eyes. When she stands, she leans close enough to kiss Noel's cheek. "Thank you."

It isn't until Flight 943 appears to have emptied out that the doors slide open one more time. A young man, burly and gentle-looking, dressed in dark green Dockers and very new sneakers, long brown hair in a tidy ponytail, steps out. Luiz. In his hands is an infant carrier that has likely seen many trips to many states. Luiz looks around, sees Eleanor, and asks the question with his eyes.

Holding her breath, Eleanor nods.

He comes toward Eleanor, huge smile on his face, the carrier bumping against his knees. Then the infant carrier turns. Pudgy fists rise up to bat at the handle. Feet kick out in black lace-up shoes. Every step or two, a quick flash of Sylvie's face. So much smaller than Eleanor expected. Like a doll.

The escort no longer exists. The carrier is placed on the floor.

"Eleanor Sweet?"

Eleanor is already on her knees. She nods.

"I'm Luiz and I'm not going to bore you with small talk.

This is your beautiful daughter." He steps back and gives her her moment.

Sylvie stills. Green eyes heavily fringed with sandy lashes blink up at Eleanor, enormous and astonished. Her caramel skin, it glows with near iridescence. Her lips part in a smile to reveal two perfect front teeth, separated by a devilish gap. Her foot kicks out in excitement and Eleanor takes it in her hand.

Noel squats down beside them, iPhone covering part of his face.

Angus's nose digs deep into Sylvie's abdomen. "Whoa there!" Luiz dives down to unbuckle her.

"It's okay." Eleanor laughs. "Angus is just saying hello."

"Go ahead and pick her up," Luiz says. "You've waited long enough."

Eleanor hesitates, then lifts the girl onto her hip—she's so light!—and takes her hand. Bounces her softly and whispers hello over and over. Hesitatingly, she kisses Sylvie on the cheek, but the child pulls away. Looks to Luiz and stretches out her arms.

Luiz looks unconcerned, points at Eleanor. "No, Sylvie. You go to Mommy now."

"It's okay," Eleanor says. "It's all scary and new for her."

"She's a laid-back kid. She'll do great." Luiz checks her ID and holds out agency forms so she can sign with Sylvie in her arms.

"Do you need anything else from me?" Eleanor gives him back the pen.

"Just a picture of the two of you to give to Cathy?"

Eleanor poses with Sylvie while Luiz snaps a quick shot with his phone. He leans forward and squeezes Sylvie's hand. "That's it, then. Goodbye, baby girl. Be good for your mommy."

Sylvie watches as her travel partner walks away. A bead of drool gathers on her lower lip. Eleanor rocks her softly. As much as it wouldn't mean anything, as much as it would be natural, Eleanor doesn't want the baby to cry for him.

She doesn't. Sylvie raises a finger and touches Eleanor's jaw, making Eleanor laugh.

"This is Sylvie," she says, turning to Noel, still filming. "My daughter."

Chapter 45

Eleanor and Ginny kneel on the bathroom floor while Sylvie sits perfectly still in a safety ring obliterated by bubbles. They hadn't started with suds clear up to the baby's chin, but when Eleanor poured in a capful of baby wash, Sylvie giggled so hard that she poured more and more while Ginny filmed it. Now the child holds her hands above the foam and pats it with her palms.

Shielding Sylvie's eyes, Eleanor shampoos her massive headful of ringlets, which seem to come in every shade from deep brown at the back to sandy blond at the hairline. Wait till this grows longer, Eleanor thinks. Her hair will likely be stunning, but, oh, the tangles.

She thought she knew, before Sylvie's arrival, what it would be to love her own child. She runs a baby store, for God's sake. But nothing could have prepared her for this feeling. That full-body melt that comes with watching your baby toddle toward you with a book, try to ride the dog, or sit in your lap and play with your collar. Nothing.

Angus is besotted. The way he stares down at her, his face a curious mix of helplessness and amusement. Eleanor is fairly certain he'd wolf down dry kibble if he thought Sylvie had poured it into his bowl.

Ginny cleans out an ice cream container with her finger and licks the digit. "When you consider it's her first night, new climate, new parent, no other kids like in the foster home, she's doing very well."

"She's probably just so stunned by it all." Eleanor turns on the faucet, fills a plastic cup, and rinses Sylvie's hair while she dunks a rubber duck under the water and holds it there. Eleanor watches as Sylvie brings the duck up for air. Sylvie grins and drowns it again.

"They all have a cruel streak; don't get freaked out by it. It's a survival thing. Wait'll my two are born. My house will be so *Lord of the Flies*."

"I'm not freaked out." Again, Eleanor saves the duck. "But I'd like to keep her out of juvie as long as possible." To Sylvie, she holds out both hands as if to pick her up. "Time to come out now, Miss Sylvie Sweet."

Sylvie plunks her hands underwater in refusal.

"Sylvie, it's bedtime now."

Ginny laughs. "Bedtime. Love that concept. Doesn't work in reality but you can't tell a new parent that. They'd effing bolt."

"Sylvie, let's go now."

Sylvie licks a handful of bubbles and grimaces.

A noise from the front hall, then Isabelle's voice. "Who leaves their door unlocked in such a building? I'm liable to stumble upon blood-soaked bodies and ruin my good shoes." She pokes her face into the room and lets her eyes rest on the bubble-covered child. "Well," she snorts. "I see you're messing her up already." Isabelle drops her handbag in the hallway and rolls up a sleeve. "Thank heaven I happened by. The two of you don't know ankle from sternum." She plunges a hand into the water and unplugs the tub. "Rule number one with girls. No bubbles in the bathwater." She eyes Ginny's swollen belly. "You of all people should know this."

"Don't take me down, Grandma. I have boys!"

"Why no bubbles?" asks Eleanor.

"It's a urinary tract thing," says Isabelle as she coos to Sylvie and offers her hands in the same way Eleanor did. This time, Sylvie grins and bops up and down in excitement. She lifts her arms and opens and closes her tiny fists. "There, there, love," Isabelle says as she lifts the child up and into a towel Eleanor has waiting. "Isabelle is here to save you from these uneducated louts, don't you worry."

Sylvie blinks at Ginny and Eleanor as Isabelle pats her dry and wiggles her into a diaper and zippered sleeper.

An hour later, with Ginny gone in search of one pizza to take home for Ted and the kids and another for herself, Eleanor stands at the door with Isabelle and watches her search her bag for her keys.

She was wonderful with Sylvie, even coaxing the child to suck from the strange new silicone nipple on her bottle—first soak the tip in formula, then touch it to her lower lip, let her smell it. Taste it. The girl darted her tongue out, hungry for more. Worked like a charm. Sylvie fell asleep while still sucking on the bottle and stayed out as Isabelle placed her into her crib.

They stay a minute, watching Sylvie in the near darkness. Finally, Eleanor thinks, she's in her bed where she should be. At long last.

"You have a wonderful daughter, Eleanor Sweet." Isabelle starts out of the room and toward the front hall. "You look very happy."

"I am."

Isabelle turns away from Eleanor and fusses with her scarf, getting involved in a far-too-complicated procedure of twisting and tucking that is in very real danger of going on all night. She's thinking about Ethan. Eleanor can tell by the angle of her head. Tilted upward as if to see above and beyond anything that might hurt her.

"Isabelle. I have some information for you."

"I do not wish to hear it."

"But you don't know what it's about."

When the woman finishes buttoning up her coat, the rims of her eyes are pink. "Try your best to keep that poor child alive until I see you again. The national adoption industry has enough to deal with without you mucking it up."

Chapter 46

At first she thinks raccoons are fighting out in the back alley again. Or there's a cat in heat. It takes a moment of blinking in the dark to realize what's going on. Eleanor sits up and kicks off the covers. Her daughter is in the next room and from the sounds of it, she's spitting mad.

Angus has already posted himself next to the crib, backlit from the moon-shaped nightlight behind him. On his face is that look dogs get when they're willing someone with opposable thumbs to take care of a problem they're unable to solve on their own. At his side, hanging onto the crib rail with one hand is Sylvie, the other hand feeling for Angus's ear, her face shiny and swollen with tears.

Sylvie catches sight of Eleanor and lifts her arms in the air to be taken out of her linen-clad prison. "Ma ma ma ma."

Eleanor knows this is a developmental stage. She knows better than to be romanced by it, to read into it. But her chest swells anyway. "Shush, shush, baby girl." She lifts the child up and holds her close so she can inhale her. Instead of settling down, Sylvie stiffens and arches her back in defiance. She is not going to be placated that easily.

"Is it your diaper?" Eleanor lays her on the change table and unsnaps the legs of the sleeper, then removes the wet diaper. Sylvie is having none of this either and tries to roll off the change table as Eleanor re-diapers her. Then, with Angus at her heels, Eleanor carries Sylvie into the kitchen to prepare a bottle—which interests the child not in the least.

After spending the next twenty minutes trotting out stuffed animals and dolls, shaking rattles that tinkle, buzz, and giggle, after turning over the cow box that moos, after reading and rereading *Goodnight Moon*, Eleanor carries Sylvie from room to room, bouncing her on her hip. But nothing can appease the infant for more than a few seconds. Finally, if only to give her aching arms a break, Eleanor straps the child into the as-yet-unused stroller and wheels her in laps through living room, hallway, and kitchen.

The motion doesn't help at all.

The phone rings. Eleanor glances at the clock. It's after midnight.

With Sylvie howling in the background, she picks up. "Yes?"

"I'm so sorry, Eleanor." Ruth. "I wanted to hear about Sylvie's first day and just realized how late . . . What's all that ruckus . . . She's upset?"

"I've tried everything. Formula, changing, distractions. Do you think something's wrong?"

"She's an infant and infants sometimes don't make sense. The sooner you accept that, the better. Besides, she's jet-lagged and in a strange environment. Totally to be expected. How are you holding up?"

"Fine."

"Don't lie to your mother."

"Okay, my back hurts, my arms ache, and I'm so jittery I could explode. She won't stop crying and don't ask if I've tried this or that. I've tried everything a person could try. I'm ready to start wailing myself."

"This is what I try to tell people. Babies are tiny dictators cloaked in cuteness. It's nature's way of ensuring the survival of the human race."

"Not helpful."

"I'm booking myself a ticket and will be there for tomorrow night."

"Ruth, you don't have to do that."

"What did you promise me?"

Eleanor smiles. "Mom."

"That's better. I'm coming and I won't listen to any arguments. In the meantime, you're going to pull out the big guns. Let her cry in her crib for a moment while you get yourself dressed."

"What for?"

"You're taking her out for a drive in the car. She'll be out cold in ten or fifteen minutes and then you sneak her back up into bed. I *promise* you, this works."

Only it doesn't. It isn't until nearly 5 a.m. that Eleanor piles Angus and the inconsolable Sylvie into the car, and after an hour of driving through the darkened streets of the city, Eleanor is spent. Her hands shake and she can barely keep her eyes open. She's nauseated with nerves and desperate for sleep.

Adopting a child on her own was the worst decision she's ever made. Jonathan was a thousand percent right. At this rate, she'll have to close the business for lack of sleep. Go on welfare. And put Sylvie up for adoption so she can go to a loving couple who will raise her in tandem. Because that's what it takes.

She stops at a red light and notices the sun is coming up. If she had the windows open, if Sylvie would stop crying, she'd likely hear birds chirping.

This baby doesn't want her.

It isn't until Eleanor sees the red tail lights of a plane landing that she realizes she's driving toward the airport. Tears blur her vision as the child she's waited nearly a lifetime for continues to wail. *Maybe subconsciously I don't want her*, Eleanor thinks as she watches another plane approach. *Maybe I don't have what it takes to be a mother.*

That she even had this thought makes her slow the car, pull to the side of the road, and stop at the base of a chain-link fence. Sylvie is fully hysterical now. Eleanor unbuckles the carrier and turns it around so she can see her baby's face. Sylvie's crying loses its force, but doesn't abate.

Eleanor offers her the bottle. Not only is it rejected, it's hurled across the seat. Angus whines.

It's steamy in the car and Eleanor opens the sunroof.

From ahead, a massive plane drones, dropping lower and lower as it approaches, the sound of the engine gaining force. Eleanor realizes, as it passes overhead, so close she can almost reach up and stroke the underbelly, the roar nearly deafening her, that she's parked at the foot of a runway.

She's never felt so small. Like a pencil dot in comparison. Eleanor spins around to make sure Sylvie isn't frightened. Sylvie's eyes, puffy and red, blink hard and fast as she stares through the roof; she isn't frightened at all. She is utterly transfixed.

"See the airplane, Sylvie? See how big?"

The child has stopped crying. Eleanor offers her a finger and Sylvie takes it, gripping hard. But once the plane is gone, she starts to sob again.

Minutes later, another plane approaches. Again, Sylvie calms. This plane is smaller, sleeker, but passes just as low and roars just as loud. Eleanor looks up at the underside of the wings, the engines strapped beneath, and turns around again, excited. "Did you see that, Sylvie?"

Sylvie, still gripping Eleanor's finger, is fast asleep.

Eleanor pulls the car to the side of the road on Newbury Street, just a half-block from her door. Sylvie appears to be in a deep slumber, but chances cannot be taken. The transfer from backseat to crib must be done with utmost care. It's nearly 7 a.m. and Eleanor is exhausted.

Bracing herself for a piercing wail followed by another three hours of crying, she shuts off the engine. Nothing. Not a sound from the baby. Eleanor, having had only an hour of sleep, would slay a dragon for another few hours of rest. She climbs out, careful not to jangle the keys, and closes the car door as quietly as possible. The sun peeks out from behind the buildings across the street and a thin layer of frost glitters from the iron railings around the sidewalk trees.

Her skin tightens in the cold as she lets Angus out of the front seat. She sees her breath. "Shh," she says to him.

She won't take Sylvie out of the car seat, she's decided. The seat will go straight into the crib, just to be safe.

In a picture of normalcy, of sleeping at night and waking in the morning, a pair of male joggers wearing mittens emerge from a side street, one adjusting his fleece headband. She feels a flash of envy, and pushes it from her mind. She has Sylvie. They come toward her and Eleanor closes the door quickly and waits until they pass, full of rhythmic chatter.

Now. No cars, no voices. It's the perfect time. She puts her house keys in an easily accessible pocket and opens the door. Folds down the passenger seat. Partway through the removal process, Sylvie sighs and shifts her head to the left, works her mouth as if sucking from the bottle, but, mercifully, remains asleep.

Just as Eleanor nears her periwinkle door, car seat in hand, a crash sounds from the right. Noel strolls out from between the buildings, carrying a dented trash can. He sees her and calls out, "You gals are up early!" Angus bounds over to him, happier than Eleanor has perhaps ever seen him.

As Noel approaches, she shakes her head. "We haven't gone to bed yet," she whispers.

He checks his watch. "Up all night?"

She nods, handing him the carrier so she can pull out her keys and unlock the door. When she turns back, he has the car seat up on his hip. He's watching the baby—her tininess, her shock of wild hair, her dot of a nose.

"Good night, Miss Sylvie," he whispers.

She carries the car seat up the stairs, Angus following closely. Once Sylvie is in her crib, Eleanor tiptoes into the kitchen and pours plain kibble in Angus's dish. For the first time in weeks, he attacks his food, right there in the apartment.

She sinks into a chair and watches. Everything is going to work out fine. Her daughter is sleeping. Angus is eating. Eleanor is surviving.

Her cell phone rings from her pocket and she jumps to

answer before it wakes Sylvie. The number is familiar, but she's too exhausted to recognize whose it is. "Hello."

"Eleanor, it's Nancy."

"Hey, Nancy. Can I give you a call in a few hours? I'm just heading back to bed."

"Listen, honey. I want to let you know what's happening. And I'm not saying it's necessarily going to present a problem. At this point we have no idea what it means, but Sylvie's father has surfaced."

Chapter 47

Well, it doesn't mean he's going to fight for her," says Ruth from where she sits cross-legged on the sofa in her luxurious hotel suite. Sylvie sits peacefully in her lap, plucking Cheerios from Ruth's palm and eating them, one by one. Her socks lie balled on the floor, where Sylvie yanked them off and tossed them upon being released from the stroller. "He didn't know about the baby and now he does. I wouldn't go getting worked up about it just yet."

"I've thrown up three times today. Domenique Beaudoin is his name, and he's originally from Haiti. Apparently he's married. Has kids, has money, a business down in California. Sylvie's mother, Tia, worked in his house as a maid. They had a thing going on the side, his wife never knew. Still doesn't, according to him. But he'd been out of the country much of the year. Tia's sister got in touch with him when he got back and she told him about Tia's death. And about Sylvie."

"Haiti," Ruth says. "Could be why this Tia gave her baby a French name."

Eleanor stares at her. "That's not helping."

Sylvie points at the remote control on the coffee table. "Ma ma ma."

Ruth sets the squirming child down so she can stand at the table's edge. Sylvie lunges for the control, holds it up to impress Eleanor and Ruth with the intricacy of it. "Listen, a wealthy man with a wife and kids is not about to destroy all that by bringing a baby born to his housemaid-lover into the picture. I'm sure it'll blow over."

"Ma ma ma."

"That's what my caseworker said. But still."

True to her word, Ruth had hopped on a flight and checked herself into the Four Seasons. Eleanor offered her mother the master bedroom, perfectly willing to camp on the sofa for the benefit of having an extra set of hands, experienced hands, during the night, but Ruth wouldn't hear of ousting Eleanor from her own room. The plan was, she'd come back to Eleanor's for bedtime, then cab back to her hotel once they settled Sylvie for the night.

Sylvie takes *Boston Nights* magazine, squeezes that and the converter to her chest, and moves along the room in search of more possessions.

"I used to give your sisters a drop of scotch in their formula on the bad nights. Did a great job of calming them down and I dare anyone to judge me."

"I mean, imagine if he decides to fight for her? I would die."

In her collecting spree, Sylvie strings Ruth's purse over a forearm and continues with her load toward the minibar. "She walks well for eleven months," Ruth says.

Eleanor leans forward to take the purse, "No, sweetie, that's Ruth's . . ."

"Nonsense. What's mine is hers." She looks at Eleanor. "And I hope it'll be Nana. Like Robbie calls me."

Eleanor smiles. Nods. Nana it is.

Ruth takes off her reading glasses and they watch as Sylvie picks them up and tries to put them on. One arm takes purchase on an ear, and the other lists to her shoulder. She blinks at Eleanor with magnified fly-eyes and clutches her loot tighter.

Eleanor pulls out her camera and tries to snap a photo, but the glasses fall to the carpet. The moment has passed. "I can't lose her."

"You're not going to lose her. It won't happen."

"Nancy said we'd know more end of day today. But it's already 3:25. I'm thinking that's not good."

The TV control drops, striking Sylvie's foot. When she wails, Ruth picks her up and soothes her, singing to her and bouncing her against her shoulder. When the crying quiets to soft whimpers, Ruth spins around sideways to show that Sylvie has fallen asleep. Eleanor moves the toys out of the way in the stroller and helps her mother settle the child inside.

"It's not going to help to get worked up before anything happens. Let's just keep calm and wait."

Ruth's phone rings from the sofa. She grabs for it and shields her voice while saying hello. Listens for a moment, then says, louder, "Well, hello to you too! So nice to hear your voice . . ." With an apologetic glance back to Eleanor, she mouths "my cousin" and takes the phone into her bedroom.

"Yes, of course," Ruth says softly from the next room. "It's been ages."

Sylvie sighs in her sleep and starts to suckle, the tip of her pink tongue darting out against her upper lip. Eleanor can't even enjoy this. What if her father takes her away? What if she never sees her daughter again?

"The wedding was beautiful," Ruth is saying. "Just the way Roxie wanted it. No, it's fine. It was a long way with your hip."

The thing is, Domenique did contact the agency in California. And they contacted Nancy's people here in Boston. That didn't happen for nothing. If he wasn't interested in Sylvie, he'd have shrugged his shoulders and carried on with his life. That he was sniffing around could not be a good sign.

"Oh, they'll travel for a bit first. I don't expect to be a grandmother again for another few years. One is plenty for now."

Eleanor stops rocking the stroller. One. The conversation continues, but her head is roaring. She can't comprehend anything else that is said. This is no wedding ceremony during which one must remain selflessly devoted to the bride's experience. This is everyday life. She's going to be Ruth's dirty little secret. Somehow if it was just her, Eleanor could handle it, but the secret is going to extend to Sylvie.

That, she will not allow.

Eleanor's eyes dart from her mother's bedroom to the front door.

Slowly, she gets up, gathers Sylvie's things, and stows them in the diaper bag. Without a sound, Eleanor pushes the stroller out of the room.

She steps onto the elevator and, just as the doors close, Ruth calls, "Eleanor? Wherever are you going?"

Chapter 48

The thing about using the car as an infant sleep aid is, sometimes you're too damned tired to navigate the streets safely. The second night passed much in the same way as the first. Sylvie slept for about an hour and a half—time Eleanor stupidly wasted showering and cooking up penne noodles because she realized she hadn't eaten all day—then woke up to scream triple murder.

There's been no further contact from Sylvie's father. With any luck, he's satisfied with Sylvie having been successfully placed and has gone back to his wife, children, and money.

After lining up the usual suspects—bottle, bath, diaper change, burping, etcetera—and failing with each, at about six in the morning, Eleanor makes peace with the situation. She turns on a movie, *My Cousin Vinnie*, and settles down with Sylvie on a duvet spread on the living room floor. Angus watches, a huge sloppy grin on his face. At least Sylvie can feel loved while she bawls. And at least she'll be safe should her fledgling mother pass out.

They both must have drifted off sometime around six thirty. When the phone rings just after eight, Eleanor, in a scratchy-eyed stupor, knows enough to grab it quickly but has no idea what to say. She goes with nothing.

"Eleanor? Is that you?" It's Ruth.

She can't speak to the woman. Maybe just for now, maybe forever. It's a decision she can make when she has had a full night's sleep. Should such a night ever arrive. Eleanor reaches out a hand, finds the receiver button, and ends the call.

Chapter 49

I t's just before eight on night three when Eleanor bundles a weeping Sylvie into fleecy jacket and sheepskin booties, and carries her and the stroller down to the darkened street. Cold rain is starting to fall and their breath puffs are quickly blown away by wind. The car is out of the question; Eleanor can barely keep her eyes open. She tucks Sylvie into the Guzzie + Guss, quilt across her legs, and covers the entire stroller with a clear vinyl rain shield. That her girl is warm and dry is all that matters.

The odd person out on the street is well bundled. A few doors up, a woman cloaked in a charcoal cape and with a tam pulled over her ears ambles out of the variety store eating a candy bar. Farther up, a man in a plaid car coat unloads crates from the back of an old truck.

Eleanor considers, for a moment, going back upstairs for a thicker jacket and her trademark scarf, but the logistics—removing the quilt, pulling the somewhat settled Sylvie out of the stroller, hauling the expensive Guzzie + Guss into the lobby lest it "wheel itself away," and climbing all those stairs—clear the idea from her head.

There is something about November in Boston that has

always enchanted Eleanor. Something about seeing the city in its bare bones, stripped of the greenery that dresses things up in the warmer months. The gnarled architecture of a tree's naked branches when seen in the foreground of a beautiful historic building is the very essence of the city. There's a certain intimacy in seeing the streets undressed like that—before December's snow and the tiny white lights and streets full of Christmas shoppers, after the flashy romance of the autumn leaves—it reminds her of Angus's collar being off. When he isn't Angus out for a walk, or Angus with proof he's been vaccinated against rabies. When he's just had a bath in the tiny tub that only comes up to his ankles and is drying off, collar-free, on the rug by the window. Himself. Raw.

Rain spatters down Eleanor's neck as they cut through the park. She shivers. Surely it's cold enough to snow. She'll walk brisker is all. She'll warm up.

Only she doesn't. Maybe the combination of not enough sleep and no jacket lining blocks the rush of warm blood to muscles. By the time they she realizes where she's taking them, they're nearing Battersea Road. Eleanor's teeth are chattering, and she can barely feel her toes. Of course maybe this is what a heart attack feels like. Her left arm is a bit numb.

As cars rush past on Beacon Street and a taxi honks its horn, Sylvie calms. She points up at the flickering gas lights with a drool-soaked finger.

"Pretty lights?" Eleanor says. "Aren't they pretty?"

Sylvie's mouth attempts the word in silence, her index finger still in the air.

❧

Eleanor did not expect the sidewalk in front of Isabelle's house to be scattered with evergreen boughs and red dogwood branches. Nor did she expect the woman herself to be outside after dark. But in the feeble light from the gas lamps and her own porch light, Isabelle teeters atop a ladder, wearing baggy jeans tucked into yellow Hunter rain boots. She hacks violently at the earth in her flower box with what appears to be a pair of silver salad tongs.

"That couldn't wait until tomorrow?" Eleanor says over the crying that resumed once they hit the bumpity-bump of Beacon Hill's brick sidewalks. "You're going to fall to your death up there in the dark."

"Just trying to give the place a bit of evergreen cheer in all this gray gloom. That's what people do outside of the slums, Eleanor Sweet. They pretty up their environs." She looks down. "Now what have you done to that child to have her cry like that?"

"She's having trouble adjusting." *Or she hates me.*

"Perhaps it's having a mother who takes her for an evening stroll in a monsoon," Isabelle calls down, wiping rain from her face and leaving a dirty streak on her chin.

Maybe it's exhaustion, maybe it's seeing Isabelle all alone and scaling the side of her house, but Eleanor is overwhelmed with the need to confess. "Would you mind coming down here a sec?"

"I'm coming down, but if this is a big, sappy thank-you, I think I'll pass. I didn't 'search' for the accolades then and I don't do it now." She steps down the ladder, but before she nears the bottom, Eleanor blurts it out.

"I drove out to Ethan's house, Isabelle. I saw his wife."

Isabelle stops her descent. "Whoever authorized you to do such a thing?"

"I left a message just like you do. A note. And she's been in touch. She wants to speak to you."

"How dare you tamper with my life." Isabelle shakes her head. "And hers!"

"Her name is Tiffany Runion and she's very interested."

"*You* are giving *me* her name? Hah!" Her hand grips the edge of the wet ladder.

"Isabelle, please come down."

"I will do as I choose."

"I just can't stand to see you like this. You'll rattle around this huge house alone for the rest of your life because you're too proud to contact his family."

"Presumptuous thing. You think because you're merging with your birth family that everyone on earth should follow suit? This is why I got out of the business. Because of people like you who get overly sentimental about the past. Some birth mothers adopt out for a reason. They don't want to see their babies ever again!"

"That's not why you quit."

"I will not be lectured to in such a fashion." She climbs all the way down and starts gathering up her branches. The salad tongs fall to the sidewalk with a clatter and she lunges angrily to snatch them up.

Sylvie's cries lessen as the patter of rain on the plastic stroller shield grows faster. Louder. Eleanor watches Isabelle pile the branches by the side of her porch. Quieter now, she says, "You got out of the business because Ethan is dead and you can't stand the guilt."

"What did you say?"

"Your plan isn't going to work. The only thing that will help you now is getting to know his family. Your family."

"I will thank you to stay out of my—"

"Don't make the same mistake, Isabelle. It may be too late for you and Ethan, but his children. His wife. Don't let a lifetime pass without meeting them."

"Go. Do you hear me, Eleanor Sweet? Go. Get off my property and leave me to manage my life the way I see fit."

Eleanor stares at her a moment, Isabelle's silver hair drenched now. Her collar flattened. Her cheeks are hollow, her eyes sunken. Her mouth grim.

Without a word, Eleanor turns the stroller around. She bumps it along the brick sidewalk back to Beacon Street, rain stinging her face like needles.

Chapter 50

On the walk back, Sylvie's crying rises in pitch until Angus is howling alongside her.

Eleanor pushes the stroller up the slope after cutting through the bowl of the park and heads straight along on Newbury. The temperature has dropped considerably since they left the apartment, and freezing rain sits like glittery slop on the sidewalks and streets. Every step Eleanor takes, her boots slip sideways.

From the end of the block, she can see busyness in front of her store and picks up her pace. Even Angus seems fascinated by the people walking this way and that, and he strains against his leash, helping propel them forward. Lights flood out not from Pretty Baby but from Death by Vinyl. A couple walks out of the shop with two black shopping bags and hold the door for three hooded teens to tumble in.

Music thumps from Noel's place and it isn't "Bohemian Rhapsody." It's something else, something frantic that Eleanor doesn't recognize right away. The Sex Pistols, "God Save the Queen." That's what's playing. She stops in front of the store and peers inside. Noel is busy at the cash, ringing in the purchase of two girls who are taking pictures of themselves with the Sasquatch. Small armies of teenagers prowl the store, and one gangly boy with a shaved head comes out of the change room curtain to model a unicorn skeleton T-shirt for his girlfriend. The skater kids gather around a phone booth kitted out with headphones and a turntable. Above it all, a disco ball turns slowly. Angus presses his nose against the window and whines, his tail wagging.

Death by Vinyl, it appears, is open for business.

Eleanor looks down at the stroller. Sylvie, who until this moment has been inconsolable, is quiet. She stares, her body hiccuping with calm, at the tiny droplets of disco-ball light creeping across Noel's ceiling.

Eleanor's phone rings from her pocket. Nancy. At this hour, it cannot be good news. Eleanor covers one ear and picks up. "Nancy, hi."

"Hon, I've been trying to get to you all day but have been battling the California office. Domenique has come forward again."

"Oh shit."

"He doesn't necessarily want Sylvie back, which is the good news. But this has come as a big shock to him. Now normally the courts won't overturn an adoption once it's taken place as it's disruptive to the baby, but in this case the natural father didn't know about his child's existence. So we're on thinner ground here."

"I can't lose her, Nancy. I can't." Eleanor's heart hammers in her chest, her throat, her stomach. Her shoulder hurts so bad she has to sit on Noel's window ledge.

"I know, sweetie. I'm doing everything I can here. A judge down there is going to hear his argument tomorrow. I don't know what to say. I don't know which way we're headed next.

Just try to stay positive in the meantime. We at the agency will do everything we can to support you and . . ."

Eleanor lets the phone slide into her bag. Sylvie smiles, points at Noel's ceiling as if to show Eleanor. She can't, she *cannot* lose her daughter.

Noel looks up from the cash, sees Sylvie in the stroller, and lunges for the stereo to turn down the music. "I'm so sorry. Did I wake her?" he says through the doorway.

"No." Eleanor feels tears sting her eyes and blinks hard. There is no way she'll cry in front of Noel.

"I opened. Almost nine o'clock at night, but I opened."

"Yeah." She nods, biting down on her lip. "That's great. Really."

"Excuse me?" A woman and her preteen son approach Noel from behind, a handful of DVDs in the boy's hands. "Are these ones on sale?"

Noel nods yes and turns back to Eleanor. "Everything okay? You don't look so good."

She stands. "Sylvie's father wants to overturn the adoption. And I want to pick her up and flee. Anywhere he can't find us. I've waited my whole life for her. I can't lose her now."

Noel pulls her close and presses her head into his shoulder. "Hey, hey. Stop that talk. You're not going on the run with your infant daughter."

It feels good, to be held again. It feels safe. She allows it, then pulls back. "I am. You'll see. I'll pack up the Bug and take her and Angus and we'll just drive. I'll change my name. I'll get some job as a bartender or a chambermaid in some isolated town. I'll—"

He pushes the hair off her face. "Eleanor. You're not running, do you hear me? Running is only going to prolong the outcome. You're going to take charge of this situation. Face it."

"Face it how?"

"You're going to call your contact at the agency and you're going to tell him or her that you want to speak with Sylvie's father yourself."

"I am?"

"You are. Now get out of here so I can serve my customers." He turns away.

"Noel?"

"Yeah?"

"Thanks." With a wave, she pulls the stroller away to unlock her periwinkle door. Holding it open with her knee, she scoops up Sylvie, whose face crumples like a paper bag. The infant lets out a sadder-than-sad moan and once again begins to sob.

It can only be me, Eleanor thinks. It's me making her this miserable. Maybe she *would* be better off with her father.

Chapter 51

At one in the morning, Jonathan slides the stethoscope up the back of Sylvie's tiny T-shirt as Eleanor holds her close and coos in her ear. The crying hasn't abated. After taking Sylvie's temperature, after writing three unsent e-mails to Nancy to explain that Sylvie is desperately unhappy and that her father is probably right to remove his daughter from her care, after contemplating driving Sylvie down to Mass General to Emerg but deciding she was so bleary-eyed she'd probably qualify as Under the Influence, she finally did it. She broke down and called Jonathan.

Eleanor rocks the whimpering Sylvie as Jonathan listens to her heart, her lungs. The child is yawning violently now. She's tired herself out. Satisfied, Jonathan wraps the stethoscope around his hand and slides it into his medical bag.

"I don't see anything at all that would alarm me. Her heartbeat's good. Ears are clear, abdomen feels normal. Breathing is clear, she has good oxygen. I think you're just looking at a bit of anxiety, combined with jet lag and a pretty major life change."

Relief floods Eleanor to her toes. She pops a pacifier into Sylvie's mouth and the child's jaw works away at it. Sylvie's eyes droop shut. She forces them open again. "It's as if she won't let herself sleep. As if she doesn't trust me or something. Doesn't feel safe."

"Nah." He reaches down to scratch Angus's back. Angus's legs nearly give out with pleasure. The dog is in ecstasy having Jonathan back in the house. He grins up at his favorite master, tongue lolling out of his mouth like a great sopping towel. Behind him is the rocking horse, which Eleanor dragged out of the closet before Jonathan's arrival. "Nothing that sophisticated, trust me." He glances around at the walls they painted yellow. "The room looks good. Cheery."

"Doesn't seem to be cheering *her*." Eleanor sets the now-calmer Sylvie into the crib. The baby looks alarmed at first, then sucks hard on the pacifier and allows Eleanor to tuck the blanket around her. When Eleanor turns on the mobile—smiling zoo animals in faded colors—Sylvie is mesmerized.

Jonathan is at her side, his hands on the rail of the crib he assembled himself. "She's even more beautiful in real life."

Eleanor nods. "Isn't she?"

"You're good with her. Better than most new moms who come in."

"You're just saying that."

"Seriously. You couldn't be more natural if she'd been born to you."

A buzzer goes off in Jonathan's pocket and he checks a small black beeper. "Sorry," he says to Eleanor as he reaches for his jacket on the rocking chair. "On call tonight. New doc's wife is in labor. I have to go relieve him."

"It's fine. Thanks for coming."

Jacketed now, he makes no move to leave. "There are things in life I regret. Being in Europe backpacking when my grandfather had his heart attack. Not going back to med school for a specialty that would allow me to work days like a regular human." He stares at her. "And this. I'm ashamed of myself."

She doesn't know what to say. A few weeks ago, she'd have taken this as an opening. He wants to come back, she'd have convinced herself.

"If you ever want to discuss things, I'd be open to that."

Always so cryptic. "You mean us? Discuss us?"

"Yes."

"Sylvie's here now. She comes with me." *If Domenique doesn't take her away.*

"I know."

"So the us you're open to discussing is the three of us."

"Yes."

She glances at the rocking horse behind him. He can be so good, Jonathan. But he's become changeable. One day he's out, the next day he's in her bed. If she allows him a major role in Sylvie's life, he could do that to her too. Easily. He could be the perfect father or he could bolt again. Even if Sylvie is removed from Eleanor's life, Jonathan remains a question mark.

Too many seconds pass.

"Okay. Gotta fly." He kisses her forehead and marches toward the door, Angus trotting in his wake. Eleanor follows them.

With a quick salute, he starts down the stairs. She remembers the "Dada" DVD. If he's even remotely open to coming back, watching the video could stir just the right thing in him. She calls, "Jonathan?"

He stops, looks back.

No. It's wrong. "Thanks for the house call."

Chapter 52

A phone call is scheduled for this afternoon. Two thirty. She's done it. She called up Nancy the next morning and told her she'd like to talk to Domenique directly. Said he needed to hear her out. And if he still felt his daughter was in less-than-ideal hands, she'd understand.

The man is Sylvie's natural father. He has a right to want the best for her.

Nancy didn't think it a great idea—she thought the situation would be better handled through the formality of the agencies and it would be less personal, less dangerous, if Eleanor and Domenique spoke through their representatives. But she agreed to extend him the offer.

Sylvie was up crying again after Jonathan left; Eleanor didn't sleep at all. By morning, she'd accepted it. The adoption wasn't meant to be. From Jonathan pulling out to people's reactions to Sylvie's unhappiness to Domenique's emergence.

Eleanor Sweet wasn't meant to have a baby.

She's all cried out. Whatever comes, she's ready for it.

The morning passes far too slowly. Somehow, on less than three hours of sleep, Sylvie is wide-eyed and chipper, but Eleanor can't eat. Can't focus. And every time she looks at Sylvie, she breaks down yet again. She'll tell Domenique when he calls. To grow up with her own father, her half-siblings—Eleanor knows now the importance of that. If Sylvie was happy, thriving under Eleanor's care, that would be one thing. But she's not. The child wants out. Sylvie doesn't deserve to see that rope swing one day and ache.

Eleanor has no more fight left. She's ready to surrender.

There are still three hours to survive.

Sylvie has been here only five days. To leave her with Ginny, even for an hour, is not something she feels good about doing right now—especially given the circumstances. But Isabelle called. She wants her dress back. Today.

The morning is cold and bright enough that Eleanor has to squint even when she steps into the clattering china sounds of the café. The place is busier than she expected. She gets herself a coffee and waits for a pair of students to gather their backpacks and cups and vacate their little round table by the window. The glare from the street is almost painful. Eleanor lowers the window shade and sips. The bitter coffee seems fitting for today.

Maybe another sort of life is fine. Like Isabelle, she can live alone and find happiness in helping other people. In preparing the mothers who come into the shop for what is to come. She knows better now. In some small way, she'll be sharing in all her customers' milestones, fears, joys.

The door opens and Isabelle walks in, prim as ever. She buys herself a coffee. Arranges herself in the chair opposite Eleanor and sips. Tries not to make a face. "Your poor child is still alive, I hope?"

The conversation cannot be about Sylvie. Eleanor won't survive it. "She is. Especially at night."

"And you? Do you have any immediate plans to brush your hair and dress in something you haven't slept in?"

Eleanor looks down at her baggy sweatshirt and leggings. It's true. She hasn't given her appearance a moment's consideration. She's gone from artful layers to survivor chic.

Eleanor passes Isabelle the bag with the borrowed dress in it. Isabelle casts a glance at the logo and stuffs it into her leather shopping tote. "The last thing I need is to have people looking at a baby-store bag, then at my face, and attempting to do the math."

"The dress pulled across the rib cage."

"Presenting oneself properly doesn't come without pain, Eleanor Sweet. Perhaps you'll try it sometime."

In spite of herself, Eleanor smiles.

"I didn't come here to collect my Armani. Couldn't give a damn about it, if you'd like to know the truth. I came to inform you that it's not all true, what I said about Ethan."

A man with a large briefcase squeezes past them to get to the table in the corner. He too closes his blinds. He too sips and grimaces.

"I was ashamed," says Isabelle. "Not unlike your Ruth. My husband married me not knowing I'd given up a baby four years prior. I couldn't bring myself to tell him. So I concocted this internal story that Ethan was better off not knowing me. The truth was that I was too ashamed to face my own son. The guilt put me into a depression. How could I sit in front of my child, knowing he's wondering what kind of mother I am? Even I don't have the answer."

Eleanor dips her finger into her coffee and draws a lumpy

S on her napkin. She never once wondered what kind of mother Ruth was. Or Diane Keaton. They were each, in their own times, her mother. Period. She was willing to forgive either or both of them anything. "It's pretty clear to me."

"How so?"

"Here's what it is to be a mother. You love your baby so much you don't know where she ends and you begin. You love her enough to do without food, without sleep. And if it costs you a relationship, it's not too high a price. And if, God forbid, it ever comes to it, you love that child enough to do the unthinkable, to give her up. If walking away is what she needs—or wants—you find the strength to do it."

Isabelle leans back in her chair and crosses her legs. "Like Ruth did?"

This Eleanor doesn't answer. She pulls a sheet of paper from her bag and sets it on the table. On the paper is an address. "Her name is Tiffany Runion and she's your daughter-in-law. Your grandsons are ages seven and ten and are named Joshua and Ben. Ben is getting nineties in school and Joshua can break an egg with one hand just like his dad. Both boys are going to camp next summer for the very first time. And they very much want to meet you. If you are interested, be at the Sidecar Diner at nine thirty Saturday morning."

Isabelle's countenance betrays no change in emotion. She takes the paper in her hand and taps it with a finger. Then crumples it up and stands abruptly. "I'll thank you one last time to stay out of my affairs, Eleanor Sweet. Have yourself a good day."

Eleanor stares out the window long after Isabelle disappears from view.

Chapter 53

The lobby of the Intercontinental Hotel has a watery echo. Eleanor shifts her weight. It's now after 1:30 p.m. She's been sitting on the ledge of a stone planter box for half an hour and can no longer feel her right leg. There's a cardiology convention going on in the hotel this weekend, according to the signs directing attendees to this table or that meeting room. Judging from the well-dressed mob in the lobby, people checking in, meeting in small groups and heading into the coffee shop, the convention is a big one.

She can't wait much longer. The phone call with Domenique is in an hour.

As guests and staff wander past, Eleanor is struck by a huge change. She no longer searches crowds for faces. She can stare out at the comings and goings of strangers and not wonder whether or not she has a genetic link to them. There's a certain peace associated with this new state. A weary peace.

It's possible she's missed her. Ruth's flight departs around four this afternoon; she could very well have gone early. Or be trolling the city before she flies home.

Eleanor checks her watch. Fifteen more minutes, then she'll leave.

She observes a man in his sixties—thick head of gray-ing hair and long, elegant overcoat—thank the concierge and turn to a woman about the same age, also in a long coat, and kiss the tip of her nose. He hooks his arm into hers and they squeeze through the revolving door in a fit of giggles.

A familiar voice makes Eleanor turn. There, coming out of the elevator, is Ruth with a woman dressed in yoga gear. Ruth sees Eleanor and stops. Brightens. It's clear that she's torn. She wants desperately to hug her daughter openly and ask for forgiveness. And, just as desperately, she wants to keep her secret.

Eleanor stands, straightens her coat.

Ruth doesn't need to ask for forgiveness. Forgiveness, Eleanor has decided, has nothing to do with it. The anger, the love and hate, the resentment, the wonder, the under-standing, it's all too big. It doesn't fit into one little word, one act. Eleanor has spent her entire life shackled by feelings too big for her. Too big for anyone. All one can hope for, she's decided, is to come to a place of acceptance. Ruth—like Isabelle did, like she's about to do—loved her enough to let go. It doesn't hurt any less or make Eleanor any stronger. But it does give her comfort.

The truth is Eleanor never considered her mother, not really. She understood that her birth mother would likely have agonized over her choice. Thought about her lost child. Maybe even pined for her. But she hadn't thought, until Isabelle really, about her mother's embarrassment. Her shame.

Moving forward with Ruth, with her birth family, it isn't going to be the stuff Diane-Keaton-waiting-on-a-private-jet fantasies are made of. This is no fairy tale, this is real life.

"Ruth," Eleanor says with a polite nod to Ruth's friend. "I just came to say a quick goodbye."

Ruth's chest heaves. Her eyes glitter with emotion she doesn't dare show. She allows herself to give her daughter a quick hug. "I'm so glad you did."

Pulling back, Eleanor takes the friend's hand and introduces herself. "Eleanor Sweet. Ruth is a dear family friend."

"Eleanor has a new baby girl," Ruth tells her friend. "Just adopted from the West Coast. I came in to help her out."

The friend, who introduces herself as Marnie, makes all the appropriate sounds of excitement and approval.

"How is Sylvie today?" Ruth asks.

Eleanor shrugs. "Beautiful. Maddening. The love of my life."

"I can stay," Ruth says. "If you need some help, I'm happy to change my flight. Let you get some rest."

The thought of her upcoming conversation with Domenique makes Eleanor's stomach flip. "I don't think it'll be necessary. But thank you."

"I'd better get going, then. I'm running late."

Eleanor kisses her mother's warm cheek. "Call me tomorrow, okay? We'll have a nice long chat."

Chapter 54

Domenique didn't call. Eleanor waited all day and never heard a word. Not from the agency, not from Nancy.

Evening at five brings no surprises. Sylvie had gone down for an hour before dinner and woke up howling. Ate some chicken and banana slices and has been inconsolable ever since. Eleanor tried a bottle, a warm bath, a baby massage, a TV show about panda bears, and a bouncy chair from downstairs. She brought in Angus for amusement only to have him pounce on her pile of stuffed animals and roll around on his back as if he'd found a rotting fish on the beach, then glance at Sylvie slyly to see if she was amused.

Angus, at least, is having a good time.

It would have been better to just get it over with, with Domenique. What he thinks of the adoption, whether he approves or not, isn't the issue anymore. Sylvie isn't happy. All Eleanor wants is for that little girl to smile.

With the sobbing Sylvie in her arms, Eleanor walks to the living room window and looks out. Maybe the moon will calm her down. Maybe she'll recognize it from back home and feel soothed. She bounces Sylvie and looks out to find no moon, but snowflakes glitter in the light from the street lamps. The snow has just started; there's no sign of it sticking to anything.

"Look, Sylvie! See the snow?"

Sylvie does look. She's fascinated enough by this white stuff that her furious wailing morphs into wet hiccups. If snow is what the child wants, snow is what she shall have.

Just after seven thirty, Eleanor backs out of the door with Sylvie in one arm and the stroller in the other. With a mighty jolt, the stroller flips open. Eleanor bundles Sylvie into it. The trees, the sidewalk, the parked cars, the street—everything is covered now in a downy layer of snow that deadens the sounds of the city. Angus, unleashed, thunders out onto the sidewalk to bite at the white stuff, grabbing a snow-covered leaf or chip bag and playfully shaking the life out of it.

Sylvie's crying has started again.

Light from Death by Vinyl floods the sidewalk again tonight and music thumps through the door—propped open by a brick left over from the completed renovations. Noel appears, wiping his hands on his jeans.

"Miss Sylvie came to see Uncle Noel?"

"Hey, it worked last time." Eleanor allows him to pick up the baby in her puffy, snowflake-dusted jacket. He bounces her against his chest, only to have her push away and howl louder. "If you get her to sleep this time, you're hired."

Angus has dropped to the ground to roll on his back, legs thrashing in the air. When he rights himself, his back and head are frosted in powder. He woofs.

"What about the snow?" Noel says, struggling to keep Sylvie in his arms. Snowflakes hitting her face seem to be upsetting her, so he ducks into the doorway. Right away, she stops squirming, stops crying. Her mouth drops open and her teary face tilts up toward the ceiling. "It's Death by Vinyl you like? The graffiti and the black ceiling? Maybe Eleanor isn't cool enough for you."

Eleanor smiles sadly. "Truer than you know."

"What's happening with the dad?"

"We were supposed to speak. He never called."

"That's good, right? He's maybe backed down."

Noel moves farther outside again and Sylvie starts to wail. He looks back at the store, frowning.

"Doesn't matter, Noel. She doesn't want to be here. With me. She's miserable, anyone can see that. I'm going to tell Domenique he needs to take her. She doesn't want this."

He opens the door and steps inside with Sylvie. She stops crying. Looks around. He goes back outside. She wails again and he returns her to Eleanor's arms.

"What are you doing?" Eleanor asks as the baby arches her back to pull away. "I get it. I get it. She doesn't like me."

He leads Eleanor inside Death by Vinyl. Immediately, Sylvie calms. Babbles and bounces happily in Eleanor's arms.

"Don't you see?" he says. "It's the silence that she hates. In here, with the loud music, she's happy. It's not you she's rejecting. It's the terrible quiet. The lack of noise. She's from a busy foster home, right?"

"Yes." Sylvie yawns contentedly in Eleanor's arms. "Six young kids. The foster dad was a musician."

"Do you think there was ever a moment of peace in a house loaded with children?"

Eleanor thinks back to the night at Ginny's place. She had to take three Tylenols to cure the headache she left with. "No!"

"She is most relaxed when surrounded by busyness. Noise."

The planes roaring over their heads at Logan. The sound was deafening. And put Sylvie right to sleep. "I think you're right."

"Of course I'm right." He bends down and pulls an old record player from a shelf, then picks out an album. "Let's go." He starts out the door.

"Where are we going?"

"To set your store up right. Forget your Bach-through-the-iPod-dock nonsense. What this girl wants is some proper sound."

Inside Pretty Baby, Noel sets the record player on the counter and bends down to plug it in. "This just may be the single greatest rock band on the face of the earth and you can't raise this child without them. Britt Daniel, the lead singer, writes lyrics so brilliant that they could be poetry."

Sylvie starts to bawl. "Whatever," says Eleanor. "Just be quick."

He turns down the lights and pulls the record, *Transference*, from its sleeve.

With great flourish, he sets it on the turntable. "I shouldn't even risk this album on a record player I haven't tested. Anything could happen."

Angus climbs up onto a big denim chair and stretches out, his great limbs dripping wet now and hanging off the edge like two-by-fours. His mouth falls open in a canine grin as he looks about at his growing family. Ginny was at least partially right. Or perhaps she was bang on. Perhaps Angus views the mighty Sylvie as alpha. She's certainly the loudest of the pack.

In the near dark, they listen to the spark and crackle when the needle meets vinyl. Sylvie grows quiet.

"She gets it. That singular greatest moment of anticipation, that hyper-charged piece of time between the needle touching down and the music starting. Not everyone can appreciate it."

"This changes everything," Eleanor says with wonder. "Sylvie doesn't hate me at all. I was so convinced."

Two sexy drumbeats. Then, together, the pluck of guitar with a slightly throaty voice that could be right there in the store with them.

"A song is never the same twice when you play it on vinyl. The way the dust lands, the smoothness of the turntable, it brings a song to life any way it pleases. You can't control it."

You can't control anything, Eleanor doesn't say. Or anyone. People let you know how much they have to give. All you can do is listen and decide where to position yourself. Some you'll stay farther away from, some closer. Some you'll keep right next to you. She squeezes Sylvie.

"Like it so far?" asks Noel. "It's called 'Out Go the Lights.'"

She nods. "I like it."

"The album was Victoria's. A birthday gift from me. Couple of months before she died." Noel drops to the floor by Angus's ankles and bobs his head softly to the beat. "I want Sylvie to have it. You know, so she grows up right."

Eleanor watches him. A smile spreads across her face. "I'm glad you moved in next door."

He leans forward to adjust a dial on the stereo. Barely perceptibly, he nods.

Sylvie reaches up to touch Eleanor's cheek. When she looks down, the child giggles. Takes Eleanor's jaw in her hands and squeezes it, then drops her head to rest against Eleanor's shoulder. She holds the child more tightly, feeling her warmth, breathing in her powdery scent. For a moment, the world is perfectly still.

Noel catches Eleanor's eye. He nods toward Sylvie.

She's fallen asleep.

As Eleanor places Sylvie in the window display crib, the bell above the door jingles. A black man walks in, tall as the door frame, and takes off a snow-covered cap to reveal short hair. In shades of brown, like Sylvie's.

"Eleanor Sweet?" His accent is West Coast. He stomps off his boots and extends an enormous hand. "Domenique Beaudoin. I am Sylvie's father."

She can think only of pushing him out the door and locking it. Grabbing her daughter and bolting out the back. She could do it. She could muster up that kind of strength. Instead she takes his hand. "Nice to meet you."

"I didn't expect to find you here. I flew in hoping to meet with you in the morning, but couldn't stay in my hotel room and took a walk." He shrugs massive shoulders. "Here you are."

Noel stands. Tugs Eleanor's sleeve. To Domenique, he says, "Can you excuse us a moment?" When the man bows his head, Noel pulls her to the side.

"Tell him I'm Jonathan. Tell him we've reconciled and you're no longer doing this alone." He cups the back of her neck and shakes his head. "Because, hey, you're not."

She takes in his earnest expression, his kind eyes, almost pleading to let him help. Rising up on tiptoes, she kisses his cheek. "Noel. The flood was my fault. She was in my store, your upstairs neighbor. We were all talking. I should have seen how frustrated she was. I should have known—"

He pulls her neck closer and kisses her hard, surprising them both. "Shut up and let me lie for you."

She steps back, smiles. Finds his hand. "I'm going to do this truthfully. I have to."

Once he's gone, Eleanor drops into a big chair, swirling with too many emotions to count. Her fingers tickle Noel's until he slides into the chair with her and lays one leg over hers.

They hadn't been in the break room long, Domenique and Eleanor. He refused, before leaving, to let her wake the child. Just watched Sylvie sleep in the window display for a while, the snow falling softly behind her. Reached up to dab his eyes. He and Eleanor exchanged contact information. They promised to stay in touch. For now, he said, he didn't want a relationship with his daughter.

"Let it be in her hands." He had put on his cap and stepped out into the snow.

"What did you say that made him leave so content?" Noel asks.

She reaches up to swipe lint from his shoulder and he grabs her hand, threads his fingers through hers. "I told him about her crying. How, even if I dropped dead from the pain,

I would have let him take her away if I thought it was best for her. But after tonight, after seeing her happy, I would stop a train with my bare hands to keep anyone from taking her away. Including him."

Noel's mouth twitches. "What did he say?"

"He said he couldn't live with himself, he couldn't relinquish his rights, until he came here in person to see for himself what I was made of."

"And?"

"He told me about Sylvie's mother. Tia. That in all his life he'd never met a woman who knew what she wanted like Tia. She was soft. She was strong. He said that she loved herself enough to make a powerful mother." Eleanor leans her head back and smiles in the dark. "He said that I was just like her."

Epilogue

Isabelle lies in the dark and claps her hands. When the light goes on, she sits up. Pulls on a robe and pads down to the kitchen to heat the kettle. As soon as it whistles she shuts the burner off and stares at the steam curling up from the spout. With a shake of her head, she climbs the stairs back to her room. She lays the robe over the foot of the bed and climbs under the covers. Honestly, she never should have let Eleanor Sweet into her life. She was managing just fine. With a loud clap, the light goes off.

"Lunacy," she says.

Right away, she claps again. Throws off the covers this time and marches into her closet. Pulls on a v-neck sweater and houndstooth trousers. A pair of boots capable of keeping her hips from shattering as she leaves Battersea Road to traipse hither and yon through the snow.

In the kitchen, she sits at the island, her purse on her lap. Here she waits for the clock to strike nine. When it does, she stands. Makes her way to the front hall, where she pulls on a wool coat. She looks at herself in the mirror, then slips a scarf from the drawer and ties it around her neck.

It's like a child raising a child, this Eleanor dousing her

baby girl in bubbles, wheeling her about the city in the middle of the night. She has all the sense of an aardvark. Later this morning, Isabelle will stop by the store. She owes it to that poor child to get involved.

But first, she has a stop to make.

The Sidecar Diner looks like a San Francisco trolley that was hoisted from its tracks, shipped across the country and fastened to the base of the Channing-Breyers building. Then, in an effort to make it feel less West Coast, less Golden State, it was coated in decidedly non-weather-resistant black paint, as evidenced by coiled strips of alkyd peeling off its body like bark from a dying willow.

Isabelle steps inside, removes her gloves and jacket. Her scarf she leaves on. Fortification.

This is no trendy reproduction diner. The black and dingy-white floor is greasy enough that she's already slipped twice. The air smells of bacon, strong coffee, cigarettes being smoked out the back door, and a mop so sour Isabelle almost volunteers to head to the store to pick up a quart of bleach.

Her eyes roam the room. There, in the last booth, sits a woman with short hair and a face clear of makeup. From the bench across from her, two freckled boys stare at Isabelle and bounce with excitement.

She pulls herself up to her full height, tilts her chin a bit higher and starts toward them.

Acknowledgments

Enormous thanks to people who helped along the way: search angel Marilyn Waugh, Deborah Jiang-Stein, Gail Konop Baker, Danielle Younge-Ullman, Barbara Annino, Evan McIntosh, Marlon Hershkop, Joseph Hershkop, Bruce Urquhart, Johnny Pigeau, Karen Elliott, Dean Andrews, Keith Cronin, Joanne Levy, Judy Merrill Moticka, and John MacDonald.

As always, to my literary agent, Daniel Lazar, and my film agent, Kassie Evashevski. At Writers House, Victoria Doherty-Munro and Maja Nikolic. At UTA, Johnny Pariseau. My brilliant editor at HarperCollins Canada, Jennifer Lambert. Also at HarperCollins Canada, Melissa Zilberberg, Leo MacDonald, Cory Beatty, Kaitlyn Vincent, Vikki Vansickle, Noelle Zitzer, and Allyson Latta.

Most of all, best of all, Max and Lucas.